THE NOW IN FOREVER

A SMALL TOWN SECOND CHANCE ROMANCE

FORTUNE FALLS

NC BARTON

To everyone that's ever been brave enough to listen to that small voice deep in your heart, this one is for you.

KEEP ON KEEPIN' ON

THREE YEARS AGO

Despite all my lists, alarms, and colorful sticky notes in my planner, time is not on my side this afternoon. I've always hated when people personify time, like it's a living, breathing thing with a fragile temperament that needs to be bounced and shushed. But today I get it. When I finally make it to the bookstore, sweat beads at the nape of my neck and I'm out of breath.

The shop is a good ten degrees hotter than outside, thanks to all the perfumed bodies packed in. I take out my earbuds, Stevie Nicks still crooning about thunder and rain. For a moment, I toy with the idea of leaving, heading back into the sunshine, putting my earbuds back in, and going to get a solo glass of wine somewhere. Because I'm a strong, independent, almost twenty-six-year-old woman. That's what I do now—stroll around Helena with empowering women in my earbuds, perfectly capable of getting dinner or a drink by myself. I never have, but I *am* capable of it.

"Name please," the woman at the door asks with a clipboard in hand.

"Hattie Stevens."

She flips to the next page and scratches a check next to my name. "Enjoy."

There's not an empty seat amongst all the neatly lined up chairs, so

I stand in the back and clutch his book in my hand, using the other to tuck my freshly dyed blonde hair behind my ear. Breakup hair; no breakup is too mundane. But *found-out-my-husband-was-sleeping-with-his-boss-hair* doesn't quite have the same ring to it. Total and utter betrayal hair? The only good thing to come out of the demise of my six-year relationship with Chad. Well, that and now I'm single.

Will Ed recognize me with the new hair?

The last time he saw me, it was brown—well, brown and unfortunately green.

I take a deep breath in through my nose and slowly out past my lips.

Of course he will recognize me. I still have the same face; the same blue eyes he once stared deeply into. There's no way he won't recognize me. Not after what we shared.

But what if he's not happy to see me?

I'm not sure what I expected from this reading. That's not true. I know exactly what I expected, more like hoped for, but it certainly wasn't this humid and crowded in my fantasies. I should've known it would be packed, since I had to get a ticket, but it didn't occur to me. All I'd thought was how amazing it's on the solstice. Exactly seven years later.

My nails dig into my soft flesh as my palm tightens. I'm spiraling. *All I can control is me, and I want to be here. I want to see him.*

The smooth hardcover in my hand grounds me. I can't believe he really did it—got his book published, and it's a wild success. *He's* a wild success. He's come a long way from that day so long ago in New Haven.

That day. My cheeks warm at the thought. Our perfect day often flits through my brain. It comes back to me the way memories often do, with no beginning or end, just flashes. The light on the water. The sweet, spicy scent of orange and clove. The sugary strawberry ice cream, salty crackers, the bitter bite of cheap beer in the back of my mouth. Soft skin. Sweat.

Sometimes I play it in a more intentional linear reel, like I'm watching a movie I've memorized every word to.

A woman with a shiny blonde bob and even shinier lips approaches the podium. "Hello. Thank you all for coming to The Nook. I'd like to welcome Ed DeArmas to the podium to read from his *New York Times* best-selling literary fiction novel, *Vex*."

The crowd erupts into applause. Everyone who was seated stands as Ed walks to the platform. His dark suit jacket is much more expensive than the one he was wearing when we met. What hasn't changed is the beat-up band shirt underneath. This time, instead of The Velvet Underground, it's Dead Kennedys. His hair is a little longer—he runs a hand through it as he surveys the crowd.

Over the heads of all the people clapping, his eyes find mine, and he stops his scan. His green eyes are as bright as ever. Adrenaline shoots to my toes in a whoosh as our moment of eye contact stretches like a strand of honey when you take a tiny taste straight from the jar.

He looks away, but the moment was unmistakable. Wasn't it?

I barely listen to the reading, too aware of my own body to lose myself. I know all the words by heart at this point, anyway. Since the book was released last October, I've read it cover to cover five times. On my third pass, Chad asked why I kept reading the same book. Toward the end, it seemed everything I did annoyed him. It wasn't about me—he was looking for ways to justify what he did.

Ed's smooth, deep voice pulls me back to the reading.

Once he's finished, the crowd claps, and the shiny-haired woman takes the microphone back. "After a brief Q and A, Ed has graciously agreed to sign copies of *Vex*. If you need to buy one, we have a display over by the register. Ed will take questions now. Please raise your hand, and we'll get to as many as we can in the time we have left."

Almost every hand in the place shoots up. Shiny hair goes to a woman near the front dressed all in black. She takes the mic, her bright-red lips curling into a smile, and I wonder if I could pull off that shade. "Do you have a girlfriend?"

The room explodes in laughter. Ed smiles, the tips of his ears turning a little pink. Once the crowd has quieted enough for him to be heard, he leans into his mic on the podium. "No comment."

There are quite a few "ahh's" and even a couple "boos," echoing my own disappointment. I want to hear the real answer to that question, and I want it to be "no." Truthfully, I want the answer to be "I actually signed up for this reading hoping to find a girl I spent one magical, perfect day with seven years ago and never saw again. She said she lived in Helena, so I signed up for all these Montana readings to find her."

The rest of the questions are much more appropriate for a literary event.

After the Q and A, Ed sets up at the signing table in the back, and a massive line forms. I stroll through the shelves of books, not wanting to get in the line yet, running my hand along the spines of the mysteries. If I'm close to the end of the line, he can suggest we get a drink. Catch up. I don't want to admit how many times I've fantasized about this day since I bought the ticket two months ago.

I wander to the romance section, still needing to buy a copy of Anh's pick for Story Club this summer. There's a little window in the corner with a table under it and a few books displayed. It's a shame. If this were my bookstore, I'd put a fluffy chair there and make a cozy reading nook.

The line is dwindling, so I step into it and start reading my new bubblegum pink book. We shuffle forward at a snail's pace. So far, the book Anh picked is absolutely delightful. I want to run out of here right now, curl up with a cool glass of lemonade and a face mask. What am I doing, subjecting myself to this level of anxiety?

"Um, I think you might be at the wrong signing."

I lower my book. Ed smiles, but his eyes stay fixed on his pen that has apparently run out of ink. He scribbles swirl after swirl on a scrap of paper. His suit jacket is hanging casually on the chair behind him, his exposed forearms flexing with each movement of the pen. I laugh, my cheeks burning, and quickly switch the book for the one under my arm, handing him my well-worn copy of *Vex*. My heart is in my throat, waiting for him to recognize me.

His lips twist into a frown. "Ah, there it is. Again."

Is he sick of looking at his own book? No. That can't be possible. If I ever publish one of my books, I'll paper my walls with the cover.

I, of course, have to complete one in order for that to happen, though.

He hasn't taken a good look at me yet. He seems a bit distracted. A woman in a navy-blue silk top and thick black pants, despite the sweltering heat, comes over and whispers in Ed's ear. His face turns taut, the muscle in his jaw clenched. He squeezes his fist, his knuckle tattoos that spell out R-E-A-D, stretching with the motion. The woman hovers behind the table.

"Who should I make it out to?" Ed asks in monotone, pen ready to scrawl away. He doesn't look up when he says it.

My chest fills with tiny pinpricks of excitement. This will do it. If he hasn't recognized me by now, he'll definitely remember my name. "Hattie."

A flicker of something crosses over his face, but I'm not sure what. Recognition? Hope? It's infinitesimal—a twitch of his lips, a little too slow of a blink.

The woman steps forward and puts a hand on his shoulder. "This is the last one, don't worry."

Ed signs the book, handing it back to me quickly, not glancing at me once. I'm frozen, staring at him, willing him to look at me. *Look at me, dammit*. His eyes flick to mine for a beat as he stands, turns, and walks toward the back of the store.

"That's all for tonight, I'm afraid. Ed has another signing tomorrow morning in Butte at Isle of Books. Please feel free to join us there."

My whole body is numb, like I've been shot with Novocain. He didn't remember me. He didn't know my face. He didn't even know me by my name. How many Hatties are there in this day and age? Five? Ten? Seventeen tops.

Feeling comes back into my fingertips, and my scalp tingles. Maybe he left me a message in the book. It probably has his number or a place and time to meet. I open the cover with shaking hands. The writing is nearly illegible, but after careful deciphering I read:

Keep on keepin' on.

- Ed

I look up, hoping to meet Ed's green eyes, for us both to laugh at the absurdity of it. He got me. It was a joke. Of course, he remembers. But he's gone.

Trudging up to the counter to buy my books, I pass a stack of signed copies Ed left. I open the cover of the top book, tears filling my eyes as I check the inscription. I move to the next in the stack and the next and the next. They all say the same thing—*Keep on keepin' on.*

CHAPTER 1
SUMMER SOLSTICE
NOW

Dust particles catch the light of the lamp and float through the air like lazy fairies, mocking my frenzied movements. It's already past midnight, and according to my color-coded schedule, I was supposed to be showered and cozied up on the couch by ten. But I still have about four boxes worth of stuff to pack.

How did this happen?

Taking in the room with the odds and ends, I notice a theme: It's all stuff that was *ours*. And according to the freshly signed settlement, it's now solely mine. It shouldn't be this hard. Chad and I split years ago. It's just now with the papers actually signed and the perfect timing of losing my job, the grief feels fresh.

Picking up a tiny glass bird we bought on a trip to Venice, my palms sweatier than I realized, it slips through my fingers onto the hardwood floors and shatters into hundreds of pieces. Metaphors normally are my life blood—filling my English teacher's heart with joy. My writing is littered with them. But the spot-on accuracy of this one is too much for me.

Wiping sweat off my brow, I sweep up the mess and throw the rest of the stuff in the donation boxes. A funny little wind-up toy, a mug that says best person, a sprig of dried lavender from our wedding day now all gone.

My purge stops when I get to the closet and run my fingers along the stiff suit jacket that's hung in the very back behind one of my grandmother's sweaters since we moved into this house. Small holes cover the shoulders, and pins, some rusted, still cling to the lapels.

If Chad ever saw this jacket in here, he never asked about it. I couldn't bring myself to get rid of it. Even after that terrible signing. It's my proof of our perfect day. Often, I wonder if that day was really perfect or if my mind has shaped it that way, like an old photograph, over-exposed and blurred, leaving only the sharpest details. Everything else faded into oblivion. Like my grandparents' wedding photo hanging in the hall of their farmhouse.

But it did happen. We shared that moment in time together, and it was beautiful. Right now, though, this jacket, my souvenir, my proof is just another reminder of my shit luck with love. Lately, shit luck with everything. It's all too much. I walk it over to the trash pile and tuck it in a bag. It's time for a fresh start.

"...TOMORROW is a new day with no mistakes in it yet," my audiobook says, and I pause it to bask in that line. My favorite line, from one of my favorite books. My comfort read...and I need some comfort.

Even with my shades, the sun is glaring, and my iced coffee is gone. I pick up the plastic cup, rattling the ice around to be sure. All rattle, no slosh. Definitely gone. My legs are that kind of achy where they need to stretch, and I feel like I've been driving for hours, probably because I've been driving *for hours.* I left at five this morning, and it's almost four in the evening now, and that's with the one-hour time difference from Helena to the coast.

Stopping at Grandma's adds a couple hours to the trip, but there's no way I can be anywhere close without stopping to say hi. My Subaru bumps down the familiar dirt road until her massive red barn comes into view, then her light-blue house—in need of a new coat of paint, but other than that, just the same as the last time I was here, a little over a year ago, for the funeral.

On the porch, Grandma's rocking in her chair. The one next to her is so empty it looks hollow. Grandpa's chair. Have I really not visited since he passed? I get out of the car, feeling the blood rush around my tired legs.

Grandma's sipping a glass of wine, the summer sun still going strong, twinkling on the red liquid and catching her white hair, making her look ethereal. There's an empty glass on the table between the chairs, and I wonder if she got it out for me or if she always has it there—a habit from all those years she grabbed two for their rock on the porch.

"Hattie-Bear."

My chest warms at the nickname. She clasps either side of the chair, her wiry forearms flexing with the motion, but I hold up a hand, hurrying up the stairs.

"Don't get up. I'm coming to you."

Her arms relax, and she sits back. I lean down to her, placing a kiss on her soft cheek, inhaling her rose-powdered perfume she's used my whole life.

"Sit. Sit. Have a glass."

I hesitate. It feels wrong to sit in his chair, so I pour myself less than half a glass—I still have a ways to drive yet—and perch at the top step, angling myself to face her.

Grandma looks at me, her face full of concern. "Where are all those kids going to go to school?"

She says it like we're mid conversation. Like we've been talking about this for hours.

I take a sip of my wine while she waits patiently for my answer. "They'll bus to schools nearby, I guess."

"It doesn't make sense. Why would they shut down a school?"

"There weren't enough kids to fill it anymore."

Grandma leans forward in her chair, her blue eyes shimmering. They're so much like mine, it's both comforting and jarring. Same dark rim around the iris, same white flecks making them look like a gem of some kind. "What's your plan, then?"

I smile, but a heaviness tugs at the corners of my lips. Ah yes, a plan. I always have a plan. "Look for another job. Chad's sure the house should sell quickly, so that's good."

A new job, a new life.

"Why is Chad handling all the house stuff?"

"He owned the house before we were married. Plus, he's staying in Helena."

Grandma's eyes narrow. I put on a big smile, hoping to calm her. "It's fine."

"You can stay here, you know. Your room's just how you left it."

I nod. "Thank you, Grandma. But Robin, Anh, and I planned this before I lost my job, even. It's going to be fun. You sure you don't mind if I store some things in the barn?"

She waves a hand at me, the gold heart charm on her wineglass tinkling with the motion. "It should be fine. For a while."

My heartbeat ticks up a notch. "For a while?"

She lifts and lowers one shoulder. "You can absolutely store your stuff. Just concentrate on what's next for you."

I'm still wondering what she meant, but if she had wanted to explain, she would've. There's no prying anything out of Grandma. "Thanks. It won't be hard to find a job."

Honestly, it might not be that easy, with budget cuts in schools across the country, but I don't want Grandma to worry.

"You know, I have a little nest egg—"

"Grandma, I don't need money." Once the house sells, I won't, anyway. God, I still can't believe I'm divorced at twenty-nine. It's definitely not how I pictured things working out. "It's going to be fine."

I hope.

The porch creaks as Grandma rocks her chair.

"Maybe you should think about a career change."

"What? Why?" I had thought about it, but what would I do? I worked as the English teacher at that high school for seven years. Teaching is all I know how to do.

Grandma's eyes light up. "This could be an amazing opportunity to change your life."

"What makes you think I want to do that?" I try to sound casual as

I ask, but my heart is hammering in my chest, because she's not wrong. I need a change.

"The past few years, you've been so run down. When you visit, you're so tired. If teaching is where your heart is, then by all means, find another job at another school."

I take a sip of wine, half hiding behind my glass, her words striking a chord in my soul. Maybe that's why I haven't been more upset about losing the job. I'm burned out. It's not the kids. I love the kids. It's the paperwork. The meetings. The new curriculum every other year.

"But if it's not, then maybe it's time to reach for something else."

"What?" I half laugh. "I've only ever taught."

"That's not true. You worked at that bookstore. You used to talk about opening up your own one day. And there's your writing. You could finish your novel."

All my dreams are staring me back in the face with each word out of Grandma's mouth. My dream to open a bookstore. My novel. But I was so close to living out my other dreams, of settling down, raising a family, and look how that turned out. I'm tired. Too tired to reach for the stars. I need to get my life back on track. Make practical decisions.

I rise, setting my wine on the table and making a show of checking my watch. "I should unload that stuff from the car."

Grandma nods, rocking her chair.

After moving what few boxes of stuff I kept into the corner of the red barn, I go inside, running cold water over the back of my neck. When I come out of the bathroom, Grandma's in the kitchen filling the kettle.

"Have you heard from your father?"

With a soothing breath, my eyes drift shut for just a moment to steady myself. Grandma's really covering all the hits today. My uncertain future, my unfinished novel, my unfulfilled dreams, and now my estranged relationships.

"Not since Christmas."

Grandma's lips purse. "Want some tea?"

"No, thanks. Robin's expecting me for dinner."

She wraps me in a tight hug. "I didn't mean to overstep. I just don't want you to feel like you have to dive headfirst into another teaching job if it's not what you want anymore. This is your one precious life. You can make it anything you want it to be."

Her hair is soft on my cheeks, and maybe it's all this talk about my life, or maybe it's the fatigue from all the driving, or maybe it's being here and having Grandpa not be, but a tear rolls down my cheek, then another, and another.

Grandma releases her hug and hands me a hanky from her pocket, a small yellow butterfly embroidered in the corner. "Come back for a visit."

"I will," I say, wiping my tears.

BACK IN THE CAR, I press play on *Anne of Green Gables*, trying to shake off the heavy conversation. Ever since the first summer Robin, Ahn, and I met, I've loved this book and always have it downloaded on my phone. Good thing, too, since the audiobook I downloaded specifically for the trip was over before I even made it out of Montana. *The Motorcycle Diaries*, Robin's pick this year for book club because it's Nathan's favorite. It was okay, way shorter than I expected. If I'm being honest, I was looking for things to dislike about it. Robin would never pick this book herself. She's always choosing memoirs and personal development books—never call them self-help; it's a thing. Will next year's pick also be one of Nathan's favorites? If they have kids, will we be reading *The Cat in the Hat*?

The phone rings, jarring me out of my silent rant.

"Anh, you're saving my sanity right now."

"As usual. How long left of the drive do you have?"

"I'm about thirty minutes away. Are you and Melissa already there?"

There's a heavy silence.

"Anh?"

"Robin didn't tell you?"

I bite my lip. Tell me? Anh can't come. The whole point of all of us staying at Nathan's family beach house for the summer is to commemorate our twentieth anniversary of Story Club. Twenty years! How can we commemorate with one third of the club missing? "You're not coming."

"I am coming, only not for a couple of weeks. I couldn't get out of work. But we'll be there for the Fourth and then again at the end of summer."

It'll be just me and the lovebirds. Not that it would be much different if Anh and Melissa were there. They've been engaged and madly in love for years now.

"How was the move?" Anh asks.

"Okay. I got rid of most of my stuff, and what's left I just dropped off at my grandma's."

"That's nuts. I can't believe you're moving."

"Yep. I applied for a job in southeast Portland teaching English at a private school."

Anh sighs. "Just like Anne Shirley."

I laugh. *Anne of Green Gables* is how we met and formed Story Club —named from the book as well. I was visiting my grandma as I did every summer, and she signed me up for swim lessons. Anh and I were both sitting on the bench waiting for class to start, reading *Anne of Green Gables*, which, in retrospect, given our age—nine—isn't that amazing, but at the time it felt like destiny. Because Robin and Anh were neighbors and already best friends, we convinced Robin to read the book, and thus Story Club was formed.

"I have to run sweetie. Drive safe."

"I always do."

Anh makes a kissy noise through the phone and hangs up.

I roll down the window. The trees are so dense, I can't see the ocean, but the salty tang in the air lets me know it's there. Sunlight spears through the branches, and I lower my rose gold aviator sunglasses. The car rounds a corner, and there it is, the ocean. White-capped waves breaking up an endless expanse of blue. I switch off the audiobook. "Cruel Summer" plays over the radio, and I put my hand out the window, relishing the fresh air on my arm while I take the exit off the 101.

On the very edge of town is a white stone coffee shop with tables out front that's closed now, but I make a mental note to go there tomorrow. I picture myself sitting at a window seat with my laptop and a perfectly made latte with a little foam heart on top, clacking away at my keys. My dual timeline mystery is coming along. I hope to have it finished by the end of summer, but how many times have I thought that before about a project? This time, though, nothing's stopping me, I have time to write.

The main street of the small town of Fortune Falls is like stumbling onto the set of a movie. Low brick buildings, mixed with others with weather-worn wooden siding, line the avenue, each business with a different color awning hanging above it, from faded red to sky blue.

The corner building is a bar with a massive, smashed sign hanging out front, only the *vern* of *Tavern* lit up. The bright-red wooden door is closed, but the neon sign in the window flashes open.

GPS informs me this is my turn toward the water. The road morphs into dirt. Finally, after some jarring bumps and clunks from my suitcases and boxes in the back, I'm at the two-story white house I'll call home for the summer. The late-afternoon sun shines on the wraparound porch like a spotlight, and bubbles of excitement fill my chest.

Stepping out of the car, I stretch my arms above my head. The house sits on a small hill, so the ocean is visible even from down here. The second-story view must be amazing.

Robin walks out, the screen door slamming behind her, and runs down the porch steps. "You made it!"

"Barely."

She throws her arms around me in a massive hug. I inhale her orchid shampoo, the same kind she's used since we were fifteen.

We part and look at each other. It's been years since we've seen each other in person—our girls' trip to Puerto Rico right after that awful book signing at The Nook.

Robin's long honey blonde hair hangs in loose waves down her back. Even though Robin and Nathan only got here a week ago, her normally fair skin is already a little tan.

Robin squeezes my hand. "It's so good to see your actual face, not on a Zoom screen."

I smile. "I was thinking the same thing."

She links arms with me, and we walk toward the house. "Let's get you a drink."

We climb the porch stairs, and I follow Robin to the kitchen, to the left of the entryway. It's delightful, with fern-colored cabinets and strawberry wallpaper. Robin pulls a bottle of rosé out of the fridge and sets it on the enormous kitchen island.

"We thought we could all go to The Vern for dinner. It's that cute little bar on the corner. Did you see it when you drove by?"

"Mm-hmm. Sounds good. Cozy table for three."

Robin takes two wineglasses out of the cupboard. "Not exactly."

"Oh, who else is coming?"

She gives us both generous pours and hands me my wine. "Actually, you're never going to guess who Nathan invited."

The cold liquid is bright on my tongue as I take a sip. She's always trying to fix me up. Robin loves love. So much, in fact, that she became a social media coordinator for a popular dating service. It's not that I don't like love. It would be great to meet someone and have something special, something that lasts, like what my grandparents had. But I'm not sure that kind of connection exists anymore. Anytime I've ever found it, it's left me worse off than when I started.

Robin is smiling widely. "It turns out he was besties in middle school with none other than…"

Footsteps come from the stairs, definitely more than one set. Nathan walks in the kitchen, followed closely by a tall, dark-haired man with eyes the color of moss in a shady forest.

My heart is in my throat.

"The guy who wrote that book you picked for Story Club."

The room tilts to the side as the wine sits heavy on my tongue. Robin's still speaking, but it sounds like it's through a paper towel tube.

My skin feels like the volume is turned up—the strings on the end of my shorts tickling my thighs, my soft shirt shifting against my stomach.

The suit jacket is gone, as are the ripped-up jeans. What hasn't changed from ten years ago is the beat-up band shirt hanging loose on his broad shoulders, this one with a little brown monkey on it.

I know this sensation of everything being more.

I know this man.

It's Ed.

SOULMATES

TEN YEARS AGO

S *oulmates.* I set the book down, and the last line I read trudges through my mind like the last mile of a long run. For a divorced woman on a journey of self-discovery, the author sure talks a lot about soulmates. Maybe she believes that to find herself, she must find her other half. I used to believe in another half. I was so sure everyone out there had that perfect person meant just for them. Just a few weeks ago, I was positive. Look at my grandparents. Up until recently I would've said look at my parents, but then they sat me down for the talk.

Not today. Today will not be brought down with such heavy thoughts. Letting out a long, slow breath, I take a sip of my almond milk latte, still too hot to drink. I should've gotten an iced one. I check the time again. Twenty minutes—I can be twenty minutes early.

Taking my coffee, I go to unlock my bike. I'm just digging the key out of my bag, deciding where to set my drink, when a blur of gray whooshes up and nearly slams into me. It weaves at the last second, catching my arm and sending my delicious latte plummeting to the ground. The cup opens up on impact. Coffee and almond milk splatter all over my sneakers and my cream thigh-high socks I bought from the boutique sock shop yesterday. Dumbstruck, I stare at my legs—my special *good luck, first day of my first job* socks are now ruined.

The blur stops a little way past me, still close enough that I catch a whiff of a faint, sweet, smoky scent. A mix of orange and clove. It's a guy, his skateboard still under his foot. The other that he used to stop looks like it's rearing to go. He's in a Velvet Underground T-shirt with a dark suit jacket over it, pins on the lapels—one that says Feminist. His eyes, the color of dewy grass that has caught the summer sun, are staring intensely at me.

"You alright?" he asks. His hair is dark but shaved close to his head. It matches the stubble, making an outline of his square jaw.

I'm so startled by his eyes, his jaw, his smell: I shake my head, unable to speak.

"Wait right here." He flips up his skateboard, picks up my cup off the sidewalk, and rushes into the coffee shop like it's all one swift movement. The threads on his jeans are almost shredded into nothing, threatening to break with each maneuver.

My socks aren't too bad. Nothing a Tide pen can't fix, hopefully. As I unlock my bike, the smacking sound of the man's skateboard hitting the concrete startles me.

"Gotta go. I'm so late, but I really am sorry."

He hands me a fresh cup then skates away, a dark blur once more. I sip my coffee; it's an almond milk latte just as I ordered before. Just below the lid is a small heart drawn in black sharpie. My lips curl up in a tiny smile. He was cute. Maybe he drew it, or it's entirely possible the barista drew it for him. As I walk around the corner pushing my bike, a tricky feat with a now full cup of coffee, I wonder what he was late for.

Neighborhood Books opens at ten, and that's when my shift starts. Today is my first day of my first job—a summer position at the bookstore in Old Town. Then I'll head back to Montana and off to college in the fall. My stomach drops into my all-white Adidas sneakers. Why is it when I'm nervous about one thing, my brain decides to scroll through all the things that make my heart want to leap out of my chest and run down the street?

When I approach the door, the sign is turned to Closed and all the lights are off. I'm still eight minutes early. I don't want to bother the opener while they're busy, so I wait outside.

Eight minutes go by. The lights are still off. The sign still turned firmly to Closed. Five more minutes. Each second that ticks by increases the erratic thundering of my heart. Did I get the day wrong?

Kat strolls down the street, her holographic Birkenstocks glinting in the sunshine. She gathers a handful of her long dark hair and puts it in a messy top knot and then waves when she catches sight of me.

"Hey. You can go in; you don't have to wait outside for me." She joins me by the entrance, her glossy lips pursing as she takes in the sign and the dark store. She checks her phone and sighs. "I see."

As she takes keys out of her *Great Gatsby* tote bag and unlocks the store, all the lights come on. She holds the door open for me, gesturing for me to go in first.

"Thanks."

Once inside, I'm greeted with "The Reigning Champ of the Teething Crowd" by Say Hi, a song I've played on a loop since I discovered it in April. The familiar melody works to ease the tension in my chest. It's not even new, and the fact that it's playing now feels like a sign I'm in the right place.

A loud noise then the smack of someone's sneakers on the hardwood floors echoes through the store. Running from the back is the man who almost killed me with his skateboard. Okay, killed is an exaggeration, but definitely the man who spilled my coffee, ruined my brandnew lucky first day socks, and possibly left a heart on my coffee cup.

"I'm here. We're open!" he yells as he passes by me to the door—my hair blows away from my face in wisps from the wind of his momentum.

He flips the sign to Open, while Kat straightens some books on the table by the entryway. She doesn't even look up as the Tasmanian ball of energy passes right by her.

"Sorry, Kat. The power went out, so my alarm didn't go off."

Now she looks at him, her dark-brown eyes shooting daggers. "The power went out? On D Street?"

He runs a hand over his shaved head; I can practically feel the prickly hair on my palm.

"It didn't go out so much as it got shut off. But I'm here now. Ready to work."

"We'll talk about it later at our meeting."

His lips set in a tight line, and I notice his Adam's apple bob with a large swallow.

"Come on over and meet Ed. Ed, this is our new employee, Hattie. You two should get along. You're both writers. Can you show her the ropes today?"

Despite all my best efforts to be a professional, Ed's lopsided smile melts my insides like butter on hot toast.

"Of course."

Kat makes her way to her office in the back and says over her shoulder, "I'm going to be doing the books if you need me."

Ed extends his hand to me, and I notice his knuckle tattoos spell out R-E-A-D. "Hattie. I was kicking myself for not asking your name earlier."

I smile and take his hand in mine. It's rough but warm. "Thanks for the fresh coffee."

"I was running late. Otherwise I would've stayed to apologize." His hand goes up to my hair and gives a strand a little tug, and my heart catches in my throat at his closeness. "I like the green."

It absolutely wasn't supposed to be green. My hair is a deep chestnut brown, and my eyes are blue. So, brown and blue are kind of my thing. I wanted a thick strand of turquoise in my hair to match my eyes, but it turned a weird, almost chartreuse color, and now it won't wash out.

"Ah, thanks." I push my hair behind my ear self-consciously.

"Come on. I'll show you how to count in."

Ed shows me where I can put my stuff and how to count the till for the day. I want to ask him if he drew the little heart, but I don't want to make things weird.

He asks, "So what do you write?"

I shrug. "Oh, I just mess around. One day I'd like to write a mystery novel, something dark, like Gillian Flynn."

He nods. "Cool."

"What about you?"

"Literary fiction, I hope. I'm finishing up my first novel now, thinking about sending it to some people."

Wow. I haven't even finished a whole novel yet, and here this guy is, already trying to publish one. He can't be that much older than me. "What's it about?"

He pulls himself up to sit on the back counter. "It's about this guy who wakes up one morning. He's out of coffee and still half drunk. He stubs his toe on his couch, and it really hurts, like the pain is so sharp the world stops for a nanosecond. It throbs all day, but what can you do for a busted pinky toe? Nothing, right? It starts a chain of events of minor inconveniences that leads to the apocalypse."

I laugh, more out of shock than the premise being all that funny. "Minor inconveniences?"

He smiles. "Yep. Turns out that's all the apocalypse is. It isn't some great rapture. Instead, it's just a buildup of annoyances, until everyone turns on each other. A sweater that shrank in the wash just enough to make you question if it got smaller or you got bigger. The store being out of the only cereal you like. Your favorite sock getting a hole in the toe."

"Socks being ruined is something I know all about." I resist the urge to cover my mouth. I can't believe I actually said that.

"From the spilled coffee?"

My shoulders rise and fall sheepishly, still a little surprised by my boldness. He hops off the counter and squats. His face is inches from my leg, his head below my carefully chosen denim skirt. My heart is hammering in my chest so hard it must actually be visible.

"You can hardly see the spots." He stands, his body close to mine. I catch the faint scent of oranges again.

A customer walks in, and he springs into action. "Welcome to the Neighborhood. Let me know if you need help finding anything."

Despite the fact that he's across the room, the heat from Ed's breath lingers on my thigh, leaving me frozen in place as my pulse starts to return to a normal pace.

CHAPTER 2
SUMMER SOLSTICE

Nathan goes straight to Robin and puts an arm around her waist and turns his attention on me. "Hey, you made it. How was the drive?"

"Long, but parts were beautiful."

"I've always wanted to drive cross country," Ed says with a sparkle in his eye.

My lips turn up. Ed has this energy that makes everything…fun—or he did ten years ago, anyway. My drive was long and boring, but seeing it through his eyes, it was also kind of cool or could've been.

I sigh. "I was so focused on making it here today. If I were to do it again, I'd make more stops."

"Yeah, got to take in the sights. Like there was probably the world's largest tea kettle somewhere along your way."

I laugh. "And I missed it trying to make good time."

Our gazes meet, and the hairs on my arms stand at attention.

"I'm Ed."

"We've met." That's not what I meant to say. I blame the long drive, the lack of coffee, the shock of seeing Ed after all these years. If he didn't remember me at the book signing three years ago, what makes me think he would remember me now?

Ed smiles, that quirky, irresistible lopsided smile that makes him look up to no good. "We have, haven't we?"

The tingles are back, like the pins and needles from my drive, but this is full body. We have. *We have?*

A cute little wrinkle appears on Robin's forehead as she asks, "Really?"

I toggle back and forth. What time should I bring up? The book event? Or should I bring up *that day*? Gulping wine, I make a quick decision. "Yeah, at one of your signings."

Ed's brow furrows as he runs a hand through his hair. "Oh?"

"In Helena. You were a great speaker. I loved the book, too."

He mutters, "Thanks," and turns to his phone.

It's like watching a garage door close, the light within slowly blocked out. I want to take it back, rewind the last part of this interaction, and do it over. Should I have brought up the day we shared together? Is that what he was thinking?

There's a beat of silence.

"I'm starving," Nathan says, rubbing his completely flat belly.

"Alright." Robin nuzzles closer into Nathan's side than looks to me. "Are you hungry, Hattie?"

Am I hungry? I can't tell. My body has gone into some kind of shock. I'm going to spend the summer with Ed.

"You guys go ahead. I need to wash that drive off. I'll meet you there in a bit."

"Rad." Nathan smiles. "Let me help you with your bags."

I throw Nathan the keys to my car. Robin shows me up the rich walnut stairs. The third one from the top creaks in a way that reminds me of Grandma's farmhouse. Her whole floor creaks at this point, not just the stairs.

"So," Robin purrs, "you went to Ed's signing?"

"I did." And it was a disaster, I think but don't say.

But him not recognizing me wouldn't mean anything to Robin. She doesn't know he's the man from *that day*. She and Anh know almost everything else about it. *Almost.* I didn't want to share his name, though. At the time, I didn't want to know if they already knew him from school or something. I didn't want to tell them his name and hear "oh yeah, he asked me to a dance in middle school" or "he's a dick that hits on all the girls." As we got older, I didn't tell them because I didn't want them Googling him or sending a DM on my behalf. I kept his name close to my chest, like a precious locket. I kept it just for myself.

"Yeah…" I answer, still deciding what to share.

Robin stops for a moment. "This is the bathroom. Straight across the hall is the linen closet. The large striped ones are beach towels, and the blue ones are for the bath. There's another bathroom downstairs, too."

I'm only half listening. Part of me is dying to tell Robin about Ed now. I clear my throat as she leads me down the hall. "You know that bookstore I worked at in New Haven?"

"Of course. Neighborhood Books. I went there the last time I visited my folks."

"Do you remember me telling you about my first day—"

"You mean the day you spent with your mystery man?" She opens the door at the end of the hall. "I thought this room would be perfect for you."

I step inside. The evening sun is shimmering through the bay window, catching the glass butterfly hanging in the center pane and throwing rainbows on the opposite wall. There's a window seat with lush velvet jewel-tone pillows. The walls are painted light blue, and in the corner by another window is a small white writing desk with a roll top cover. A lush white comforter covers the bed along with more velvet throw pillows. It's beautiful. Calm and luxurious. "I love it."

"What were you saying about the bookstore?"

There's a commotion in the hall, and Nathan walks in holding one suitcase, followed by Ed holding the other.

"Nothing," I quickly mutter.

Robin opens a door in the corner, showing me the small closet. "This house is a little quirky. The walls are super thin, so when you wake up at the crack of dawn as per usual…"

I laugh. "I'll be quiet."

Nathan and Ed set down the suitcases inside the room, near the door.

"Who's in the room next door?" I ask.

Robin crooks her thumb at Ed.

He smiles—what is it about that smile?—his green eyes catching the light. "Don't worry. I won't blast Bowie at all hours."

Having to hear "Golden Years" is the least of my worries.

They all head downstairs. After the door clicks shut, I kick off my Vans, flop onto the bed, and exhale all the air out of my body. This is wild. Ed is going to be living next door to me all summer. Sleeping, writing, fidgeting tatted-knuckled hands all over the place.

And yet he doesn't seem to remember me or our perfect day together. Maybe he thinks I don't remember. I'm the one who brought up the signing, after all. But if he didn't remember me then, why would he now?

Maybe he had more to drink during our perfect day than I thought, or maybe he's suffered a traumatic brain injury. Of all my theories over the years, that's the one I go back to the most. My least favorite, and most likely, theory is none of it meant as much to him as it did to me.

Eventually, I drag myself off the softest bed in the world and unpack my clothes in the closet. Grabbing a blue towel, I get into the shower. The hot water untangles the mess of knots in my shoulders from the drive and possibly from the stress of running into Ed and having him not remember me once again.

It's fine.

I exhale and lather my hair, the rose and ginger of my soap calming me. We'll carry on like that day ten years ago never happened. After my shower, I take extra care with my makeup. Nothing over the top, but I want to look good, *really good*.

The bar is a short stroll. I take my time, enjoying the ocean breeze on my bare legs in my blue sundress that I've been told brings out my eyes. The Vern is busier than I expected for a tiny town bar, but it *is* a Friday. The inside is dark with rich wood, hanging Tiffany lamps, and red vinyl booths. In the back is a pool table and behind that a dim hallway, but I don't see Robin, Nathan, or Ed anywhere.

The bartender finishes pouring a pitcher of light golden beer as I approach the bar. After handing it and a stack of glasses off, he comes over. His kind brown eyes crinkle at the corners as he smiles, black hair slicked back in a style reminiscent of Superman, a few grays salting the sides, and a nose that looks like it's never backed down from a fight. "What can I get for you?"

"Oh, um." I'm momentarily caught off guard. You have to actually order when you're standing in line for a drink. "Wine? Do you have any that aren't terrible?"

I smirk so he knows I'm joking, mostly.

"Nope, nothing but Boone's Farm here. Gals seem real fond of the strawberry flavor, but Blue Hawaiian is half off." His smile widens and I realize he's kidding. "We sell local wines by the glass."

"Oh, thank God. The summer was looking bleak there for a second."

"I'm Kyle." He slides an impressive wine list across the bar.

"Hattie." I take the menu in my hands, the paper well-worn and smooth under my fingertips.

"It's nice to meet you. Are you staying around here?"

"Yeah. Some friends and I are just down the street for the summer."

"You'll be in here a lot, then."

"I'm trying to save money, so not that often." I select a Cabernet out of the Willamette Valley, one of the less expensive ones on the list.

"Saving for what?"

My uncertain future, my lack of knowing where my next paycheck will come from. Instead of getting too deep with this person I just met, I shrug. "Life."

"Lucky for you"—Kyle takes a corkscrew to the bottle— "tenants within a two-block radius get a discount."

I laugh. "Really?"

He shrugs. "If they order from me, they do."

Heat rises to my cheeks. Is it my imagination, or is he flirting with me?

"I'm actually looking for my friends. Have you seen a tall woman with long blonde hair, in cutoffs and tank top?"

Kyle hands me my glass. Our fingers brush and our eyes lock. "Robin? They went out to the patio. It's out that way."

He points to a hall on the other side of the bar.

After thanking him, I take my glass, and feeling quite good about myself, I head past the pool table, down the dark hallway, to the open door lighting my way.

I step into the waning sunshine to a gravel yard filled with wooden picnic tables, bright-yellow umbrellas, and a fire pit in the corner surrounded by Adirondack chairs. Happy chatter and laughter fill the air with an almost imperceptible sound of the ocean underneath it, like someone forgot to turn off the white noise app on their phone.

Robin half stands from a table in the corner. "Over here!"

The table is full of food. There's a plate of fries, a hummus platter, nachos, a pitcher of beer, and both Nathan and Ed have burgers in front of them. Robin and Nathan are sitting next to each other, which leaves me the space on the bench next to Ed. My heart pounds in my ears.

I can do this. I can sit next to the man who's held a piece of my heart for years and doesn't even know it.

Setting my wine down first, I slide my legs into the picnic bench as gracefully as one can. The person who invented picnic tables and the person who invented short flirty sundresses should've had a little chat.

Ed turns his body slightly so he's half facing me.

"Hattie's also a writer," Robin says, holding her wine in one hand and a chip in the other.

I hate when she does this, pushing a connection. Plus, calling me a writer when I haven't finished a novel feels disingenuous. "More like an unemployed English teacher."

Robin makes a raspberry, waving me away. "You'll find a new job, no problem."

Ed smiles, warm and wholehearted, as he shifts his body on the bench so he's facing me even more. "What do you write?"

I'm mid drink—trying to hide behind my glass—and swallow a little too quickly. The wine goes down the wrong pipe. I sputter for breath, my cheeks flaming hot, eyes watering. Ed pats my back, sending electric pulses all the way to my toes.

"You alright?"

Am I alright? I just need to pretend that I don't remember our day together, either. Only, I've never been good at pretending things aren't the way they are. With my parents pretending to be in love for "the sake of the family" for so long, you'd think I'd be a pro. It had the opposite effect. I'm a terrible liar.

Should I just bring it up? What's the worst that could happen? He could not remember our day together at all, instead of just not realizing it was me, and what's left of the romantic in me would be splattered like one of the many casualties on my windshield. I'll live the rest of my days alone. Maybe I'll get a cat or a fish. I will leave all the boxes on my dream life list unchecked.

Nope. I'll just pretend.

"I'm good," I manage to whisper. His hand falls from my back, and my skin feels cold in its absence.

There's mischief in the upturned corners of Robin's lips. "Ed was asking what you write?"

I glare at her. She's trying to fix us up, in her extremely unsubtle ways. "Murder stuff."

Ed's eyebrow arches. "Like true crime?"

"No, mysteries, sometimes thrillers. There's always a murder."

"Anything I may have read?" Ed asks as he dips a fry in ketchup and pops it into his mouth.

There's a beat of silence that threatens to swallow me whole as the last question runs circles in my head. I'm nearly thirty and not published yet. Being a writer and owning my own bookstore were my two dreams growing up, and I haven't done either.

Robin rushes to fill the gap in conversation. "We read your book, you know—"

I will Robin not to say it. *Don't say it.*

"Hattie picked it for book club." There it is. Now he's going to think I'm some kind of super fan, going to his signings, talking about his book in Story Club.

He finishes chewing. "Which one?"

Which? I hadn't realized he wrote another one. After that signing, I stopped searching him on the internet, and I quit all social media after high school.

"*Vex*," I answer.

"Sounds about right. What's on the docket for this month?"

"It's not a monthly club. When we were little, Hattie used to visit every summer—"

Ed is nodding slowly. "From Montana."

My heart is beating fast. Did I say I'm from Montana? Robin and Nathan could've mentioned that's where I drove from today. Honestly, I'm so tired I may have said it, and I don't remember. I set my wine down, deciding I don't need any more tonight.

"Right." Robin smiles brightly. "We each pick one book for the three months of summer."

"What are the books this time?"

"*The Motorcycle Diaries*," Robin says.

Nathan tips an imaginary hat. "You're welcome, by the way."

Robin snuggles into Nathan's side as she finishes, "*The Likeness* by Tana French and *Beach Read* by Emily Henry."

Ed makes a face—not one I can entirely read—as he chews a large bite of burger.

"You want in?" Robin asks.

I gasp—I can't help it. We don't let people into Story Club. It's the three of us, that's it. No boyfriends, no girlfriends, nobody else. Why would she invite Ed?

"I have to work on my book. It's due to my editor at the end of the summer, but I'll read one if I have time."

I'm relieved he basically politely declined. "What are you working on?" I ask, proud of myself for pulling it together enough to join the conversation.

"It's a novel about a time slip. A man meets a woman, and they slide through a vortex to the future."

"Ooh, that sounds interesting." I grab some pita.

"Yeah, it does." He laughs. "But so far, it's not. At all. I have a lot of work ahead, and I'm not sure if I should scrap the idea and do something else."

"I know what you mean. I've hit a point in my mystery, too, where I don't know where to go with it. It feels flat, and I can't quite put my finger on it."

Robin slams her wine down on the table, her hands flapping. "Oh my God. You guys! You should do a genre switch, just like that book we're reading!"

Ed backs up reflexively, but there's only so far you can go at a picnic table.

Robin's enthusiasm can be a lot for some people, but it's one of the things that I love about her. "The Emily Henry one?"

"Yes." Robin points to me with her bright-red, sensibly short nail. "You write a speculative literary fiction book." She turns her finger on Ed. "And you write a mystery. It solved all their problems in the book, and they fell madly—"

My glare stops her from finishing that sentence.

"It might shake up your writing process anyway," Robin says then takes a healthy drink of her wine.

I know she's trying to find ways to throw us together, but this isn't a terrible idea.

Ed's dark brows are knitted together in a look of deep thought. It's so sexy, I bite my bottom lip to stop myself from taking a finger and smoothing out the wrinkles.

"Hmm. A mystery." Ed nods slowly. "Might make for a fun summer."

I DON'T WANNNA GROW UP

TEN YEARS AGO

Patient is not a word I would've associated with Ed when he ran into me on the street. But as he shows me how to enter an inventory number for the third time, it strikes me that he is. After I successfully enter in a tiny plastic frog and we delete the sale, we move on to shelving books.

"If you don't know the genre, you can leave it on the cart behind the counter and let someone else put it away."

"I think I can figure out the genres of the books, Edward."

"It took me longer than I'd care to admit to figure out some of them, Harriet." He laughs. "My name is not Edward, though."

"Ed's not short for anything?"

"Oh, it's short for something, just not Edward."

"What's it a nickname for?"

A tiny smirk pulls at the corner of his mouth, but he doesn't say.

"Come on. You can tell me. I'll tell you who I'm named after."

"Harriet Tubman."

"Nope."

His green eyes search the ceiling and send a tiny buzz straight to my toes.

"Huh. I'm not sure I know any other Harriets." He snaps his fingers, and his face lights up. "The turtle."

"The turtle? Like a Ninja Turtle? Wasn't the girl one named Ashley? I never got into that cartoon."

He scoffs. "Um, no. The girl was April O'Neil, and she wasn't a turtle. She was a reporter who helped them. Either way, that's not what I meant. I was talking about the little turtle that learns all the lessons. He has a younger sister."

Ed runs away, off into the children's section. From my spot at the counter, I can see into that section perfectly. He goes right to the shelf, pulls a book, and then he's back in a blur, quick as he left, this time holding a copy of *Franklin's Baby Sister*.

"Truly impressive detective work, but no."

He slumps on the counter, burying his head in his hands. "I give up."

"*Harriet the Spy*. It was my mom's favorite book as a kid." I always hated my name growing up, wishing I'd been named Taylor or Hannah or Madison. But my mom said I should be grateful for a unique name. Her name is Sarah, and she had five other Sarahs in her kindergarten class. When I was young, though, I would've given my bike away for a name that just blended into the crowd.

"Huh." Ed says, startling me out of my thoughts. "I don't even know what my mom's favorite book is now, let alone when she was a kid. She's more the *have a few beers in the backyard to relax* kind of lady. That's rad, though."

A small swell of pride blooms in my chest. It's *rad*. Maybe Mom was on to something. "Your turn."

He blows out a long breath and heads back up to the counter as I follow.

"Come on. I won't tell a soul."

He smiles wide again and grips me by each arm, looking deep into my eyes. *He is touching me. Ed is touching me with his large hands and looking at me with his mossy green eyes.* My knees are jelly. If I swooned right now, would he catch me?

His voice is low. "You promise not to tell anyone?"

I nod.

"Promise?"

"I don't even live here, so who would I tell?"

He lets me go, and it feels like getting to the other side of a loop de loop on a roller coaster. Suddenly, the world is right side up again. He still doesn't say his name, though.

"I promise."

He lets out a long breath. "It's short for Edgar."

"Edgar?" I laugh. Of all the names I thought he might say, that one didn't occur to me. I thought maybe Theodore, or Edmund, but Edgar?

He nods with his eyes closed, like it pains him to admit it.

"With a name like that, you should be writing horror. Is your middle name Allen?"

He ruffles my hair, and my scalp tingles at his touch. "And you should write middle grade."

I stick my tongue out at him.

"What did you mean, you don't live here? Where do you live?"

"Montana."

"Hell of a commute."

I laugh. "I stay with my grandparents for the summers. Have since I was a baby. She lives here—well, just a little outside of town on a farm."

"Ahh. Why get a job if you're visiting? Couldn't you just loaf at your grandparent's? Eat their food, watch movies…"

"I'm saving up for college. Anyway, spending all day in a bookstore sounds more fun."

"Really?"

I shrug. "I love bookstores. Someday I want to own my own." My cheeks burn at the admission. I only ever talk about that with Mom, Grandma, Anh, and Robin. I actually took a gap year, thinking maybe I'd skip college and open my bookstore instead, but Mom talked me out of it. Said I should see what career options there are, try some things. She said she'd help with tuition.

He smiles as he gets a stack of books to put away, and I notice the tattoos on his other hand that spell out W-R-IT-E on each knuckle, the tiny *I* and *T* sharing his ring finger. "Bookstores are pretty rad."

A woman walking hand in hand with a small boy with curly brown hair walks in. The boy drops his mom's hand and runs straight to Ed. "Is it time? Are we late?"

Ed's eyes go wide as he looks at his watch. "Nope, you're early. We'll start in about twenty minutes."

More adults with children come in and head back to the children's section.

Ed whispers to me under his breath, "I almost forgot about story time today." His lips turn up at the corners. "You distracted me."

I straighten the Post-it pad on the counter, take a pen out of the cup, and then put it back. "Me? I'm super busy working."

He laughs. "I'm going to grab my guitar from the back. If anyone asks, we start at 11:30. Just point them in that direction."

"Got it."

He moves past me, but his spicy sweet scent lingers. Ed is cute, and funny, and he does story time for kids. Is he even real, or did he leap off one of the pages of one of these books?

At 11:33, Ed perches on a tiny purple chair in front of a horde of kids of all ages and sizes sitting with their families. The little boy with the curls is right at Ed's feet, his face shining as he stares up at him.

"Okay, little dudes and dudettes! Do you know what time it is?"

"Story time!" they all scream.

"Yep." Ed holds up *Dragons Love Tacos* by Adam Rubin and begins to read. He does voices, makes faces, and the kids eat it up. Once the story is over, he grabs his guitar to the cheers of the children. The light coming from the window highlights the strong planes of his face as he tilts his head to look at his fingers. He turns the knobs this way and that then starts to play.

The chords are familiar, but I can't place the song at first, until he gets to the line that gives it away.

"I don't wanna grow up."

The kids are dancing and hopping around. Ed stands and stomps his foot on the wood floors to the beat. It's glorious, so amazing in fact, I realize I've been ignoring a customer trying to ask me a question.

"Sorry. What was that?"

I try to focus on the customer, on doing my job, but my eyes keep drifting to Ed. He catches my gaze and winks.

CHAPTER 3
SATURDAY, JUNE 22ND

It's against my nature to sleep in. Even if I'm up until three a.m., my body still wakes me up promptly at six eleven. Why six eleven? Who knows? Because of the time difference, I am up this morning at five eleven, early even for me. I guess circadian rhythms don't adjust for time zones.

Ed's door is closed. I press my ear to the door, holding my breath as I listen to him breathing deeply. After I wash my face, I grab my neon blue running backpack. Of all the gear I've acquired since I started trail running a few years ago, this is by far my favorite. It has a bladder of water with one of those little hoses, a small pocket for a snack, and a side pocket where I can easily reach my pepper spray. Out in Montana, I carried it mostly for bears, but it'd work on a man too. It's always best to err on the safe side as a woman running alone. I lace up my trail shoes, sling the backpack over one shoulder, and get in the car. Nathan said it wasn't that far to the trailhead, but I want to save the miles for the trail itself.

The sky looks like a painting, a thin layer of clouds veiling the blue and gold beneath and a light mist hovering over the ocean. The sun is strong, though, and will probably burn through the haze soon enough.

With the GPS, I find the trailhead easily and pull into a gravel lot with a carved wooden sign saying Crescent Trail. I stretch a little and put my headphones on, the kind that sit over the ears so I can still hear my surroundings, and turn on my new audiobook, *Darkslide*. Ed's second book. I bought it last night after dinner with Grandma and listened to it on the drive back. So far, it's good but slow.

Pressing Play, I start my run—the dirt soft and springy under my feet, like running on clouds. The trees are massive, the morning sun peeking through them. I find a rhythm with my feet and breaths. Through the gaps in the trees, I catch glimpses of the ocean, waves rolling in. One thing I love about trail running is how much you can lose yourself in your surroundings. I never feel as close to nature as when I'm sweating through it.

The trail goes up, and I pump my arms to help my momentum. In the background, footfalls thud down the path. I stop. They're getting louder. Probably just another person out for a morning run. But the other, less rational voice inside me pipes up. *Or a serial killer out hunting.*

As the footfalls get louder, the less rational voice wins out, and I duck behind a tree, pepper spray in hand. The sound stops right next to me on the other side. *Oh shit.* They know I'm here. They know I'm hiding. *I'll take them by surprise.* I jump out, pepper spray at the ready.

Ed raises his hands and stumbles back. "It's me."

I lower the pepper spray. "What are you doing?"

"I was out for a run, and I saw you duck behind the tree. I was going to make sure you were okay but then thought you might be… um…indisposed."

My mouth falls open. "You thought I was pooping!"

Ed laughs, holding up both hands in surrender. "I wasn't sure. Things get moving sometimes when you run."

"Ew. I'm aware, but also, ew. No, I was just…" Hiding—no, he doesn't need to know my excessive true-crime-documentary watching has me worried about serial killers. "Nothing."

He wipes his brow. "Want to run together?"

My heart leaps as my mind flashes to Ed and me traveling around New Haven, me on my bike, him on his board.

"Sure." I try to turn off the audiobook without Ed seeing my phone. I don't want him to know I'm reading his second book. Switching off my headphones instead of turning off the audiobook, it comes blaring out of my phone speaker at full blast. I fumble and eventually shut it down.

Ed's smiling. "Those words sound familiar."

I sigh. "I'm reading *Darkslide.*"

He's beaming, but he quickly changes his face to a serious expression. "Ah."

We run together up the trail, finding a pace that works for both of us.

"So," Ed begins. "How many mysteries have you written?"

Six. Six unfinished novels, each with a piece of me that will never see the light of day. Maybe someday I'll go back and write the last chapters. Only one was ever to a place I would call done. Still, I wouldn't let myself type the words "The End." There's always room to improve, edit, polish. I shrug. "A few."

I glance over at him, trying to read his face for a reaction. He nods, opens his mouth to speak, but then closes it again.

"What?" I say. "What is it?"

"That's awesome. I've only written the two. *Vex* and *Darkslide.* Well, and I'm working on my third."

Part of me hates him for this. Massive best-seller, literary darling, on his very first book. For him, it was just that simple. It doesn't hurt that he's extremely easy on the eyes, but his work is also...exceptional. It's stupid.

Not that my writing is bad. It's finishing it. I get to the end of the book, and suddenly I'm paralyzed with fear. What if I wrote it all wrong? What if I'm not starting in the right place? How can I move forward if I don't fix those crucial things first? The one that I nearly finished once it was finally to a place that anyone would consider complete, I sent to beta readers, and the feedback was clear. It was nowhere near done.

My thoughts are swirling, so I run my way out of them, charging up the hill, setting my destination as the guardrail and a break in the trees up ahead. Ed increases his pace, but I still make it to the rail first. Not that it was a race, although if it had been, I would've won.

We're both sweating and panting. I place my hands on the rickety, weathered rail, careful not to put any weight on it. If I did, I'd probably end up on the rocks below, the waves taking my body swiftly out to sea. Ed's doubled over with his hands on his knees, trying to catch his breath. Since my runs are usually at high altitude, I have a slight advantage.

Once Ed catches his breath, he leans against the railing, and my stomach lurches. He has a twinkle in his eyes, one I recognize from *that day*. "I have an idea."

My stomach tightens. Is it excitement? Anxiety? A mix of both? He said those exact words ten years ago before one of the most memorable nights of my life.

I nod, unable to look away from where his body is making contact with the old wood rail. "You shouldn't lean on that. I don't think it's sturdy."

He moves away with a small smirk. "We can help each other."

"How?"

"I'm not suggesting we do a genre switch or anything, but I'm into the idea of adding a mystery to my book. Well, you're reading *Darkslide*. What do you think of it?"

"Um..." I falter. "I'm just at the beginning."

I start to run again, this time back down the trail and at a slower pace. Ed follows.

"It's slow as shit. Barely anyone read it, and the people who did most likely fell asleep."

He's not wrong. "How can I help?"

"Well, you can help me with the tension. You're the mystery expert. What makes a page turner?"

I nod slowly. I can do that. Pacing is actually one of my strong suits. "And how are you suggesting to help me?"

"I can get you published."

My heart skips a beat, picturing holding one of my books in my hands. But how can he promise that? Maybe I misunderstood.

"What?"

"I mean, not directly, but I can help you polish your manuscript and help with your pitch package."

Concisely, talking about my novel is definitely not my strong suit. I'd rather write an entirely new novel than a one-sentence pitch. But I'm still not sure about this plan. I'm not sure I'm ready to let myself get close to Ed again.

"I can also introduce you to some people. My friend has a book launch party in Portland in July. You can come with me. There will be a ton of industry people and other writers there. You'll like Bill. He's a good dude. And there's the Oregon Book Awards at the end of the summer. You can be my date."

I laugh. "Your date?"

"Not like a date-date, but you can come with me. There will be a ton of agents and editors there. I can even steer a few conversations to the amazing novel you're working on."

"How do you know it's amazing? You haven't even read it."

He smirks, and my stomach somersaults. "If it's not already, with my help, it will be. We'll make our own writer's workshop."

I would love to go to that dinner. And I wouldn't mind a fresh pair of eyes on my manuscript, especially attractive green eyes. I sweep that thought away. *No.* I'm not going down that road with him again. What I meant is best-selling, been through the publishing process, professional eyes.

"Okay."

Ed's smile lights up the trail. "Okay?"

"Let's do it."

He jumps, fist in the air—so reminiscent of the final shot of *The Breakfast Club,* I laugh.

We shift focus to the task at hand, running the rest of the way in silence. Moss hangs off the trees in great swaths, catching the morning sun and making everything look like we are in an enchanted forest. When we make it to the parking lot, it's still just my car.

"How did you get here?"

"I ran. There's a trail down that way to the beach. It's not too far.

Hard, though. You always see people on TV running gracefully on the beach, but it's a real slog through all that sand."

"'If this were only cleared away,' they said, 'it would be grand.'"

Ed laughs, a booming belly laugh that fills me with joy and pride that I made him do that.

"*Alice in Wonderland*?"

I make an exaggerated frown. "*Through the Looking Glass*."

"Ah, of course. I stand corrected."

I dig my key fob out of my bag and point it at my car. "Want a ride?"

"Yeah."

In the car and back on the road, we work out the details of our workshop. First, we'll swap manuscripts and give each other feedback. Then we'll go from there. It's not as detailed a plan as I usually make, but I'm going with the flow. Living in the moment. It's better to just leave the past in the past.

WHAT'S YOUR SIGN?

TEN YEARS AGO

After shelving more books, I head back to the counter, and Ed is chatting with a young guy with shoulder-length bleached hair. They clasp hands in that dude way that makes it seem like their hands are hugging rather than a shake. "See you there."

"You know it."

Ed turns his green eyes on me. "What are you doing later?"

"Today?"

He laughs. "Yeah."

"I'm not sure."

"My friends are having a little thing for me… It's at the beach. Anyway, do you want to come? You have your bike, right? We could ride together; there's a paved path that'll take us all the way there."

I nod but keep my lips tightly closed. If I open it, the butterflies that are wildly flapping in my stomach may fly right out of my mouth. We arrange to meet at the park after I'm off work.

Ed heads into the Westerns section, a stack of books in his hands.

I send two quick texts under the counter. The first to Grandma:

Me: I'm going to sleep over at Robin's tonight. :)

And the second to Robin:

Me: Met a cute boy. He asked me out tonight, but I think it's a friend thing. Can I sleep at your place?

Then I put my phone back in my bag. Kat comes out of the back and lets me know she has to run some errands, saying she'll be back in a bit. She props the doors open when she leaves. The cool breeze on my warm skin is refreshing.

Taking a stack of books, I fumble around trying to find the right places to put them. I'm about to put away the last book in my pile, an astrology book in the New Age section, when a crocodile puppet pops out from around the corner of the shelf, sending my heart to my throat.

"What's your sign?" Ed asks in a Muppet voice, making it look like the crocodile is talking.

"Libra."

He comes out from around the corner. "Libra, huh? I'm a Pisces."

I open the book in my hand and flip to Pisces. "Let's see… You are empathetic—"

"Debatable."

"Creative—"

"Hopefully."

"Generous—"

"On a good day."

"Idealistic."

"Sounds about right."

"Lazy, closed-off, moody—"

"There I am. Wow, these books are uncanny. So accurate." His eyes widen in exaggerated shock.

I laugh.

"What's it say about you?" He takes the book from my hand, and our fingers brush the slightest bit as he does. It's like his skin is a live wire. It sends a shock straight to my core. I pull up my knee socks that haven't slipped at all, just for something to do.

He smiles, a slow, sexy grin that intensifies the electricity running through me. I'm suddenly hyper aware that we're alone in the store together. "You're romantic…"

My cheeks burn, and I hope they aren't as pink as they feel.

"Charming, artistic, diplomatic, good listener."

I shrug. "Maybe."

"Indecisive, vain, manipulative, and you hate conflict."

The word conflict immediately brings my thoughts to my parents. It's not wrong. I do hate conflict, and so do they. Which is why they lived for years being miserable together. Until I graduated. They didn't want me to go through high school with divorced parents. So, they waited until the day after graduation and then told me they were splitting. They don't love each other anymore, haven't for a long time. My dad reconnected with his high school girlfriend on Facebook —his true soul mate. I immediately deleted all my social media. It's all fake anyway, just like my parents' marriage was. They lived a lie for years so they didn't have to confront the truth or at least until graduation.

Ed's looking at me with soft eyes. "Hey…"

He throws the book over his shoulder like it's a wadded-up piece of paper. "It's just a silly book. It doesn't know you."

I laugh and can't quite believe he just threw a book. Crossing the store quickly, I kneel on the hardwood floor to pick it up. "I'm not sure I buy all the astrology stuff."

"Me either." He pulls out another book off the shelf. "I'm much more into palm reading. Far more accurate science." His smile is infectious. "Come on."

He carries the book back toward the counter, and I follow on butterfly wings.

Ed opens the palm-reading book on the counter and uses the pen cup to keep the side that keeps curling closed open.

He reads for a minute. "Uh-huh, okay. Yes. Let me see your hand."

Suddenly, there's concrete in my throat. I swallow hard to try to get it down, but it's still there. I offer my hand, and Ed takes it in his. He squints, moving his face extremely close to my palm, his breath hot on my hand.

He moves his face back and takes his finger, softly tracing the line from my thumb to the base of my palm. Heat rushes straight to my thighs, and my cheeks warm at his touch, so light it almost tickles. I want to pull away, and I want to lean into the feeling at the same time. I want to snap the air like a cat that's had too many pets.

"Hmm. I think you have water hands, but they could be air."

"What's the difference?"

"Well, your fingers are spindly like air hands—"

"Spindly? Who you calling spindly?"

He smiles. "But they're soft and narrow like water. Let's say they're water." He consults the book again and reads aloud. "You are fueled by compassion and imagination. You're also extremely sensitive, and your feelings are easily hurt."

I frown, embarrassed how shockingly accurate that all is. Ever since I was a kid, my mom always said, *You're so sensitive, Hattie. Lighten up.* Like my feelings were heavy. She was right—they were—but telling me I should feel them less just made me lonely and anxious. So, when I was sad about something, not only was I sad, I was also worried that I was being too sad.

Ed traces a line near the base of my fingers. "This is your heart line. It tells about your relationships, both romantic and friendship."

I hold my breath, waiting to hear what my palm reveals about my love life.

"Since it starts below your index finger, you are content in your relationships and tend to have long, lasting ones."

"That's true of my friends."

"But not your boyfriends?"

My face is on fire. "I haven't had a serious boyfriend."

"You haven't?"

I shake my head.

"No fella back in…where again?"

"Montana—Helena. No. I mean…there was this one guy, Brandon…but he moved so…We kept dating for a while. We were in love. We promised to text and call all the time, but it turned into me texting him, waiting for a reply."

"That's shitty."

I shrug, wanting it to seem lighter than it felt. "We were young."

Ed moves on, tracing another line so delicately, it brings me back to the bookstore.

"This is your lifeline. It's a deep groove, suggesting that you have full rich experiences."

I think I have full experiences. I *try* to live in the moment. Once, I read that living in the present is the key to true happiness. I won't bore you with how many times I have to remind myself of this while I'm ruminating on some mundane detail from the past—something everyone else has long forgotten that I'm still running circles around in my head. Like the boy who never texted me back. So, it's still a work in progress.

Ed traces another line, bringing me back to the present that I strive to live in.

"This is the line of destiny. Hmm… Yours is narrow and a little faint, so you are not likely to be bound by a common destiny."

"That sounds terrifying."

Ed laughs and drops my hand.

"Wait, what about you?"

He holds out his palm to me, and I consult the book.

"You definitely have air hands—square palms and long fingers." My hand is starting to sweat. "It says you are easily distracted and can be anxious if not properly stimulated."

"What was that? I wasn't paying attention."

"Ha, ha."

"I think you were saying something about being properly stimula—"

I cut him off, not able to handle the rest of that sentence while holding his hand in mine. "Your heart line starts at your middle finger, so you are restless in relationships."

Ed takes his hand back. A customer walks in, and he says, "Let us know if you need anything."

My hand feels cold and weightless. He swipes the book and goes to put it back on the shelf. I wonder if the last thing I said hit a nerve.

CHAPTER 4
SUNDAY, JUNE 23RD

When we get back to the house, I hop into the shower. By the time I get out, there is an email at the top of my inbox from Ed with his manuscript attached. I pad downstairs and grab a cup of coffee and a banana. Then I head back up, tuck myself in the window seat with my baby blue writing journal, open the Word document, and dive in. Ed's use of language is astounding, and this is just an early draft. It makes me a little jealous. But he's right—the pacing is off if he wants people to keep turning pages. I add comments to the document, making sure to note things I like as well as things not quite working for me, and jot down some thoughts in my journal.

I'm not even sure how much time has passed when there is a knock on my door. "Come in."

Robin walks in with a cup of coffee, a freshly washed face, and bright eyes. "You look hard at work for a Sunday."

Closing my notebook, I shrug. "I guess."

"We're going to go to this glass-blowing place then stop for lunch on the way back at this cool bar on the top of a cliff called the Hideout. Do you want to come?"

I stand and stretch my muscles, feeling stiff from the run and then the complete inactivity that followed. "That sounds great."

Robin claps. "Yay. Ed is coming too." She sings the last word, and her meaning is clear. "You two went for a run together this morning, I hear."

I nod but don't say anything, just dig my sandals out of the closet.

"Both runners, both writers, both smoking-hot single people." She waggles her eyebrows and has an absolutely devilish smile.

"Don't."

She raises both hands like a criminal surrendering. "Don't what? I'm just saying a little romance wouldn't be the worst thing that could happen this summer."

Nathan and Robin are nearly engaged, clearly headed that way, but no one has popped the question yet. Anh and Melissa are engaged. Melissa asked Anh in the most romantic Valentine's Day proposal earlier this year, spelling it out in rose petals on the hardwood floor of their glamorous condo in LA, the kind that only two lawyers can afford. And I am the lonely friend. The divorced friend. The one they're always trying to fix up with somebody—sometimes it feels like with *anybody*.

They don't understand. It makes it harder to put yourself out there after being so thoroughly squashed. But I want a family someday. I want to check one thing off my list of life goals. I want to find love, like the one my grandparents shared.

But not with Ed.

I can work with him on our writing. I wouldn't even mind running together again, but I will not let myself fall head over heels for him. Not this time.

"Please don't try to fix me up. I just want to spend the summer finishing my book and looking for a new job. Okay?"

Robin's smile falls. "I worry about you, honey. I know Chad broke your heart, but that was years ago."

"It's only been three years. Either way, this isn't about Chad."

"Then why haven't you had a boyfriend since then?"

"I haven't met the right guy."

Robin puts a hand on my arm. "Maybe Ed's it? He could be the one."

I turn toward the window so she can't see the flush in my cheeks. "He's not. Trust me, he's not."

The faint sound of a door closing makes my heart leap into my throat.

Even if it was Ed, what do I care if he heard me? It's better he knows up front; there will be no hookups involved in our writer's workshop.

I grab my bag. "I'm ready to go when you are."

NATHAN OFFERS to drive since he's the only one who's been to the Hideout before. Robin takes shotgun, naturally, which leaves me in the back with Ed. The SUV is large. There's no real danger of my leg accidentally brushing his, but we are close enough that I can smell him —clove and orange, spicy and sweet, just like he smelled a decade ago.

The drive up the coast is as windy as it is stunning. The sky clouded over, making the water a deep gray blue. Large rocks jut out as wave after wave of foamy white water crash against them, like a fly buzzing in the ear of a Clydesdale.

Birds dive dangerously low to the cars as we drive over an iron bridge into Washington State. We pass a road sign for Cape Disappointment.

"Wow." I laugh. "They really didn't pull any punches when they named this place."

Nathan chuckles. "Some people say they named Fortune Falls as a direct response."

Ed sits forward in his seat, his eyes lit up. "Like look how much luck we have down here in Oregon, while you're all up there in Washington, disappointed and shit."

We all laugh.

"Exactly," Nathan says.

"Why were they disappointed?" I ask, looking out at the water again. "No one could possibly be unhappy with a view like this, could they?"

"He thought it was just this bay, and he was looking for the mouth of the Columbia. He was wrong, though; he just didn't see it."

"He fucked up, and now the cape must forever suffer his disappointment. Terrible," Ed says as he furiously makes notes on his phone.

We pull into a gravel lot of a small building that looks more like a mechanic shop than a tourist destination. It has a wide garage door, rolled open. Ornate, colorful glass balls, some large, some tiny, surround the building; a narrow path into a garden is lined with them.

We get out of the car and enter the shop. A wave of heat rushes to my face. Even with the open door, it is sweltering in here. There is an older couple browsing the shelves of glass ornaments, the woman smiling from ear to ear. A red-haired man dressed in blue jeans and a heavy-looking khaki apron approaches us, a face mask pushed up on his forehead.

"Welcome in. Feel free to look around. Any green ball is on sale today, fifty percent off."

Robin smiles. "We'd like to learn how to blow glass."

"Grand. All of you, or…"

Robin is nodding while Ed is shaking his head, still typing on his phone.

Nathan grasps his shoulder. "Come on. Don't be a spoilsport. Yes, all of us."

"Great. Look around, and I'll let you know when I'm ready for you. You'll all have to decide who goes first. It's a one-at-a-time thing."

We decide I'll go first, and Robin will go next, then Nathan, and Ed is going to go for a walk.

"Alrighty—who's up?"

I step forward while Nathan and Robin look around hand in hand. Going through all the motions, I learn step by step how to mold the molten glass. I haven't made anything with my hands like this since the last time I spent any real time with Dad. I'm embarrassed about the tears forming in the corner of my eyes.

Muttering my thanks, I rush into the fresh air without a word.

THE GARDEN IS like something out of a fairy tale. There's a wooden bridge with a small creek babbling under it. On the other side, there are pockets of wild roses, lavender, and daisies lined by colorful glass balls. I let the tears fall. I'm alone, so what does it matter? But then I hear a deep voice that sends shivers to my toes.

"Oh, come on. It couldn't have been that bad." Ed smiles from a wooden bench, holding his phone in both hands.

I swipe at my tears while he moves over on the bench.

"What happened? Do I need to fight somebody?"

Taking a seat, I run my palm on the arm rest, the painted wood smooth under my palm. "No, nothing like that. I used to make pottery with my dad. Growing up, he was always throwing clay on the wheel in the workshop behind our house. He would've loved this."

Ed dips his head in understanding. "Oh, I'm so sorry for your loss."

"No," I say quickly. "He's not dead."

Ed's brow furrows in the most adorable wrinkle. He has a very serious face most of the time—strong jaw, prominent cheekbones, piercing eyes—but when he's confused, he looks more like a sweet wrinkly puppy.

"Text him, then. *Dad, try glass blowing*...yadda yadda."

"We don't text much."

"Why not?"

I shrug. "When I graduated from high school, my parents got divorced. They sold the house, and my dad moved across the state. He has a new house, a new wife, new kids. When I visit, I feel out of place. Over the years, we slowly lost touch. Like a thread on a sweater that was pulled one day, until suddenly you wake up cold. You know?"

He smiles. "That's a very writer brain analogy. It's good though. You should write it down."

My cheeks warm at the compliment. "Are you close with your parents?"

He purses his lips. "I was close with my mom when I was a kid, I thought. But I've never met my dad. He left when I was a baby."

"I'm sorry. I didn't know." Had he told me that on the perfect day and I forgot? I know I told him about my parents getting a divorce. I was positive I remembered every second of that day, but now I'm not so sure. Not that it matters. Ed's clearly forgotten the whole thing.

"It's fine. I was a handful." He chuckles.

"Still are, I'm sure."

"Heyyyy."

We both laugh, but it fades quickly. I put a hand on his arm; his skin is warm from sitting in the sun. "Every baby is a handful."

He nods absently, but I can tell he's not really hearing me. I try changing the subject so he doesn't lose interest in the conversation all together. "What are you doing on your phone?" I raise my eyebrows. "Candy Crush?"

"Candy Crush? What year is it? No."

I laugh.

"I got an idea from Cape Disappointment. What if one mistake marred not just the life of the person who made it for eternity but everyone they ever came in contact with? And what if, in this case, it was a murder?"

"Hmm, sounds interesting. What about the time travel manuscript?"

"Yeah, so instead of going into the future. These two people have to go back in time to solve the murder. If they can find out who did it, they can fix the terrible future. They fall in love along the way. But if they solve the murder and stop it, the pair will also never meet."

Goose bumps rise on my arms. "Ooh, that's good."

His smile is so wide, I expect a cartoon twinkle to appear.

Robin pops up on the path. "You two ready to roll?"

We get back in the car and drive up, up, and up a windy patch of road that eventually gives way to gravel. We make it to the top just as car sickness is about to sink its teeth into me. Usually I'm fine in the car. It's just all the twists and turns. I hop out, gulping the fresh air.

The building looks like something Frank Lloyd Wright would be proud of, all sharp angles. The deck juts out over the cliff. There's no sign, nothing that denotes this is a restaurant instead of a private home, except the full parking lot and the sound of voices and cutlery coming from the deck.

"Wow."

Robin smiles and links arms with me. Nathan and Ed are already at the door speaking to the hostess. We follow them through the dining room to a high-top table on the deck. The view is breathtaking. It looks like we're floating right above the ocean; the waves crash on the rocks below. We order drinks, wine for Robin and me, a beer for Ed, and a Coke for Nathan, who's offered to drive back too.

"Well, glass blowing was a lot of fun, but did you notice we were the only people in there under sixty-five?" Nathan asks, grabbing Robin's hand.

She laughs. "Stick with me, babe. I'm nothing if not adventurous."

I smile. "What's next? Antiquing? Pottery? Knitting club?"

"Those all sound great to me. It can't all be your wild, perfect day."

My stomach sinks to my toes along with all the blood in my body, and I nearly drop my wineglass.

Ed puts his phone down, tuning into the conversation. "Perfect day? When was this?"

Nathan raises an eyebrow like an obnoxious older brother.

My throat turns as dry as sand. I take a sip of wine while everyone stares at me waiting for my answer. "I don't really remember when it was. It was a long time ago."

Robin is looking to the clouds, searching for the answer. "It must have been…ten years ago. Wow, has it been that long? It was the summer you worked at—"

I cut her off. Ed and I are getting along. It's fine that he doesn't remember *that day*. He certainly doesn't need to now.

"It was so long ago. We don't have to talk about it."

Robin nods, getting the message.

A deep groove appears between Ed's brows. "I had a day like that once. It was a long time ago."

My heart stops, but I don't say anything, waiting if he'll say more. He has to be talking about us.

He says, "What made yours perfect?"

"It wasn't about what we did." My heart rate spikes at the use of the word *we*. I quickly clarify. "I mean the guy I was with and me. None of it was particularly special or even things I would've chosen for myself. It was—I don't know how to describe it. It was the vibe, I guess."

Ed is nodding like he understands what I'm saying, even though I just said a bunch of incoherent gibberish. The vibe? I'm a writer, and that's the best I can come up with?

Nathan asks, "Who was the guy?"

Robin shakes her head. "Don't even try it."

"What? Is it girl secrets?"

"She won't even tell Anh and me," Robin says. "And we've tried all our tricks. Letting her come to us. Nope. Margaritas. Nope. She's taking it to her grave."

My cheeks are burning. "Come on. We have all summer to swap secrets."

Can't we just move on?

Nathan frowns. "Well, until Ed goes to LA. When are you leaving again?"

"In a couple weeks."

He's leaving. Again. Fuck. Why didn't he mention this when we talked about our plans for the summer? The book party. Trading manuscripts.

"But I won't be gone long. Plenty of time for secret swapping." Ed raises his glass. "To secrets."

THE STORM IS YOU

TEN YEARS AGO

I check my texts behind the counter. One says:

Grandma: Have fun, Hattie Bear. I hope your first day is going well. Love you. -G

The second says:

Robin: Call me if you can! I need deets. If not, I'll just see you tonight.

Excitement fizzes in my chest. *I'm going to hang out with Ed tonight.*

Quickly, I shove my phone back into my bag as another customer enters the store—salt and pepper hair with a full beard, red hipster glasses, and a scowl on his face. He approaches the counter with a book and receipt in hand. I push my shoulders back. Smile widely. "Hi. How can I help you?"

Ed weaves behind the counter, sticking price tags on some Jane Austen action figures. The customer does not return my smile. "I need a refund for this book. I'll take cash."

"Oh, um…"

Ed steps up. "Do you have the receipt?"

"Right here." The customer hands a yellowed receipt on top of a clearly used book to Ed.

He squints at the fine print on the bottom of the paper. "It's past the thirty-day return window."

Then he moves the receipt to uncover the book. "*Kafka on the Shore.* Why do you want to return it?"

"It's gibberish."

Ed barks out a laugh. "Gibberish?"

The customer puffs out his chest, his plaid shirt stretching with the motion. "Yes. Complete and utter garbage. Most of it doesn't make any sense at all, and the parts that do are boring as hell."

Ed furiously flips the pages, shaking his head as the man keeps going.

"Plus, they're always drinking milk. Who the fuck drinks milk? It got to a point in the novel where I decided I'd rather gnaw off my own leg than keep reading. And I'm a vegan."

"Didn't you return *Virgin Suicides* two months ago? This is not a library. Did you even give it a fair shot? Really? Here, listen." Ed stops on a page and starts reading. "*Sometimes fate is like a small sandstorm that keeps changing directions. You change direction, but the sandstorm chases you.*"

The customer rolls his eyes, the gesture magnified by his thick glasses. "Look, dude—"

"It's gorgeous. A modern masterpiece. Just listen." Ed reads louder as he hops up to standing on the counter, his voice rich and full of something. It's like a deep sadness. His foot brushes against the cup of small frogs, and they skitter to the ground like some kind of plastic plague.

The customer has his arms crossed, a scowl on his face.

I've read this book, these words, before but never felt the power of them. It's like witnessing the storm he's talking about, both breath-taking and terrifying.

"*This storm is you…*"

The sidewalk draws my attention, a shadow moving ever closer. I try to catch Ed's eye, but he's so focused on the book. He's lost in the prose.

"*…walk through it, step by step.*"

Kat comes in, but Ed doesn't hear her footsteps on the hardwood floor, or if he does, he doesn't look up. It's like watching a tornado rip the roof off a house. I should look away. I should find something to do, but I can't.

Kat slow claps—that gets Ed's attention. He looks at her, his face going almost green as he hops off the counter. She clears her throat and points to the hipster. "Hattie, give this man a full refund."

I stare at the register completely baffled how to do that but sensing now is not the time to ask.

"Ed, pick those up and then come with me to my office."

Scooping the frogs back into the cup, Ed gives me a weary smile. "It was nice knowing ya."

He marches in the direction of the office.

Giving the man cash back, I put the receipt in the register to remind myself to ask someone how to ring it in.

An eternity passes. I straighten the books on the table. I finish putting price tags on the Jane Austen dolls. Finally, Ed comes out of the back, skateboard in hand. I want to ask if we're still meeting tonight, but I don't want to be insensitive. He heads straight for the door, puts his skateboard down and, right before he steps on it, looks my way, and we lock eyes for the briefest moment. It almost looks like he winks, but it could be the early evening sun shining through the window, catching his eye. Then he steps on the board, skating out of the store and down the sidewalk.

CHAPTER 5
MONDAY, JUNE 24TH

Monday morning, I pop out of bed, put on my running gear, and decide to try the full run from the house to the trail and back. I'm filling the bladder in my backpack when Ed comes into the kitchen, also in running tights.

He points to me. "Great minds. Want to go together?"

We head out the door. I catch the screen on our way out and help it close gingerly so it won't wake Nathan and Robin. They were up late last night, and they both have to work today. Ed was up late too. I could hear him typing away when I passed the door. Okay, more like pressed my ear against it, but still. I read most of his pages. They're good. On a line level, he is extremely talented, but I can see some places where the plot is lacking momentum.

We walk to the beach, warming up, and once we hit the sand, we start to run. The air is misty. A dark-blue light bathes everything: the sea, the sand, Ed's chiseled face, and his messy bed head hair. The sand is thick and shifts under my feet, making my thighs and hamstrings work harder to power forward. My pace is slower than usual.

Ed says, "Doing okay?"

I nod, catching my breath enough to talk. "The Walrus and the Carpenter were right. Fuck this sand."

Ed laughs. And screams into the wind toward the crashing waves. "Fuck this sand!"

We find a comfortable pace, and my breaths even out. The sun is rising and turning all the deep blue into lollipop swirls of pink and purple. I want to ask him when exactly he's leaving, and at the same time, I don't.

"Are you ready to share notes today?" Ed asks, hardly out of breath at all.

"Yep."

We run a few more minutes. He swings his arms back and forth gracefully, fists loose at his sides, and I can't help but picture the young man in ripped jeans, skating like a maniac through the side streets of New Haven. Was he a runner back then? "When did you start running?"

Ed smiles. "A couple years ago. I've always had a lot of energy to burn. I used to skate—sometimes I still do. But I landed funky on a backside nosegrind. Caught myself right at the bottom of some stairs, sprained my wrist. I was on a deadline too, with the edits for my second book. My editor was very nice about it all, but I could tell she was pissed. So, I started running. I can do it anywhere, and when I find cool trails like this one, it's not so bad."

I look out at the deep-purple sky, the smattering of clouds lighting up with a golden glow. "Not bad at all."

He laughs and pushes the pace a little faster.

After our run, I shower. As I lather up, my chest feels as light as the bubbles. When we're dressed and ready, we're going to meet at the kitchen table to go over our notes for each other's pages. I pick out a chocolate brown tank top that matches the highlights in my hair and some light-blue denim shorts and throw an oversized cardigan on. I slip on my sandals, grab my notebook and laptop, and head to the kitchen.

Robin is bustling around, humming and stirring some eggs on the stove.

"Morning."

Robin spins around, putting a hand to her heart. "You startled me."

I set my stuff down at the table. "Why are you so jumpy?" I pour myself some coffee then rummage through the fridge for the oat milk I bought yesterday.

"I'm not jumpy. Why are you so sneaky?" Robin turns back to the skillet. "Are you hungry? There's plenty of eggs."

I smile and walk over. "Sure. They look great." I plant a little kiss on her cheek, and she beams. "Where's Nathan?"

"Still in bed. He has to get online in like an hour, though, so he's going to have to wake up now." Robin gets out three plates and scoops some of the scrambled eggs onto each of them. There's still some left in the pan. She grabs the toast out of the toaster and plops it on two of the plates then adds some strawberries.

"Wow. Breakfast in bed. Check you out. Girlfriend of the year."

Robin smiles, but there is something very serious in her eyes. She lowers her voice. "Hattie, I think he's the one."

I purse my lips and nod. *The one.* What does that even mean? The one for right now. The one until you get sick of each other or bored? Until one of you stops returning texts or cheats, or the whole thing just falls apart like a pair of leggings that have been washed one time too many? But Robin, with her giant blue puppy love eyes, doesn't want to hear any of that. "That's great."

Ed walks in, laptop in hand, a worn in pair of jeans hanging off his narrow hips, and a light gray T-shirt with *The Trucks* printed across the middle, little white hearts around the words. It looks so soft, I want to run my hands along it. Robin pauses, looking into my eyes for one last meaningful moment, and then walks past Ed with her plates of lovingly prepared breakfast in hand.

"There're eggs on the stove if you want some."

"Thanks." Ed sets down his computer and grabs some coffee and the rest of the eggs. My appetite has suddenly vanished after talking to Robin. Out the window, the tall yellow grass blows in the wind. What is wrong with me? Robin is my best friend. I should be happy that she is happy. Not prophesying her relationship's eventual end.

And my grandparents found true love. Maybe Nathan and Robin did too.

"Hattie? Earth to Hattie."

I spin around. "Yeah?"

"You alright?"

"I was just lost in thought." I sit down at the table with my coffee and open my laptop. "Let's get started. Who should go first?"

Ed takes in a large deliberate breath and says, "I was wondering… well, there's something…"

My stomach drops.

Then Ed smiles. "Never mind. It can wait. Let's do mine first. Rip the Band-Aid off."

Sifting through my notes for Ed, I start with what's working. A lot of it is, so that takes a while. Honestly, if he wants to write a literary fiction novel, what he already has is excellent. But if he wants his book to have more commercial appeal, I have some thoughts on areas that could have more propulsion of the plot.

Then it's Ed's turn to give me feedback. "The mystery itself is great. I have no idea who the killer is. And you have some nice lines in there."

He stops and takes a sip of coffee, and I brace myself for the "but."

"The writing needs work on a line level in some places."

I open my mouth to say something, which is technically against our rules—we agreed to listen completely and not get defensive—but he holds up a hand to stop me. "I know you're probably not to that point in the draft yet, and that's totally cool. Just mentioning it. I also think…" He moves his leftover eggs around on his plate, the dried-out yellow blobs making me queasy, or is it waiting for the rest of his critique? "Well, the story is told linearly. Does it need to be? Maybe you could get more tension with a little more back and forth, maybe some creative editing. Like, did you ever read that one where the story is told backwards? I'm not saying do that, but it needs something."

It needs something, but backwards? I'm not Megan Miranda.

"And one last note." He checks his notebook as if having to decipher it from his chicken scratch. With his eyes still on his paper, he says, "It seems like maybe the main character is a stand-in for you." His voice trails off at the end of the sentence. Then, in full volume, he says, "I think that's about it. Do you have any questions?"

A frown settles on my face like quick dry cement. "Could you say that last part again?"

He sighs, a world-weary, I-knew-this-was-coming kind of sigh, that makes me want to flip this table in a Hulk-filled rage. "The main character is obviously you. And that could be problematic."

"How? How is she me?"

Ed sits back a little in his chair, crossing his leg, bringing his ankle to his knee. He starts ticking things off on his fingers. "Let's see… Her name is Hallie. She has brown hair and robin's egg blue eyes. She's thoughtful, observant, a rule follower, and she's a vegan." He puts his hand down. "Should I go on?"

How dare he presume to know me? He doesn't even remember our day together. So, he only knows me from a signing where he barely said two words to me and the past three days. "I'm not vegan. You just watched me eat eggs."

He sighs. "Aren't you a vegetarian?"

I stand, closing my laptop. "What difference does it make?"

Ed closes his notebook and looks at me with a soft expression. "It's your book. You can write it however you like. I'm only saying when we put ourselves into the book, we might not be able to go deep enough to write a fully formed character. Characters need flaws and pain and depth. And sometimes when you *are* the main character, well, we end up writing what we wish we were. On top of that, we lose all objectivity when it comes to edits. I can't tell you to change parts of Hallie, because it would be like me saying there's something wrong with *you*."

What he's saying makes sense, and in all honesty, I hadn't intended to write myself into the book. My face is hot. It's probably beet red. It's such a rookie mistake, and I've been writing for…too long to admit. "I need some air."

Ed is clicking at the keys on his laptop. "I sent you the rest of my notes. Look at them when you're ready."

I nod.

"Hattie. I liked the story."

His words bounce off me, a Super Ball on hard concrete.

Seizing my tote bag, I head out the door, walking toward the main road to see other people, hear other voices than Ed's negative comments echoing in my brain over and over.

Critiques are the worst. I'd thought over the years, with various writing groups, I'd gotten better, but this one was a special kind of torture. Why should what Ed thinks matter so much? Is it because I know he's right?

I trudge farther down the street than I have before and look towards the water. On the end of the small block, a large circular sign swinging in the breeze catches my eye.

Painted in loopy cursive, arced on the bottom of the circle, is the word *Books*. I follow it like a siren call. The building is an old dusky blue Victorian house with a large porch. From the steps, there's a perfect view of the ocean from the railing. More space than even my grandma's porch. There's worn spots on the wooden slats, like there used to be tables and chairs out here, but now all that's left is the scuffs.

On the large bay window is a For Sale sign and a phone number. I step forward, cupping my hands on the glass. Inside is lit only by the ample windows. It's enough to see the rows of shelves with books still on them. Floral-patterned wallpaper covers the walls, peeling here and there. A large chandelier hangs from the center of the room above a large circular table, empty at the moment, but I can imagine the displays that could adorn it.

The red front door has an oval glass and lead window in a floral pattern. I twist the knob quickly. Locked. Not that if it wasn't, I would go in. I snap a picture of the sign then head down the stairs and take a picture of the building itself, excitement stirring in my chest and an idea percolating. I head back to Main Street.

After a long walk, I end up starving and realize it's past lunch and I still haven't had anything today but coffee. Maybe that's why Ed's critique stung so much, because I'm hangry.

The Vern is the closest place and the only one I know so far. The bartender comes over, the same one from Friday night—Superman with brown eyes.

"Would you like a Cab?"

He remembers. That's sweet, but if I have a glass of wine on a stomach full of nothing but coffee and spite, I will wretch. "Food. I need some food."

He laughs and hands me a menu. "We have that."

I order a hummus plate and a club soda with lemon.

Stirring the squeezed lemon carcass around my glass, I replay my conversation with Ed over and over in my head. *It needs work on a line level.* I'm not even at that stage. I have to finish it first.

I open my phone to the Word app and look through his comments. There's a particularly nice metaphor in chapter three that he's marked with a question. "Would this character wax poetic about sunflowers?"

He's right. That line would work better in one of the other POVs. Most of his comments are irritatingly spot on. I slam the phone down.

I shouldn't even be messing around with my writing until I have a job lined up.

Kyle sets my plate in front of me. "Here you are."

I try for a smile, but I'm too surly, so I just nod.

"Do you want to talk about it?"

I sigh.

"Is it man troubles?"

"Sort of, but not the way you mean. Have you ever wanted something so bad, and tried so hard, and then you see someone else, and they do it like it's nothing? Like when you strain and nearly pop a blood vessel in your eye trying to open a stupid jar of pickles, and someone comes along and opens it like it wasn't even stuck. Like you're a weakling and it just takes a normal amount of strength to crack the jar right open. And all your effort is just a waste."

Kyle is scratching the back of his neck, looking confused. "You want pickles?"

"No, well, kind of now, but that's not what I meant."

"They probably opened the jar because you loosened it for them."

"No, it's their jar. I haven't touched their jar." Too many hot flashes of *that day* come uninvited into my brain. This metaphor is running away with me. Stupid writer brain.

"You know what can affect jars? Everything. Humidity, air pressure, the way it was sealed at the factory. Their jar was probably easier to open to begin with or the conditions were perfect when they tried. Sometimes when things look effortless, it's because we had some well-timed help or approached it at the right moment."

I sigh. "Timing."

The door opens, sunlight momentarily blinding me.

Kyle crooks a thumb to the door. "Here's your boyfriend now."

It's Ed. He takes off his sunglasses, and when he spots me at the bar, his electric eyes lock on mine.

"He's not my boyfriend."

STICK AND POKE

TEN YEARS AGO

At seven, Kat shows me how to close, and after sweeping the store, I head out into the summer evening. The sun's still going strong, and the air is thick with humidity. It feels like I have to swim, rather than walk. Unlocking my bike, I ride the short way to Boulevard Park with my heart in my throat. Ed probably won't be at the park, not that I can blame him. He did just get fired.

And I'm right. No one is there. That's inaccurate… There are a ton of people. People rollerblading like it's 1996. People eating ice cream from the stand set up in the corner of the park. People smoking weed, trying to be discreet, but the skunk smell gives them away. Tons of people, but not the one person I want to see.

Ed.

I lean my bike against the back of a bench that faces the water and sit down. Maybe I'll run into him again this summer. New Haven's not that big. Although in all the summers I've been here, I've never run into him before.

As I gaze into the water, looking for seals, behind me I hear the sound of small hard wheels on concrete. I turn, but no one's there, and the sound has stopped too. A few minutes later, I smell clove, orange, and strawberry.

Ed is standing there, his suit jacket gone, his skateboard tucked in between his back and his backpack, with a strawberry-vanilla swirl cone held out to me.

He's here.

Sparklers glimmer in my chest. Not only is he here, but he has my absolute favorite flavor of ice cream. I take the cone.

"How'd you know I like strawberry?"

He pulls a chocolate-vanilla swirl cone from behind his back. "I didn't. Covered all my bases."

Taking a lick, he sits on the bench close to me, so close our thighs touch if one of us moves. So of course, I can't sit still.

We eat our cones, listening to the chatter of the crowded park and the water lapping far below. Eventually, I break the silence. "Sorry you got fired."

He crunches his cone and says through a mouthful of sugar, "Couldn't be helped. I'm not cut out for retail."

I want to ask a million questions, like how will he pay rent? Will he get another job? Is he going to be okay? But he doesn't seem worried about it, so I shouldn't be either. Instead of asking any of those questions, I take a lick of my ice cream as he watches me the way a wolf watches an elk, and to my surprise, I like it. A lot. "What's the plan?"

He stands and holds out his hand to me. "Plans are overrated."

I take his hand. "Um, no they're not. If anything, plans are under-rated. More people should have a plan."

He shrugs. "What truly good thing in your life came from plan-ning? Did you plan to meet your book club friends? Did you plan to write the first story you ever wrote? Did you plan to meet me today?" He pulls out his board, and I grab my bike. "The universe has its own plans. Let's just see where it takes us."

He hops on his board and skates away, fast. I get on my bike and pedal hard to keep up. The water sparkles as we ride the trail, dodging walkers, strollers, dogs, and other people on bikes. We ride into town and through the back streets, stopping at a light-green house, the paint so dingy it's almost gray. There's a ratty plaid recliner on the porch next to a massive glass ashtray overflowing with cigarette butts and a charred action figure. The door is wide open.

"You can put your bike up on the porch or inside if you want," Ed says.

"Will it be safe on the porch?"

Ed purses his lips. "Bring it inside, and then we don't have to worry about it. We won't be here long; we just need to grab snacks."

Ripping a paper off the door, he reads it as he goes inside. The living room is surprisingly clean—filled with light, house plants, and an adorable yellow floral couch. We walk through into the kitchen, where a girl with a short, bright-pink pixie cut is holding the arm of a man with dark-black hair and light-brown skin. He's looking away, almost wincing as she takes a needle and pokes his arm, stopping every now and then to dip it in ink.

"Hey, Sasha. Hey, Lenny," Ed says.

"She's torturing me," Lenny cries.

"Oh please. You asked me to turn your ex-girlfriend's initials into a ghost, and that's what I'm doing. We're almost done."

Ed sits at the table to watch. I take the open chair next to him. He crumples up the paper in his hand and throws it on the table. "Did you both see that?"

Sasha frowns. "You're leaving tomorrow anyway, right?"

He's leaving?

Ed clasps his hands on the table. "But what will you both do?"

Lenny shrugs. "We'll figure it out."

"This is Hattie." Ed smiles at me.

"Hey," they both say.

Sasha is quick but careful. After a few minutes, Lenny is done. "Voila."

He holds up his arm and shows us the cutest little black Pac-Man ghost tattoo.

"I need a beer." Lenny heads off through an open door to the kitchen.

Sasha looks at Ed then me with a gleam in her eyes. "Who's next?"

Ed raises his hand. "I am." He looks at me. "Unless you want a stick and poke?"

"A stick and poke?"

Sasha nods. "It's what we call these homemade tattoos. They don't hurt."

"Speak for yourself," Lenny says from the kitchen, cracking open a can.

I don't have any tattoos at all, let alone a homemade one. "No, you can go."

Ed takes the chair in front of Sasha and holds out his forearm like he's about to give blood. He points to a spot a little beneath his elbow crease. "Right here, please."

"Okay," Sasha says. "What do you want?"

"Something to commemorate the day." He looks at me, his green eyes shimmering.

I picture him holding that book, bellowing out the prose—a force of nature—and speak without a second thought. "A tornado."

The corner of his mouth quirks up on the side. "Easier than a sandstorm."

The tattoo is simple, and Sasha is swift. Ed shows me his spiral line of a tornado once it's finished. It's perfect. A snapshot of him.

Sasha looks to me. "Sure you don't want one?" Part of me falters for a second. I could get something small, maybe on my ankle. A heart —no. A book? A little book would be sexy, adventurous.

"Can you draw a book?"

Sasha smiles. "Yep."

Ed catches my eye. "I'm going to grab a beer. Want one?"

"No, thanks."

Taking Ed's seat, I push down my sock to the top of my foot.

Sasha grabs a new sewing needle and dips it in the pot of India ink. I inhale sharply, bracing myself as she brings the needle to just below my ankle and punctures the skin. It doesn't hurt, necessarily, but it makes a small dot. A black dot that I will have forever. What if this turns into a day I don't want to remember? What if someday I don't like books? That's a little ridiculous. But the permanence of this act hits me all at once, and my head swims. I stand up abruptly, hitting the table and knocking over the ink in the process. "Sorry."

Sasha grabs a towel off the chair. "No worries. I have more ink. Did it hurt?"

I run my fingers through my hair, my unintentional green streak catching my eye. "It's forever."

Sasha nods her eyes soft, almost all knowing. "Forever is composed of nows."

Deep in my ribs, a bell rings.

Sasha's cheeks turn a light shade of pink. "I'm a lit major. It's—"

Lenny bursts from the kitchen with an unopened can of Rainier and hands it to Sasha. "Are you quoting Emily Dickinson again? We've talked about this… No Dickinson in the house."

Sasha bolts from her chair. "Oh right. And I'm so obedient. 'Since I could not stop for death, he kindly stopped for me.'"

Lenny chases Sasha into the living room and up the stairs.

Ed emerges from the kitchen zipping his backpack. "Got the snacks. They 're a little warm. Fridge isn't working. Ready?"

I nod, noticing for the first time there are no lights on and remember what Ed said earlier about his power being shut off. I'm a little dazed by our entire time in this house.

As we walk out the door, Ed yells upstairs, "We're going to the bonfire. You guys coming?"

"Later," Lenny calls back.

I get my bike. Once Ed shuts the door, I ask, "Are Lenny and Sasha a couple?"

Ed shrugs. "Some days. They don't believe in what you would call a typical relationship anymore. They're not monogamous, but they enjoy each other's company."

We walk down the sidewalk. My mouth feels dry. "Do you have a girlfriend or girlfriends like that?"

Ed looks me in the eye. "No. When I'm with someone, it's just me and them."

Relief washes over me.

Ed keeps going. "When I was little, my dad cheated on my mom. And one day when I was still a baby, he left with one of his other girls. I never got to meet him."

"Ever?"

Ed shrugs. "It's okay. I don't even remember him. Except…"

He stops himself and rubs his hand on the back of his neck.

"What?" I ask.

He gives me a sheepish smile. "I have this one memory of him holding me—it must be from a picture I saw. He left when I was like two. But I can smell his leather jacket and his sandalwood cologne, feel the cold metal of his ring on my leg, the rain splattering against the window." He shakes his head. "It's not like that's what Lenny and Sasha are doing; they both know they sleep with other people. It's just open relationships aren't really my thing."

"Mine either." I smile, warmth spreading down my neck. I take a deep breath, gathering my courage. "Hey, what did they mean, you're leaving?"

"Oh…" Ed runs a hand over his shaved head. "I got into a writer's residency in Crested Butte, Colorado."

"That's… Wow. That's amazing."

"Yeah, I leave tomorrow." Ed puts his skateboard down on the ground and starts to skate toward the water.

Tomorrow? I just met him, and now he has to leave.

CHAPTER 6
MONDAY, JUNE 24TH

E d approaches the bar. "I didn't know you were here. Do you want to be alone?"

I did, before. But now that he's standing here, I really don't. "No. Have a seat, if you want."

Kyle comes over, and Ed orders a beer and a turkey sandwich.

I idly stir the lemon in my drink, thinking about all the comments Ed left on my manuscript. If it was printed in red ink the way we did it in my Intro to Long Form Narrative class, it would've been bloodier than the murder in my book.

"Look, I didn't mean to be harsh in my critique."

I nod but don't look his way. Kyle comes back with Ed's tall can of Pabst. Ed takes a sip, and the silence stretches in front of us.

He sets his beer down on the bar. "There's a lot to like in your book. It's exciting. I couldn't put it down. Literally. I stayed up late reading it on my phone. And the stuff that needs fixing, that's easy stuff. It's only my opinion. Writing is so subje—"

"I swear to God if you say subjective, I will throw this lemon wedge in your eye."

Ed laughs. "Okay. I'm just saying sometimes it's easier to let the negative sink in and the positives slide off. Let some positives sink in."

He has a point.

Kyle brings over Ed's sandwich and gestures to my empty soda glass. "Want a refill?"

"I'll take that Cab now."

Kyle brings my wine over. Ed holds up his can in a cheers. "To the positives."

I clink my glass, the contact with his half-empty can making a dull thud.

"Easy for you to say, Mr. New York Times bestseller."

Ed laughs. "Yeah, how many years ago? You're only as good as your last book, and mine wasn't great. In fact, one Goodreads reviewer called it a 'shameful waste of trees.'"

"You look at your Goodreads reviews. Oh, you're bad."

He smiles, that devilish twinkle in his eye. "Do you like bad boys?" He says the last part in a mock breathy voice.

I sip my wine to hide how wide my smile is and how undoubtedly pink my cheeks must be. "Mmm-hmm."

"It's on my phone. I can't help reading them. Literally, all I have to do is go to a little app, and I can see what people are saying about me."

"Your writing." I correct.

"Same difference."

"I can see how it would be hard. Not that I would know, but I can imagine."

Ed puts his hand on my leg, his palm warm against my bare thigh. "You're a good writer, Hattie. You're going to get published."

Instead of deflecting or making a snarky comment, I let his words sink in.

He moves his hand, and my leg feels cold in the spot where his hand is now missing.

"This is what I think we should do. We should sit with each other's critiques, let them percolate, throw them against the wall, see what sticks."

"Are the crits coffee or spaghetti in this analogy?"

He shrugs. "Take your pick. We'll sit with them for a week then get back to work. In the meantime, I think we should get a little day drunk and play that pinball machine in the corner."

I look past the pool table to the *Twilight Zone* pinball flashing neon. I turn back to him and steal one of his French fries.

Ed looks at me expectantly. When I still haven't agreed, he says, "Drinks on me."

"Let's do it."

Ed buys some quarters from Kyle and orders himself another round. We take our drinks over and set them on the sticky little table by the machine. Ed puts the quarters in and presses the button twice for two players. He motions to the table with an exaggerated sweeping of his arms, and for a second, it's like I'm back on the beach with him. I'm stunned still.

"Unless you want me to go first?" he says with a confused wrinkle creasing his brow.

"I can go. It might be quick though. I don't think I've played pinball since I was a kid, and honestly, then I didn't know how to play. There was a machine at the Red Robin out by the mall, and sometimes I would play with my dad."

The memory is so vivid, I can practically smell the seasoning salt.

Ed steps a little closer to me, putting his arms around me to the machine. He pushes the buttons on either side, the loud clacking mimicking the wild beating of my heart. "Keep pushing the flippers, and you'll be alright."

He moves away, and I resist the urge to ask him to show me one more time, just to feel his body next to mine again. My first ball goes straight down the gutter but is auto-saved.

"Lucky save. Flippers, flippers," he instructs.

My next attempt is better, but not by much. I try to focus on the ball, but Ed is bopping around next to me, and my eye catches sight of the tornado tattoo on his forearm just as the ball sinks right through the middle.

Ed does much better on his turn.

"So, you're a shark?" I say while he hits ball after ball as the game blinks and flashes.

"Figure if the writing thing doesn't pan out, I can go pro." Two balls sink one after another. Then a third out of nowhere. Ed tries to save it, but it goes down the side. The table is silent.

"Hmm." I frown. "Better stick to your day job."

After a few games, we make our way out onto the patio, sitting near the unlit fire pit. Now that I've noticed Ed's tattoo, I can't help but sneak glances at it every so often. He catches me and holds it up to get a better look.

"It's a sandstorm."

I smile. "Looks more like a tornado."

"Same difference." He sips his beer, leaning back in his chair. There's a mystery in his smile. It's a little far off. I wonder if he's thinking about *that day*. How can he remember it but not me? Have I changed that much? I don't feel like I've changed at all.

"Do you have any?" Ed asks, bringing me out of my thoughts.

"Any...?"

"Tattoos."

"Oh, um. One, kind of."

"How do you have a *kind of* tattoo?"

"It's a long story."

Ed props his legs up on the rocks of the fire pit. "I have time. I love a good story. I have one from the day I got this you might want to hear."

My heart jumps to my throat. Oh God. Is he going to tell me a story about me? Or is he playing? Does he know? I'm suddenly not ready to talk about it. What if it breaks the spell of whatever is going on now? Looking desperately for something to change the subject, I notice two interlocking hearts on Ed's other arm and point to it. "What's the story with that one?"

Ed instinctively touches it. He finishes his drink and stands. "I'll grab another. You?"

"Sure."

Was he really going to tell me about our day? Maybe I should've let him.

Ed hands me my wine, startling me out of my daydream. He sits back down and props his legs on the rocks. I kick off my sandals and attempt to do the same, but my legs won't reach. I try to scoot the chair a little closer, but the things are made of solid wood, and all I wind up doing is splashing some of my wine onto the rocks.

Ed laughs. "What are you doing?"

"I want to prop my legs up like the cool kids."

Ed shakes his head, but I can see a tiny smile twitching at the side of his mouth. He grabs my ankles, shocking me so much I nearly spill the wine completely. Propping my feet up on his lap, his warm hand finds my shin. The heat spreads all the way up to my chest. "Here. Now you're super cool."

My legs feel stiff at first, but after a few minutes, I relax into it.

"How's the job search?"

I swallow my sip, feeling a tightness in my chest. That's what I should be doing, looking and applying for more jobs. Not drinking wine in the middle of the day. But what about that bookstore? Could that be my new job? My new career? My new life?

"That good, huh?" Ed says, his brow furrowed, and I realize I never answered.

"It's slow. Actually, I'm thinking I might want to do something else. Something different."

"Like what?"

"Open my own bookstore. Maybe here, even."

Ed frowns into his beer.

"What? Don't you like it here?"

Ed lowers his voice, leaning in. "It's fine for a vacation, but it's so small. Won't you get bored? Do you want to be tied to this tiny town for the rest of your life?"

I shrug. When I picture myself opening the bookstore, staying in Fortune Falls, it feels more like planting roots, not being tied down. But I can see his point. It is small.

We drink in stillness for a couple minutes until Ed breaks the silence.

"So, tell me more about this perfect day."

I cough. "Why?"

"I'm a writer. I'm curious."

"Like I said before, it's not really anything we did. It was just a feeling. Anyway, it was dashed pretty quickly. A day is over before you know it."

"Hmm. What ruined it?"

"You ask a lot of questions and answer very few."

Ed sips his beer and stares into the unlit fire pit. He holds out his arm for a second to give me a good look at the heart tattoo. "I was in love." He lowers his arms and lazily traces the bone of my ankle. "Dated long-distance. We weren't even together when we got these tattoos. She drew it, and we went on the same day. Texted each other pictures of red inflamed skin and ink, but we weren't actually there for each other during the pain. I should've seen that as a sign. She asked me to move into her apartment in Brooklyn. I moved all my stuff into my buddy's storage unit and moved in with just a suitcase, my laptop, and my skateboard. She was away a lot. Then I was away for the book tour. But when we were together, it wasn't the same as when we wanted to be together. Does that make sense?"

I consider it, tilting my head to the side. Maybe it's all the wine, but it really doesn't.

Ed laughs. "We got so used to missing each other. Pining. We were great over text. Even the"—he lowers his voice—"sex was better long-distance. It's like when we were together, we didn't know how to touch each other."

My skin is hyper aware of him touching me right now.

"We didn't know how to talk. Once the longing was gone, there wasn't anything else there. I should've known all along that it wouldn't work. She was too good for me."

Too good? I'm unsure how to respond, when he says more brightly, "Your turn. Tell me about this perfect day."

I sigh and take a large sip of wine, stalling. "It might not have been as perfect as I remember. I've just built it up in my head over the years. Anyway, if I ran into that guy on the street, he probably wouldn't even recognize me."

Ed holds my eye contact for a long, charged beat. "I don't see how that's possible."

"You'd be surprised."

"Hattie, I..."

Footsteps approach on the gravel, and Robin and Nathan come out holding drinks. I quickly move my legs, sitting up a bit and tucking my hair behind my ears.

"We didn't know you'd be here," Robin says with a smile and gives me an "oooh" look.

Ed chats with Nathan while Robin whispers in my ear. "Are we interrupting?"

I brush my hair out of my face. "Of course not..."

"You two looked cozy."

"We're just friends." But even as I say it, the words are bitter on my tongue. I don't want to just be friends with Ed. I want his hands on me, his fingers tracing my ankle, going up my legs. I want him. But how many times can one heart be broken? I roll back my shoulders. Friends is fine. "Just friends."

MELTED CHOCOLATE KISSES

TEN YEARS AGO

We make it to the beach, underneath the railroad bridge. There's a group of people set up around a bonfire built in a circle of rocks on the sand. I lean my bike against one of the massive pillars of the bridge. Ed interlocks his fingers through mine, and the butterflies in my stomach go wild. He introduces me to some people, none of the names I remember because I'm so hyper-focused on Ed's hand in mine, his palm rough, his fingers warm.

It's cool that he's leaving. We can still stay in touch, and if somehow that doesn't work, we can still enjoy this night together. I'm going to live in the moment.

We find a spot a little ways away from the main group—out of the smoke of the fire. Ed lets my hand go, and I almost let out an audible disappointed sigh but catch myself. He unzips his backpack, pulls out a green and black–striped Mexican blanket, and spreads it out on the warm sand. Making a grand motion with his arms, gesturing to the blanket like a magician completing a trick, he's smiling from ear to ear.

"After you," Ed says in a terrible fake British accent.

"Why thank you, kind sir," I say in my best Cockney, which is also terrible.

We sit crisscross on the blanket, so close the loose threads from his ripped jeans tickle my knee. Ed goes back into his backpack and pulls out two ham and cheese Lunchables, the kind with the little Hershey bar as a treat, and hands me one.

"Your dinner, madam."

I laugh. "Wow. It's so elegant. You didn't have to go to so much trouble."

"No trouble at all. They were a dollar at the NHGO."

"You got these at the Grocery Outlet?" I check the expiration date.

"Hey. These things will outlive us all. At the end of time, it'll just be these and Twinkies we're left with." Ed's eyes spark. He grabs his notebook and scribbles away. "I might add that to my book."

"What's it about again?"

Ed tells me all about his book, which sounds wild but intelligent and interesting—a lot like him, really. He trades me my ham for his cheese. The savory orange squares combined with the salty crackers are surprisingly delicious. I open my chocolate. It's melty from the heat of the day and sticks to the wrapper. I try to put it in my mouth without touching it, and I'm mostly successful. Ed is laughing, watching me maneuver the wrapper open and into my mouth.

"What?" I ask through a mouthful of chocolate.

He shakes his head. "Nothing. Very graceful."

I'm about to wipe the melted chocolate left on my lip, when Ed raises his hand to my face. He cups my cheek gently and runs his thumb over my lip, wiping the chocolate away.

My heart literally stops, and this is how I die. From Ed touching my face.

He licks the chocolate off his thumb. I am a puddle of lust.

Ed leans in, and our lips connect. I half expected his lips to be rough, like his hands, but they are soft and light as feathers floating on a summer breeze. Needing more, I increase the pressure, losing myself in our kiss, until we both hear a wolf whistle and someone shouts, "Get a room."

We break apart.

Ed hands me his Hershey bar with a devilish smile. "Want mine?"

After we finish our Lunchables, Ed fishes two beers out of the backpack and hands me one. I hate beer, especially the cheap light stuff, but when in Rome… I crack it open and take a sip, the liquid light and filled with bubbles popping on my tongue. Someone brought a guitar and is softly playing "Oh You Pretty Things," the sound of the waves from the bay lapping beneath making the song perfect. Ed sips his beer, the waning sun illuminating his green eyes and highlighting his strong jaw. He is breathtaking. I'm struck by how odd it is that I didn't know him yesterday. He catches me looking at him and winks.

"Bet you don't have sunsets like this out in Montana."

"Believe it or not, we have sunsets there too."

He laughs, giving my thigh a little push. "Smart-ass. Not many bays though."

I nod, taking another sip of my beer. This time it's not as biting, a little more refreshing. "This is true. No bays, no ocean."

There's a long pause, and then he says, "I think I'll always live next to the sea."

"Okay, Ahab."

He smiles but gazes out at the water. "Har, har. But honestly, I don't think I could live far from the water. It's so soothing, you know? I get some of my best ideas just staring out at the waves."

We both stare out at them, the rhythmic swells and contractions hypnotizing in its pattern. Ed reaches over on the blanket and finds my hand, holding it in his. His hand is warmer than the air around us. With the sun dipping below the horizon, and the breeze of the water, it's gotten a little cooler.

Ed tears his eyes away from the view, turning to face me. He lies on the blanket, propping himself up on his elbow but still holding my hand lightly, tickling my fingers and palm. "Tell me more about this book club."

I sigh. "Not much to tell. It's with my two best friends, Robin and Anh."

Ed nods. "And you've known each other since you were kids?"

"Yeah. I visit every summer, so I get to see them then. And we read our books, hang out."

"It must be lonely having your best friends live a couple states away."

I start in on my usual deflection. "I have other friends." There's a whole rehearsed speech that comes after this about how it's good for us. We get to be our own people, and we have things to talk about when we come back together. But it's not the truth. Not really. I lie down, matching Ed's posture, propping my head up on my elbow but still fiddling with his fingers with my other hand, tracing the letters on his knuckles.

"It is lonely. Anh and Robin are together all year long. They share classes, they went to prom as a double date, and they pop over on Christmas to say hi. Sometimes I feel like a third wheel. They're a grade ahead of me too. Anh's birthday is in April, and Robin's is in July. Mine's in October. They both started high school before me. They both graduated before me."

Ed nods, showing that he's listening, but he doesn't try to fill any pauses in my confession.

"Sometimes I worry that if I lived here full-time, we wouldn't be friends. Like the novelty of me would wear off."

Ed frowns. "I know that I have only known you—" he looks at his watch, a large leather band with a cracked glass face "—not even twelve hours, but you are not a novelty. I don't think anyone would see you that way, ever."

His words warm my chest, a heat that slowly spreads through my body. "I bet you say that to all the girls."

He smiles, a crooked mischievous smile that I want to kiss off his face, but I'm not bold enough to make that move yet.

Someone runs over, popping our bubble and kicking sand onto the blanket. I sit up, and so does Ed. The guy offers a joint to Ed. "Nah." He turns to me. "Want some?"

"No, thanks."

"Cool, cool." The guy leaves as fast as he came, sand flying all around him.

"You could've..." I motion to the people smoking. "I don't mind."

He slices his hand through the air like an umpire signaling you're out. "Nope. Every time I smoke, I think I'm dying, and the only thing that helps is watching episode after episode of *SpongeBob*."

I smile. "*SpongeBob*?"

"I find Patrick very soothing."

The sun blazes on its last descent, lighting up the sky in deep oranges, pink rippling the clouds above as purple takes over the sky. We watch the sunset, holding hands, sitting close enough I can feel the warmth of his thigh through his tattered jeans. As soon as the last twinkle dips below the water, Ed whispers in my ear, "Let's get out of here."

"Where?"

Even in the dark, his eyes glimmer. "I have an idea."

I hesitate, and he grabs my hand. "Do you trust me?"

Searching my body for the answer, my limbs feel warm and light. Even though I've only known him a handful of hours, something in me trusts him. I smile. "I do."

CHAPTER 7
MONDAY, JULY 1ST

I spent the last week trying to unravel some of my plot problems and avoiding Ed. Not that I'm upset with him, really. I just needed some space after the critique. And it felt like he was going to talk about our long ago day together, which means then he'd want to talk about six months later, and I'm not ready for that. I needed time to process my feelings without being influenced by his electric eyes and intoxicating citrus scent.

Waking up extra early so I wouldn't bump into him on my runs, working in my room, at the coffee shop in town, and at The Vern. Kyle even started plugging my laptop in for me behind the bar when it was running low on battery. Every time I sit to work on fleshing out my main character, I hear another voice instead. A young woman working at a bookstore, desperate for something to shake up her life. I push the voice away. She won't work in my mystery.

I applied to three more jobs, most of them in Portland. One closer to my grandma, for a middle school, and I honestly don't want it, but it would be nice to be close to her.

Work on my novel has been slow. Rereading Ed's comments, I realize they are annoyingly insightful, well thought out, and just stupidly right. I don't know how I couldn't see it myself. My main character needs a fatal flaw. Right now, she is too perfect, too flat, one dimensional.

I've been working on an exercise where I'm writing her diary from when she was a kid. None of it will make it into the manuscript— probably not, anyway—but hopefully it helps me understand her better, and while we may share some of the same traits, I need to make her separate from me. I was up late last night working on it and am getting out the door for my morning run a little later than usual because of it.

Warming up with a little, stretching and a walk on the beach, gets the blood pumping. Too excited to wait any longer, I begin my run. The sun is already lighting up the sky in streaks of gold, with one long bloodred cloud slashed across the horizon. I'm staring at it and nearly run into Ed standing in the middle of the beach, phone pointed at the horizon.

"Whoa!" I stop mid stride, arms windmilling like a cartoon. I usually think of myself as a pretty graceful person, but around Ed, it's like I'm doing a bad impression of Mr. Bean.

Not that it matters, because Ed doesn't seem to notice, his eyes fixed on the sky. "Look at that."

"It's beautiful."

I continue running, and he falls into step next to me, tucking his phone into his waistband pocket. "And a little terrifying. It looks like the end of the world."

Looking again at the red slash, dark gray clouds rolling in from far off in the distance, it does look ominous.

Ed keeps talking. "You know the saying? Red sky in the morning, sailors take warning?"

"You think everything looks like the apocalypse."

Ed laughs. "You got me there."

We run in silence until we get to the trail. Ed clears his throat. "Have you been avoiding me?"

"No," I say automatically, but even to me it doesn't sound convincing. Robin and Nathan went on a trip to visit Nathan's family. They left yesterday but should be back for the Fourth. Anh and Melissa should be here by then too, and we'll finally all be together. So far, this celebration of our twentieth year of book club has been lacking in girl time. It's just been Ed and me in the house since yesterday, and it was pretty blatant I was trying my hardest not to be in the same room with him.

"Are you pissed about my comments on your work?"

"I'm not mad." I sigh, not sure how to explain without making him sound like a jerk or me sound like a baby. Maybe I *am* being a baby. It's not really what I'm upset about at all, but I'm going to take the out. "It takes me a while to acclimate to feedback. I've just been letting it sink—"

And just like that, I'm airborne. I wasn't looking where I was going, too focused on choosing just the right words, and my foot hit a root. Bracing myself, I thud to a stop on the dirt trail, my bare knees taking the brunt of the fall. I roll onto my back, and Ed is by my side in the dirt before I even open my eyes.

"Holy shit. Are you okay?"

My pride stinging more than my scraped knees, I open one eye, then the next. "I'm fine." I go to sit up, and Ed put his hands gently on my arms.

"Slowly. Did you hit your head?"

"No. I just tripped on the root."

Ed runs his hand up my calf slowly to the delicate tendons behind my knee, and suddenly my scrapes don't hurt as bad, my body distracted with other more pressing sensations. My breath catches in my throat. He blows the dirt off my knee lightly, and goose bumps cover my arms.

"Does that hurt?"

I don't remember what pain feels like anymore. "No."

When I study his face, it's the same as that day ten years ago but so different. Somewhere along the way, his jaw got squarer, his face and body less gangly and more muscular. He looks like a man. He *is* a man.

His eyes are fixed on my knees. He grabs his water bottle from his running belt. "I'm going to pour a little of this to get the rest of the dirt off, okay?"

"Okay." The cold water stings my knees, and I suck in a breath as he does the right and then the left. There's the pain. I remember what it feels like now. Ed pries a little rock off the left knee.

"Just scrapes. I think it'll be okay. We should probably walk back and get you a Band-Aid or three, though," he says with a warm smile.

He stands and offers me his hand to help me up. As I take it, I'm surprised how unsteady I am on my feet. I pitch forward, and Ed catches me in his arms. His hands are on the small of my back, mine are on his chest, his muscles solid under my palms. I look up into his face, just inches from mine. His citrus and spice scent, his warm arms, and the pain in my knees scrambles my brain. I lean forward, reaching my lips up to his. Ed's eyes are warm, but he quickly pulls back.

"Can you walk?" he says, keeping his hand out for me in case I can't. I trudge a few steps, my cheeks burning. I can't believe I was going to kiss him. And he's going to pretend like it didn't happen, like I didn't just try to make out with him on this trail.

"I'm fine." I stride ahead, with a little limp in my step, but for the most part okay. Physically, anyway.

"Hattie."

I whip around; his face looks pained. "What is it?"

Ed rubs the back of his neck. "Nothing."

We return to the house, and I shower, the hot water stinging my knees. After I dress and grab some breakfast, I open my laptop and dive into revisions. My story is about a woman named Hallie who works at a bookstore. She finds her boss dead in his office. Ed suggested adding another employee into the mix. Maybe they could even team up. I wonder if he recognized the bookstore as the one we worked at together in Old Town. No. Probably not. He seems to have the memory of a goldfish.

I try incorporating some of the character traits I've come up with through the journal exercise, but to be honest, I'm sick of the sight of these words. This story isn't working, and it feels like no matter what I add, it's missing that spark of magic.

Closing the document, I open a new one. Usually, I'm an intense plotter and never start a draft until I have all my beats meticulously planned out, but today feels different. It feels like I've stepped outside my life, sitting at this window seat with ominous black clouds rolling in. I give in to the voice that's been whispering to me. I type a new story.

I write for hours, until my leg falls asleep and my stomach snarls at me for food. It's after four already. I skipped lunch because it hadn't occurred to me. Shutting my laptop, I stand up. I already have three new chapters and the beginning of a love story. It's a story about love but also about our attachments, how we see ourselves, and timing. June finds an old book hidden underneath one of the shelves. It's stuck, so she pulls it out, and when she does, a man appears. He is handsome, tall, with dark messy hair that looks like he's attempted to tame it with styling product, but it still escapes over his brow. His cheeks are high, his jaw razor sharp, his eyes mossy green. Okay, so Ed may have been some of the inspiration.

But it's not a straightforward love story. She can only see him when the book is open.

It's new for me. A whole book and not one murder—well, at least I don't think there will be. Sliding my sandals on, I grab my bag and head to The Vern for some food, lightly tiptoeing past Ed's door. There's no need. His room is wide open, and he's nowhere to be seen.

A huge gust of wind nearly yanks the door right out of my hand as I open it. I grab an oversized wool cardigan with large wooden buttons from the coat rack and head out, ducking my head against the weather. The walk takes me twice the amount of time, partly from the wind, partly from my banged-up knees. The Vern's door, which is usually wide open, is shut tight and for a moment I worry they're closed. But the door is unlocked. Kyle spots me and smiles. He motions to the empty stool in the corner, and I have a seat.

"Let me guess, a hummus plate and lemon water or wine?"

I frown. "Am I that predictable?"

Kyle shrugs. "I don't know if I'd say predictable. You like what you like, and there's nothing wrong with that." There's a spark in his brown eyes when he says this, and not for the first time it occurs to me Kyle might be flirting with me. I bask in it. After this morning's humiliating display, it's nice to have a man, an attractive man, show open interest in me. But it's nothing. He probably flirts with everyone.

I inhale deeply. "You know what? Today is a different day. I'd like a margarita on the rocks and the black bean nachos."

Kyle raises his eyebrows. "Okay. Coming right up."

He puts in my food order then gets the tequila while he asks me, "What makes today different?"

"I started writing a new story, in a new way."

"You're a writer?"

He hands me my drink, and I take a sip, the tartness biting the back of my jaw. I always hate talking about my writing to strangers. Honestly, I'm shocked I brought it up today. I never know what to say. I write stuff. Does that make me a writer? But I haven't published anything except a handful of short stories when I was in college. I take my craft seriously though, and I think some of the novels I've started are great.

"I am. I teach English—well, I did before my school closed. Anyway, it's not my job, but I do write."

"That's cool. I've always wondered what you were doing on your laptop. So, what made today different?"

I shrug. "The storm. It's like there's a new smell in the air. It feels charged."

Kyle's face shifts, and he excuses himself. He goes straight from behind the bar down the hallway to the patio. I sip my drink and idly scroll my phone. After a few minutes, people file in from outside, drinks in hand, some with plates of food. Kyle must've closed the patio.

One of the last people to file in, holding a sweaty tall can of Rainier, is Ed.

BEFORE SUNRISE

TEN YEARS AGO

We ride through the local college campus, the sound of the skateboard wheels on the brick ground so loud it echoes through my head. Sculptures cover the campus—bright-orange ones, odd, shaped wood monstrosities, and unassuming walls with plaques announcing the art. Ed weaves his board between two massive wrought iron slabs, momentarily disappearing. I ride in circles around this one, clearly a modern masterpiece, but in this light, it looks a lot like a half-finished dungeon with giant rusty rivets covering the edges.

"Ed! Ed! Did the sculpture swallow you?"

He pops out the other side and wheels away fast, headed right for some stairs. I veer to the left for the ramp, but Ed keeps barreling straight ahead, faster and faster, toward the stairs. My stomach lurches as I picture him falling down them, reaching the bottom a mangled mess. Maybe he doesn't even see the stairs at all. I'm about to call out to warn him when he bends then leaps up, his arms outstretched at his side like a bird, the board magically stuck to his feet. It's the stillest I've seen him, flying through the air. He hops over the entire staircase and lands at the bottom, rolling away on the board, moving his left arm behind him in an arc. Cool as can be. I've never really had a thing for skater boys, but I do now. His movements are so graceful, but strong. It's like watching a dancer on wheels. I'm a runner.

I started running track in my sophomore year of high school, so I'm fit and relatively strong in a wiry, long-distance runner, hate-to-do-my-weight-training kind of way, but Ed's strength is explosive. He can fly.

The ramp is the longer way down, and I catch up to him after a couple of minutes. "Fancy moves."

He shrugs. We ride about a mile farther up a windy road. Ed stops at the edge of a field and hops off again. There are tall pine trees surrounding a chain-link fence. I lean my bike against one, and we walk along the fence until we come to a part that has a hole. Ed holds it open a little wider, making a door. "After you."

I take a deep breath, not quite knowing what will meet me on the other side. There is a small grassy area beyond the rows of cars parked in front of a large flickering screen. It's a drive-in. Ed joins me and grabs my hand. "Do you like movies?"

"Yeah. How will we hear it, though?"

"Leave that to me." Ed pulls me to the edge of the grass. We're still in the shadows. The lights from the concession stand don't reach this far. Ed spreads out the blanket again, and I take a seat. He sits next to me and pulls out a small handheld radio.

"That's like a Mary Poppins bag."

Ed smiles. "You don't know the half of it."

He unfolds the antenna and scrolls until the sound matches the action on the screen. Parker Posey is yelling at a group of freshman girls; it's somewhere in the middle of *Dazed and Confused*.

"Do they always play older movies?" I ask.

"Nah." He points to the other screen. "That one is showing the new Marvel movie. But Richard Linklater is releasing a new movie soon, so they're doing a marathon. A double feature every Friday."

"That's so cool."

Ed lies down and props himself up on his elbow, patting the blanket in front of him. Stars fill my veins. I snuggle down on the blanket, the small spoon to his little spoon.

"Was your high school like this?" I want to ask him where he went, but I also don't want it to be where Robin and Anh went. I don't want to pop our bubble. Today feels like a dream, like we're the only two people who exist. If he knows the same people as I know, it might bring that crashing down.

"No. Well, sort of. In senior year, everyone hung out a little bit more from different groups, but they didn't do the hazing freshman thing. What about your high school?"

"Everyone pretty much hung out with everyone. The school was too small not to."

"Were you a cheerleader?" Ed asks as he traces a line from my hip down my thigh and back. It feels lazy and charged all at the same time.

"No. I ran track and took AP English. What about you?"

"I wasn't a cheerleader, either. Mostly skated. Went to some classes."

"Some classes?"

Ed laughs. "School felt optional."

"It's not supposed to be."

"Well, I still ended up graduating, so it was fine."

"Didn't your mom care?"

"She cared, but she was busy..." He trails off. I'm about to say something, ask what he means, but he continues. "When she did catch me skipping, she'd drag me back to school. Usually when I went, it was because I didn't want her to worry."

The movie ends and another begins. It's getting late, but I don't want to move. Ed doesn't make any attempt to get up either. His hand still traces my leg as *Before Sunrise* starts. Even in these still moments, he's moving.

On one of his trips back up my leg, he takes my hip in his hand and gives it a firm squeeze. Warmth spreads through my body like lava rolling downhill. I turn to face him and whisper, "You're distracting me from the movie." In all honesty, I've seen this movie a million times.

A smile slowly spreads across his plump lips. "Am I?"

I lean in closer. "Mm-hmm."

He says, almost into my mouth, "They make a pact to meet each other again in a year. Now you know the end."

"Actually, it's six months. They couldn't wait a whole year."

He smiles then kisses me, his lips soft and firm. His hand on the small of my back pulls me closer to him. I run my fingers over his shaved head, the short hairs soft and prickly under my skin. His hand moves so he is tickling my thigh again, this time going higher up. I move my legs so he can go even higher, under my skirt, just barely touching me but setting my skin on fire every centimeter higher he goes.

We watch the whole movie snuggled together, stealing touches and kisses. As the credits roll, Ed whispers in my ear, "Up for another adventure?"

CHAPTER 8
MONDAY, JULY 1ST

E d walks to the bar sipping his beer. He motions to the stool next to me. "Mind if I sit?"

I shrug.

"Kyle closed the patio."

"Probably worried about the storm."

Ed runs his hands along the bar, the tattoos on his knuckles drawing my attention. "So far, it's just a little wind."

"A little?" I laugh. "It nearly blew me down the street when I was walking here. If I'd had an umbrella, I would've Mary Poppinsed right out of here."

Ed laughs. The lights flicker, and he stops laughing abruptly. "Shit."

I sip my drink in an attempt to calm my nerves. "It's just a summer storm. We'll be fine. Right?"

Ed nods. "Yeah, sure."

The lights sputter again then go completely out. There are a few cheers and a couple of boos from the crowd.

Kyle clears his throat, but it does nothing to quiet the chatter. He rings a bell hanging on the wall loudly. "Folks. We have to close. Please finish your drinks quickly and go home. Be safe."

Ed puts his beer on the counter, the aluminum making a hollow along as he does.

Kyle comes over to me. "Are you going to be okay? If you stick around, I can walk you home."

I'm flattered that Kyle is concerned. This whole bar is full of people, and he's worried about me getting home safely. It feels good. "I'll be fine. We're walking together. What about my tab?"

Kyle shrugs. "Come back, pay it later."

I smile. "Okay."

Once we're outside, the wind whips my hair from my face. I squint so sand doesn't get in my eyes. But I can feel it smacking against my legs in swirls. Walking feels like pushing against a heavy door. The light is odd too. It's a bright golden yellow with dark gray, almost black clouds so heavy they look like suspended mountains, unmovable rocks. Then the sky opens up, and rain pours down, soaking into my heavy cardigan, dripping down my legs. We run the rest of the way, but it's no use. We are both soaked.

I get inside, and then Ed shuts the door behind us. The lights are all off. The power's out here too.

Brushing off my legs, I shrug out of my cardigan, heavy and waterlogged and smelling a lot like a wet dog. The storm has made it a good ten degrees colder, and the house isn't providing much warmth. The rain is so loud, it sounds like it's inside. It dawns on me. "The windows."

"I'll check downstairs."

"I'll go upstairs," I say, jogging up the hardwood steps. I stop at the hall closet and grab a towel, drying my hair off.

I shut the open window on the landing and use the towel to wipe up the droplets that got in. I peek into Ed's room—the windows are closed up tight.

There is a window cracked in what will be Anh and Melissa's room when they come this weekend. My bedroom has the last window to close, the one by my desk. I throw on a dry sweatshirt and some leggings, feeling a little warmer.

Downstairs, Ed has been busy. Lit candles are all around the room, and a couple flashlights are on the coffee table. There is a blanket on the floor by the stone hearth with a bottle of wine, two glasses, a plate of saltines, a small tub of cream cheese, and a knife. Ed is crouched at the fireplace, his T-shirt stretched tight across his strong shoulders.

"All closed up."

Ed turns, flames jumping behind him, and smiles. "Great."

I motion to the spread. "Fancy."

He takes a corkscrew to the wine. "Crackers and cream cheese. Can't beat it. Care to join me?"

I cross the room to sit on the blanket. With each step closer, my heart beats that much faster in my chest. It's the same green and black–striped Mexican blanket from *that day.*

Ed notices my hesitation. "I can see if there're other snacks if you're not into cream cheese. I looked, but there weren't any Takis."

I laugh and sit, running my fingers over the familiar texture. "Crackers are fine. Where'd you get this blanket?"

"I've had it forever. I always take it to the beach."

He hands me a glass of wine; it glows a shimmering ruby red in the firelight. The rain smacks against the window. Wood crackles in the hearth. It would all be so romantic if I could stop thinking about ten years ago. Does he remember our time on this blanket before?

"How's your book going?" I ask, trying to jar myself out of this funk.

"So-so. I added in a murder, but I think I may have to start over. Something about it feels off."

I know what he means. It's like this cozy little picnic. It should be fun, exciting, idyllic even, but something is off. The conversation is stilted, moving in odd ebbs and flows. All I keep thinking about is the last time we were on this blanket together. I run my hand along the soft fibers, and I can almost feel tiny grains of sand on it. Oh, I actually do. I stare out at the rain streaming down the windows, putting me here now and not back on that clear summer night.

"How's your writing?"

I tear my eyes away from the rain-streaked windows to Ed's face. Dark stubble covers his strong jaw. It's so rough, such a contrast to his soft pink lips. His face is a study in contradictions. His fingers are playing with a stray thread from the blanket, still always moving.

"It's okay. I've digested some of your notes and made some changes. But I started something new, something different."

"Oh, really?" Ed scoots a little closer to me on the blanket.

"It's a love story. Trapped in time."

"Ooh, trapped in time? That sounds intriguing."

I tilt my head. "I think it will be. Hopefully. We'll see. I haven't plotted it out, which in itself is new for me."

Ed nods knowingly. "Ahh, you're a plotter."

I laugh. "And you're a pantser."

Ed sings out in a vibrating old timey voice, "Let's call the whole thing off."

Grabbing a pillow from the couch behind me, I half lie on the blanket, feeling more comfortable.

"Why did you decide to change your process?" Ed asks, lying down too.

"The definition of insanity is doing the same thing over and over and expecting a different result, right? If I've plotted every single novel I've ever written and never finished one to a place where I feel it's good enough, then maybe it's time to switch it up."

Ed nods, setting his wine down, looking deep into my eyes. "Why haven't you ever felt like one of your stories is good enough?"

I sigh and lie back. "You know that uber critical voice in your head you need for editing? It's like I get stuck there, and all I can see is the story's flaws. Then I think of a new idea and start a new book."

"Yeah, I get that. That voice never shuts off for me."

My stomach sinks at the thought of that. "Ever?"

"No. I thought it would once I got an agent. But it didn't. Then I thought once I got a book deal." He shakes his head. "I just keep moving the bar. Maybe someday it'll feel like I did something right?"

A stray hair falls into my face, and Ed moves it, his closeness making my heart hammer in my chest. The fire crackles. Ed's hand lingers, moving along my cheek, down to the back of my neck. His touch is electric.

I lean forward, and so does he, the moment stretching like salt-water taffy warmed by the sun. He runs his tongue lightly along the edge of his lips, and a loud crack of thunder startles us both. Ed knocks over his wine on the hardwood floor. "Shit."

He jumps up and runs toward the kitchen, and I lie back, feeling everything all at once, my heart still beating wildly. I want Ed. I want his lips on mine, but that's not all. I want him on top of me, inside me —to what end? This is probably just a rainy-day distraction for him. He'll leave, and I'll think about it for the next decade. Compare other men to him for years to come.

Ed strides back with a paper towel and wipes up the wine, a few tiny drops splashed on the blanket. I hope they stain. Then every time he uses this blanket, he'll have to remember this night.

He sits back down, upright this time. I sit up too, taking a sip of my wine, trying not to show how stung I am he didn't lie down and go right back to where we were.

"Can I ask you a question?"

"Sure." I grip my wineglass in my hand, the cool surface grounding me.

"Are you and the bartender seeing each other?"

A laugh bubbles out of me, even though it's not particularly funny. "No, I'm not dating anyone."

He traces the mouth of his empty glass. "It's none of my business. It's not even what I wanted to ask. It just popped out."

"What do you want to ask?"

Ed looks up, the fire lighting up his green eyes. "Hattie, how long are we going to pretend like we don't know each other?"

TIME OUTSIDE OF TIME

TEN YEARS AGO

E d stops in front of a light-blue house with a white picket fence around it and holds open the gate in the fence to the backyard.

I'm confused. I thought we were at his house earlier. "Whose house is this?" I whisper as I wheel my bike into the backyard, smelling a sweet floral scent and cut grass.

"It's my mom's." He points to a window on the second floor. "That was my room. It has her art studio in it now."

"Is she here?"

"Nah, she works nights."

He leaves his skateboard by the fence, so I follow suit and lean my bike against it. There's a large tree in the middle of the yard. It's too dark for me to tell what kind. Oak, maybe. Porch furniture is arranged on the concrete near the sliding glass doors of the house. Once my eyes adjust, the yard isn't so dark; the moon is nearly full and casts an eerie light on everything. There are roses planted along the back of the house. I lean my face into a blooming pink rosebud. It smells almost like lemonade. Ed fiddles with something next to the house, and behind me, the tree lights up.

Before, where it was all dark branches and leaves, it's now a large tree house, the windows lit up from the inside, a ladder nailed into the sturdy trunk.

"It's amazing."

Ed smiles. "Thanks. I built it when I was twelve."

"All by yourself?"

He nods. "Mostly. I've made some improvements over the years. Wait until you see inside." He motions to the tree. "Shall we?"

"Is it safe?"

Ed puts a warm hand on my back. "I wouldn't take you up there if it wasn't. Come on. I'll go first."

He climbs the rungs of the tree, and it supports his weight fine. Not that he looks like he weighs a lot, but if it will hold him, it'll hold me, hopefully. I climb up after him. Golden Christmas lights and a pink lamp softly light the small room. There's a record player on a milk crate in the corner, with another crate next to it filled with albums. Covering the floor is a large carpet with pastel pink flowers that looks like it belongs in a nursery, rather than a skater dude's tree house. A small bed neatly made with a dark-blue blanket is off to the left side. In the center of the room is a couple of mustard yellow corduroy floor pillows and a dark wood coffee table with gold hair pin legs.

"This is so cool."

Ed beams in the golden light. "Thanks. I found most of this stuff in free piles." My face must give my apprehension away, because he quickly adds, "I cleaned it all."

I take a seat on one of the floor pillows, running my hand along the frayed seams, while Ed puts on a record. "La Vie En Rose" fills the tree house.

Ed joins me, taking the other pillow.

"I bet you bring all the girls here."

He runs a hand over his shaved head, and I imagine the feel of it under my palm. "I don't. You don't have to believe me, but only a few people have been up here."

"Really?"

He nods. "I moved out right after high school. My mom told me I could stay and go to college, or I could get my own place if I chose not to. I barely got through high school in one piece. No way was I ready for college. And all I wanted to do was write. So, I moved out. But I still come here to write some nights when my mom isn't around."

A pang of jealousy hits me. I've always wanted to make my own writing space, somewhere other than a lap desk on my bed. And he built himself one when he was twelve. And now he's off to a fancy writing residency. It's amazing. I gaze at his chiseled face, staring at the walls of his own creation. He's amazing.

"I'm more of a morning writer. I like to write before my day has started. When it feels like time outside of time."

Ed smiles, a slow, lazy smile like he's enjoying the sound of my voice. "Time outside of time. That's a little what today has felt like, for me at least."

"Me too." The Christmas lights are highlighting the lines of his face. He is the most beautiful man I have ever seen.

He catches me looking, and we lock eyes. Edith Piaf sings low in the background, the smell of roses waft from the yard, and I take a mental snapshot of this moment. I never want to forget how lovely it is. He scoots his cushion a little closer and gently tugs my strand of green hair.

I laugh. "Hey."

He reaches for my hair again, this time running his fingers through it and cupping the back of my head, gently moving down the sensitive skin of my neck. We lean in, and our lips meet, soft, tender, light as a feather at first. I open my mouth, and he does the same, our tongues exploring each other. Desire spreads through me like warm honey.

My hands drift down the sides of his back. He moves his hands down around my waist and lifts me up onto his lap, while we kiss like if we stop, some spell might break. I adjust myself on his lap, moving my legs over and hiking my skirt up so I'm straddling him. I'm never this bold, but something about tonight feels different. *I* feel different with him. Bolder, sexier. He lets out a moan as I feel how excited he is. He slides his hands up my back.

I break our kiss to lift my shirt up over my head. His eyes drink me in like a glass of cold water on a sultry day.

"You're so beautiful," he says, his voice husky.

"You are," I whisper into his ear and nip at his soft earlobe then make my way down his neck, kissing and licking as his hands move over my bare back.

"Ed!"

The yell from below startles me.

I gasp and hop off him as if the voice came from inside the tree house.

"Ed, is that you?"

Ed clenches his hand into a fist. "Shit. She's supposed to be at work."

He goes to the window and leans out. "Yeah, Mom. I didn't mean to wake you. I thought you were working."

Putting my shirt back on, I try to stay low so she can't see me.

"Not today. Not anymore. Come in. I'll make us a drink."

"Mom. What do you mean, not anymore?"

Ed pulls his head back inside. "I'll be right back." He moves close to my face and says in a hushed voice, "Don't go anywhere."

He gives me one last look before heading down the ladder.

I sit on the bed then try lying down. Arranging myself with my legs crossed just so, lying on my side so my tank top gives me some cleavage that normally I don't have. I look sexy. Ed will stop in his tracks when he comes back up. The record player is still playing Edith Piaf softly, and I close my eyes for just a second while I wait.

The slam of a door wakes me up. I bolt upright, not remembering for a second where I am. Then it all comes back to me at once in a whoosh. I wipe my chin and am grateful Ed didn't find me asleep and drooling in his bed. So much for my come-hither arrangement. The ladder creaks, and Ed pops his head up, his brow wrinkled. I quickly move off the bed.

"How it go with your mom?"

"We should probably go," he says, completely ignoring my question. "I can skate with you home."

"Oh." My heart sinks like a lead anchor in the ocean. Of all the things I thought he might say, that wasn't one of them. "I can find my way to my friend's house. You don't have to—"

"I'm not going to let you go alone. It's too late—or early at this point. I'm not sure. Where does your friend live?"

"Near Clark's Point, just past Old Town."

"Full circle for us, then."

I nod, still feeling like my heart is underwater. I don't want this night to end, but of course it has to sometime. I grab my bag and check my phone. It's already after four. I was asleep for longer than I thought. "I'm ready." I'm not. "Let's go."

We ride through the night. Everything is quiet and still aside from the sound of my tires and Ed's skateboard wheels. Not a breeze rustling the leaves, not another soul in sight. The bar crowd is long gone.

The ride takes us around thirty minutes, and by the time we get to Robin's neighborhood, I'm sweaty and drained. I don't want the sound of the skateboard to wake up Robin's parents, so I stop a couple of blocks away. Ed stops too, his chest heaving with effort. He wipes his brow with the sleeve of his suit jacket, which he put back on when we left.

"I can make it from here."

He reaches for my fingers with the tips of his. "Feel like watching the sunrise with me?"

My smile is so pure, I can feel it radiating off my face. "Yes. I would like that."

Ed's smile matches mine. He glances around at the large houses, all in the multi-million-dollar range. "This isn't really my neighborhood. I'm not sure where to go."

The sky is starting to lighten; we have to go somewhere close. "I know just the place." I get back on my bike. "Grab on."

Ed grabs my seat, and I pedal, pulling him on his board behind me.

CHAPTER 9
MONDAY, JULY 1ST

My mind is spinning. What does he mean, *know each other*? Is he talking about the signing? Or does he really remember *that day*? He keeps talking.

"Ten years ago. Neighborhood Books. We met up after work, after I quit."

I scoot back, sloshing the wine in my glass. "Wait, you quit?"

A slow smile spreads across his face like syrup on hot pancakes. "You do remember."

"I remember you yelling at a customer and getting fired."

"Kat might've been going to fire me, but I quit. I found out I got into the writer's residency in Colorado late, like super late. My roommates didn't give me the letter, and I wasn't great about checking e-mail. Anyway, I had to quit. I had to leave the next day."

We sit there silent for a beat. He'd quit. How did I not know he'd quit? What else is different than I thought it was about *that day*?

"I'm so relieved you remember," Ed says and refills his glass of wine. "When we met in the kitchen and you just brought up the signing, I thought... Well, for a minute I wasn't sure it was you. Then when I was, I thought you had forgotten the whole thing."

Fire fills my veins. "Me? You thought *I* forgot? I've always remembered. And even after everything, I went to your book signing, gave you my name, and you didn't even know it was me."

Ed opens his mouth like he's about to say something, but nothing comes out. There's a knock at the door, making us both jump. I cross the room, but Ed stands, grabs a flashlight from the coffee table, and strides in front of me.

"Let me get it."

He opens the door, and a gust of cold wind instantly blows in. Anh is standing in the doorway, suitcase in hand, her black hair wet and plastered to her head.

I leap forward. "Oh my God. Come in, come in."

Water is running down her face, but as I get closer, I see it's not just rain but tears.

"Anh, what happened?"

She comes inside and sniffles. "Melissa left me. We called off the engagement."

"Oh, no."

Anh and Melissa have been together for six years. Engaged for three of them. Just this year, they actually set a date for this October and started planning the wedding. How did this happen?

She takes the glass of wine in my hand and downs the rest in one go. "Is there more of that?"

I point to the blanket. Anh lets her wet coat fall to the floor and takes my glass to the living room.

After shaking the coat out a little, I hang it up. My mind is spinning in a million different directions.

Ed says, "I'm going to head upstairs and give you ladies some privacy."

I nod but don't say anything.

He puts a light hand on my shoulder, and I look into his eyes. "Can we talk about this later? I'd like to... Well, I can explain."

My stupid heart leaps, like a prima ballerina on opening night. But my more practical senses tamp it down. What can he possibly say?

"Can we talk tomorrow?"

I shrug. "Okay."

Grabbing another glass from the kitchen and another bottle of wine, I join Anh on the blanket.

She's completely still, staring into the fire. I nudge her foot with mine. "Do you want to talk about it?"

Her whole body slumps on an exhale. "No. Never. But also, yes."

Fresh tears start to fall.

"We don't have to if you're not ready. We can just sit, warm up, drink wine."

"She met someone else. In a CrossFit class. They do Cross-fucking-Fit together. Isn't that stupid? Of all the places to meet someone? They're happy hot lesbians doing CrossFit together. They probably go to the farmers' market and make smoothies. They'll probably get a stupid dog and name it Burpee. Melissa has always wanted a dog. I should've let her get one."

I put a hand on Anh's knee. "Honey, you're allergic. That's not your fault."

"I could've taken Allegra." Anh sniffles. "She moved her stuff out last week."

"Last week? Why didn't you tell us?"

Anh's shoulders slump, and she closes her eyes. "I called. I was going to. But I didn't want it to be real. If I told you and Robin, then it was really happening, you know? I was hoping she'd come back, change her mind."

We talk into the night, and Anh drinks quite a bit more wine. I try to be present, to be there for her, but my mind keeps wandering back to Ed.

Around one in the morning, the power comes back on. I help her up the stairs and put her into bed. There's a light streaming from under Ed's door, but maybe it came on when he was already asleep. I put my ear to the door to listen but can't hear anything.

I crawl into bed but lie awake. If Anh hadn't interrupted, would we have kissed? I frown at the ceiling. It's a bad idea. We shouldn't have slept together a decade ago, and we shouldn't now either. Ed became this impossible dream that I measured every other man I was ever with against. My heart has belonged to a ghost, a phantom, my entire adult life. And now he's here, licking his lips in front of roaring fires. But there's nothing he could possibly say to make this right. It's time to let it go, let my fantasy of him go.

IN THE MORNING, I wake up extra early. *Wake up* is a stretch. Mostly I give up trying to sleep. The wind has died down, and outside looks peaceful. The ocean is a calm expanse of blue. I throw on my running stuff and check on Anh. She's still sleeping, her arm flung over her face.

I sneak out the door and run in the gray morning light. When I get back to the house, Ed is making coffee in the kitchen, sweaty in his running gear. Did he go for a run too? How did I miss him? Did he take another route? Is he trying to avoid me?

He turns around. "Hey."

I smile, but my stomach twists. "Good run?"

"Yeah, I checked out the other way on the beach. Running on sand is getting easier."

Of course it is, for him.

Ed hands me a steaming mug of coffee, the aroma ironing some of the wrinkles in my brain out. He lowers his voice. "About last night—"

"I thought I smelled coffee." Anh comes into the kitchen, her long black hair tied up in a messy bun.

Selecting a pink mug with white flowers on it, I pour her some coffee. "How are you feeling?"

Anh blows on her drink, the heat wafting off in waves. "Like I was steamrolled by a giant bottle of wine. I'm never drinking again."

I laugh.

She turns to Ed. "We haven't officially met. I'm Anh. My girlfriend left me for a CrossFit lover."

"I'm sorry to hear that." Ed holds out his hand. "I'm Ed. I'm Nathan's old friend."

"Now that we're on a first-name basis, I fully expect you to hold my hand through this breakup. So, what are we doing today?" Anh asks, sipping her coffee.

Ed laughs. "Well, Anh, I have to go to Portland for my buddy's book launch party." Ed turns to me. "Do you still want to go?"

My heart sinks. I do want to go, but I can't leave Anh all by herself.

"A party in Portland sounds perfect. When do we leave?" Anh gets up from the table.

"Whenever." Ed shrugs.

"I'll shower." Anh heads off, taking her coffee with her.

Ed is still dripping sweat from his run, and so am I, but our showers will have to wait, I guess. "Is it okay if we both come to the party?"

Ed nods. "Sure. I booked us two king rooms at Posh downtown, but I could make it three rooms."

Posh is one of the fanciest hotels in downtown Portland. "No, we can share. But we can just get a room at The Jupiter or The Quality Inn or something.

Ed shakes his head. "Nah, this place is great. I got it."

I want to protest, to say of course I'm going to pay you back, but the house hasn't sold and I'm uncertain where my next paycheck is coming from and when. "Are you sure it's okay if we come? We can stay here—"

"It's cool." Ed pulls out his phone and starts tapping away. "I'm pretty sure I can get us another invitation."

"Are they going to be sticklers about invites?"

"It's at the Pittock Mansion, so maybe. But I'll figure it out. It's black tie. Should we stop somewhere in Portland to pick up clothes?"

Posh, black tie, mansion? Now it really feels like we're party crashing. "Anh and I should just stay here."

Ed startles me by putting his coffee down and taking my hand in his. "I want you to come. Please."

I try to slow my breathing. "Okay."

Ed's phone lights up in his hand. He drops my hand and answers it, "Bill! Happy book release day."

He takes his coffee in one hand and his phone in the other and walks out of the kitchen.

A COUPLE HOURS LATER, we're all showered, dressed, packed, and in Ed's car headed to Portland. Ed insisted on driving since he invited us, but my car looks far more reliable than his white Datsun Hatchback. Anh needs to sit shotgun; the roads are windy, and she gets car sick even on days when she's not hungover. So, I'm sitting in the back, the ocean whizzing by, feeling the cracked leather seat underneath my fingers. A couple of empty cans of cold brew rattling around on the floor next to me. "I really think we should've taken my car. It's not too late to turn back."

"Don't be silly. This car is a tank."

Anh's head is leaning against the window, her soft snores almost matching the beat of the song on the radio.

"Must be my riveting company," Ed jokes softly.

He pushes in an actual cassette tape and pulls onto the highway, Tom Waits droning out of the stereo. It's so perfectly music he would listen to, I laugh.

"What?"

I bite my lip, finding his eyes in the rearview mirror. "Tom Waits is just very on-brand for you."

"Come on, now. I'm going to take that as a compliment." He points to Anh's seat. "There's a whole box of tapes under there. You pick something."

I sort through Dolly Parton, The Clash, Sonic Youth, and a mixtape. I read the list on the paper insert—a lump in my throat forms as I land on the first song by Say Hi. I hand it to Ed, and he pops it into the player. As the first track plays, I wonder if he'll recognize it from when we met in the bookstore.

He nods as the soft notes hum through the car. "I love this song."

"Me too." I smile. "So how long does it take to get there?"

"Probably around two hours or so? Actually, will you turn on the map on your phone so we're sure we're headed the right way?"

I type in Posh Hotel Portland, and the little blue line pops up, two hours and twelve minutes. Placing my phone in the center console, I settle back into the seat and watch the landscape change as we leave the coast behind and head through the forest, mossy trees on either side.

The song changes, deep base filling the car.

Boom—boom boom. Boom—boom boom.

Ed smacks the steering wheel to the beat.

As the first words come over the speaker, we both sing along. Unplanned synchronicity. It's so good. In the chorus, Ed's voice goes so low, it rumbles something deep in my core.

"Just Like Honey."

When the song is over, Ed clears his throat. "Hattie, about that night."

My pulse ticks up. Now? Ed wants to talk about this now, with Anh sleeping in the front seat? "Ed it's fine. Let's just forget it, okay?"

"Forget it?"

"Yeah, that night just didn't mean as much to you as it did to me, and that's fine. It's been years. I'm over it. We don't have to rehash it all."

"But it did mean *a lot* to me. Wait, you're over it?"

The car hits a pothole, jostling the vehicle. Anh stirs in the front seat. "Ugh. Mind if I change this?" Anh reaches into the back, and I hand her the box of tapes.

"Knock yourself out."

Anh puts on Fleetwood Mac's *Rumours* and turns it up. "Remember that summer you played this nonstop?"

I nod. "The summer after Chad and I split."

"Right. That was the same summer we went to Puerto Rico—oh, and you changed your book club pick. The only time we ever allowed it. What was the first one you chose called? Do you remember? It was that one about the guy that stubbed his toe and started the apocalypse."

Ed and I both say it at the same time. "*Vex.*"

"Yes! That was it. You know it, too?" Anh asks Ed.

"I wrote it."

Anh laughs, a bubbling giggle that fills the car. "No. You didn't."

Ed chuckles. "I did."

"I loved it," Anh says, frowning slightly as if she's still deciding.

"You don't have to say that."

"No, I did, but it wasn't *light* reading."

"So I've been told."

Anh turns in her seat; she points to me and back to him quickly. Either implying we should hook up or asking if we have, I'm not sure which. I shake my head because it's not happening. He did just say our day together meant a lot to him, though. But those are just words. If it had meant that much, then it wouldn't have ended the way it did.

RIGHT PLACE, RIGHT TIME

TEN YEARS AGO

The water is dark in the approaching dawn. We ride for a while until the paved trail stops then trek a little farther, finding an opening in the trees off the path. Ed lays down the blanket, and we both sit facing the water as the sky turns dusky shades of pink and deep blues.

He holds my hand, intertwining his fingers with mine. I shiver a bit, my skin cooling down fast after the ride and probably the long night. I always get cold when I'm tired. Ed notices and shrugs off his jacket, placing it on my shoulders. It smells like him, sweat and citrus and spice. I tear my eyes away from the light show to look over at Ed, who is staring at me. His eyes are warm, his lips slightly parted. He licks them, and I feel a pulse of want shoot through me so strong, I'm momentarily stunned by it.

I lean forward. Our lips meet soft and unhurried, like we have all the time in the world. But we don't. I know we don't.

He reaches up into my hair, and tingles shoot from my scalp all the way to my thighs. I lie back on the blanket, and he follows me, never taking his lips off of mine. The weight of him on top of me sends fresh electric pulses through me. He keeps a hand firmly on my waist and runs his other hand down from my neck to my collarbone, tracing it lightly, then continues his path, skimming my breast down to my stomach. He plays with the edge of my tank top as my breaths get heavier. I arch into him, and he moves his hand up through the fabric as goose bumps erupt on the sensitive skin of my stomach. He finds my breast and runs his thumb over my nipple through the silky bra. I let out a moan, and he squeezes tightly.

I roll so that I'm on top of him and sit up, shrugging off his coat, taking off my shirt, and then undoing my bra, the cool morning air making my nipples almost painfully hard. I don't remember a time I've ever been naked outside like this. It's not like me, too wild, but this morning, it feels right. I feel bold.

Ed is running his hands up my ribs. "You're so beautiful."

I tug at his shirt, helping him get it off. His abs flex with the motion of throwing it to the side. Ed is all wiry muscle and tattoos. I trace one on the side of his ribs, a small baby deer curled up in on itself.

He smiles and wiggles. "That tickles."

I smirk. "Does it?" I run my fingertips up both sides of his waist lightly, and he squirms.

"Oh, I wouldn't start that."

He squeezes my hip bones, and I wriggle under his touch. Laughter bubbles through me.

I lean down and kiss him, feeling his soft skin and hard muscle on my breasts. I whisper in his ear. "Do you have a condom?"

He scooches, with me still on his lap, toward his backpack, reaching out his long arms and digging around in the front pocket. He sets the little foil package nearby.

We roll so we are side by side. He runs his hand from my shoulder to my waist and slips in through the gap in the waistband of my denim skirt. My heart catches in my throat as his fingers find the place I've been longing for him to touch since the tree house, since the movie. Honestly, I've imagined it since he read my palm in the bookstore.

The rest of the world falls away. I am all nerve endings and desire as we explore each other's bodies, nipping and licking, finding out what each other likes. It turns out I like all of it. Ed's hands are strong. I never want them to stop touching me, and he doesn't, not until we're both a sweaty, tingling mess. Just a pile of skin and bones intertwined, our souls hovering somewhere above our bodies, looking down.

Ed is the big spoon to my little spoon as we watch the color of the sunrise fade into just another summer day with a bright-blue sky and fluffy white clouds. Ed pulls half of the blanket over us. A hazy worry about someone seeing us passes through my mind, but I can't bring myself to care.

I'm a little shocked. This is all so unlike me. But something about this day, about Ed, it feels right. I can't imagine it going any other way. Like it's destiny.

Ed points to the clouds, and a dark bird swoops by. It soars in a large arc—its wings outstretched, its body perfectly still slicing through the blue sky. "Every time I see an eagle, I always feel like it's the universe telling me I'm in the right place at the right time."

I snuggle closer into him, my back against his chest, and let his words sink deep in my bones. We both silently watch the eagle fly until it disappears into the trees. My eyes are heavy, and with the blanket over us, it's warm and cozy. I shut my eyes for a moment, but Ed pokes my side.

"Don't fall asleep."

"Why not?" I turn my body to face him. "It's warm and you're so cozy."

He laughs. "I don't think anyone has ever said that about me, *ever*. You can sleep if you want. I just thought you had work today?"

My whole body slumps under the truth of his statement. "I do. I have to open, since somebody had to go and yell at a customer."

"I wasn't yelling at the customer. I just got a little carried away. It's *Kafka on the Shore*."

It occurs to me that it would've been his last day either way. Since he's leaving. I lay my head on his chest and listen to the thump, thump, thump of his heartbeat. "I don't want this night to end."

He runs a hand through my hair. "It already has."

Panic snatches my breath, and I look into his green eyes.

"I just mean it's already morning."

My stomach clenches as if preparing for a blow. Needy is the absolute last thing I want him to think about me. I don't want to be the one to ask if we're going to see each other again. But the question hangs in the air between us.

We get dressed and trudge back down the path, through the fancy neighborhood, to Robin's house. I stop a couple of houses away. I don't want Robin's parents to see us if they're already up and moving around the house.

A soft tug on my green streak brings me back to the moment. Ed's hand brushes my cheek as it drops to his side. I smile, but I feel like crying. This can't be goodbye.

Ed runs a hand over his shaved head. "Tonight—last night, I mean. It was the best night of my entire life."

Joy bursts in my chest. "Same."

"Do you think I can get your number?"

I picture myself, us, messaging back and forth. Me waiting for him to text—just like with Brandon. I've been down that road before, and it only leads to heartache.

"No."

His smile falls from his face.

I put a hand on his arm, excitement bubbling in my chest. "It's just, I have a better idea. You're going to be so busy with your writing, and I'm getting ready for college. What if we plan to meet? Just like in the movie. Are you busy in December?"

The smile is back on his face as he shakes his head. "The residency is over in early December."

"I could visit my grandma for Christmas break."

Ed's eyes brighten. He wraps me in his arms. "Let's meet then. *Before Sunrise* style. When? Where?"

I get out my phone and pull up the school schedule I have saved. "My break starts December twentieth."

Ed's smile is so wide it reaches to the corners of the earth. "Six months from now. It's perfect. Let's meet on December twenty-first. Where?"

I'm nodding, equally elated and deflated. This feels like a brilliant idea and also so dumb. "Boulevard Park. Where we met tonight? Seven p.m."

"It's a date."

It's also the most romantic thing that has ever happened in my life.

Movement in Robin's upstairs room draws my attention. The curtain is pulled back at the corner, and Robin's angelic little face is peeking out, but I don't think she can see us over here. "I should go."

Ed leans down, putting his full lips to mine. I channel all my mixed emotions into this one passionate kiss. We pull apart and stare at each other for one last charged beat. Then Ed lets me go. My body misses his hands already.

"See you in December."

"See you then."

Ed gets on his board and skates away, a blur of movement once again. An unstoppable force. I realize I'm still wearing his suit jacket, but he's too far gone for me to call after him. I'll give it back in December.

CHAPTER 10
TUESDAY, JULY 2ND

W e pull into the hotel roundabout, *Rumours* still blasting. The valet approaches, and Ed hands over the keys. A bellman dressed in a black suit with gold piping whisks our luggage away.

Walking into the lobby is like walking back in time. It's art déco swanky, with high-backed leather chairs, a rich red Persian rug covering a black and white–tiled floor, mirrored walls, and a long, low, black shellacked bookshelf serving as the front desk. The ceiling is a true work of art; it's all hammered copper.

Ed strolls up to the front desk, and Anh and I follow.

She takes my arm and whispers, "Is something going on with you two?"

I don't know how to answer, so I just shush her instead. We get to the desk, and Anh pulls a book off the shelf and holds it up. Of course they have a copy of *Vex.*

"Put it back," I whisper.

She purses her lips and sets it on the desk instead. "You should autograph it for them."

The desk clerk's eyes go wide. "Oh, my goodness. I knew I recognized your name." He hands Ed a pen. "Would you mind signing it? It's such an honor to have you staying with us."

I resist the urge to roll my eyes. *An honor.* He wrote a book; he didn't save lives in some third-world country.

Ed smiles, but it's not his usual *take over his whole face, make his eyes crinkle in the corner* kind of smile. It's an uncomfortable grimace disguised as a smile. He signs the book quickly. *Keep on keepin' on.*

"Here you go, man."

The clerk nods. "Thank you. Here are your keys." He hands us each a small leather case with a keycard inside. Leather. I've had keycards in little paper sleeves before, but never in a leather case. How much does this place cost?

A bellhop ushers us in the elevator and shows us to our rooms. Two black doors with gold-plated numbers, right next to each other all the way at the end of a hall with a patterned carpet to rival the one in *The Shining.* Before we head into our room, Ed says, "Should we just meet in the lobby around six?"

Anh waves. "Sounds great," she says then walks through the door. I can hear her oohing and ahhing over the amenities.

Ed leans in closer to me. I can smell his citrus scent, and my chest warms. "Hattie..."

He looks at me for a long, drawn-out beat, his warm green eyes snatching my breath away.

"The thing is, I don't think I *can* forget it."

I search his face and give him a nod. "We'll meet you at six, dressed to the nines."

He smiles, the real one this time.

The room is truly amazing. Dark hardwood floors, covered by a massive white fur carpet. A white leather couch and two golden velvet chairs sit in front of a marble fireplace, already lit with a fire. There is a low coffee table, with a marble top to match the hearth and geometric gold legs, a gold bucket of champagne on ice, and two glasses. Anh runs to the fireplace and turns a knob. The fire goes up. She turns it the other way, and the fire goes down.

I laugh. "The magic of gas."

She beams. "And that's not all."

It feels so good to see her happy. She opens the double doors to a bedroom with a fluffy king-sized bed, gold geometric wallpaper, and a wall of windows with a door to a balcony.

"Wow."

"You're telling me. This must be costing your boyfriend a pretty penny."

I ignore her and step out onto the balcony, the late-afternoon sun warming my face and casting an amber light on downtown Portland and the Willamette River beyond it.

The champagne cork pops inside. So much for never drinking again. I take a seat in one of the gold metal peacock chairs with blue fur cushions positioned on the deck. It looks more like a throne than patio furniture.

Anh brings out two glasses of champagne, handing me one and clinking it with hers. She sits in the other chair and sighs. "I could get used to this."

"You could probably afford places like this with your fancy lawyer salary," I say, sipping the light bubbly liquid.

Anh laughs. "Yes, I probably could. It's the vacations I don't usually get to take. This is the first time off I've taken in…" She pauses, searching the clouds for answers. "God, in two years. That can't be right." She sips her drink and nods slowly. "Two years. When Melissa and I went to Cabo." She lets out a sound somewhere between a sob and a laugh.

I sit forward in my chair, putting my hand on her arm.

"It's no wonder Melissa wanted someone more fun. She actually told me that. She said Stephanie's lighter, less serious. She said we never laugh anymore."

"Honey, you both work a lot. You can't beat yourself up for being good at your job."

"Sure. At what cost, though? For years, I was so focused on trying to make partner. I just never thought it would cost me mine."

I rub a hand on Anh's back.

She looks up. "You know what else? I haven't actually read one of the books for book club since we went to Puerto Rico."

I drop my hand, more out of shock than anything. "Really?"

"I've just been so busy, and I read all day for work. When I get home, I just want to throw on sweats and watch *Below Deck*. I don't want to think anymore." She puts her head in her hands.

I rub her back again. I can't believe she never read the books. On the Zoom calls, she always spoke so eloquently about them. But now doesn't seem the time to bring it up. "It doesn't matter."

We sit silently for a minute, but then, I can't help it. I ask. "You didn't even read the ones you picked?"

Her whole body slumps, fresh tears welling up in the corner of her eyes again.

I quickly add, "It's okay. It's fine."

After Anh calms down, we head out to find dresses for the party. We stop in a nearby boutique, and Anh finds a gorgeous purple silk dress that falls on her tall frame like it was made for her. She doesn't even look at the tag before trying it on. I peek at the prices, swallow back my discomfort, and head to the small sale section. There is a black backless dress with complicated spaghetti straps in the front that's a reasonable price. I try it on, and Anh purses her lips.

"It's alright."

"Gee, thanks."

"I mean, you look great, as always, but the straps are a little dated."

She flits about the store, bringing me three other dresses, again not even checking the tags. I try on the light-blue chiffon dress, which has a long sheer layered skirt and plunging V neckline with a matching one in the back. The blue almost exactly matches the shade of my eyes and makes them stand out even more.

I come out of the dressing room to look at it in the three-way mirror. It's stunning. Truly. I feel like a fairy princess and twirl, the soft skirt flowing around my calves.

Anh gasps. "That's the one."

My stomach drops when I check the tag. Why didn't I check it before I tried it on? I can't afford this.

"It's not really me."

Anh, sharp as a tack, shakes her head. "I've never seen any article of clothing that is more *you*."

"I... I don't know."

Anh frowns. "I'll buy it."

I open my mouth to protest, but she holds up her finger. "No arguing. I'm on vacation."

***

ANH GETS ready first then scrolls her phone with a glass of champagne while I have my turn. I take extra time with my makeup. I'm trying to decide if I should put my hair up or leave it down, when I hear a gasp from the other room, then a large clatter and shattering glass.

I run out. Anh is heaving, her white knuckles wrapped tightly around her phone, a collection of glass shards and champagne in a puddle on the floor near her feet.

"Oh my God, what happened?" I lead her away from the broken glass. "Are you okay?"

Anh shows me the screen of her phone. "No. I'm not okay. Look, look at this."

It's Melissa's Instagram account. There is a picture of her looking rosy-cheeked and happy sitting next to a beautiful Latino woman with gorgeous chestnut hair, a pristine aquamarine pool behind them, cocktails held up in a cheers. The caption reads, "I am beyond grateful this incredible human was born on this day twenty-six years ago. You are the love of my life, the light of my days, the star of my nights. I'm so excited I get to do this life with you."

Yikes. I'm stunned and also thankful I'm not on any of these sites. Chad probably posts all the time.

"You need to unfollow her."

Anh nods and grabs the champagne, taking a swig right from the bottle and sitting on the floor in her beautiful gown. "I know. I know. I should. But the thing is, then I won't see them—see her. I won't know what's going on in her life anymore."

I check the time. We're supposed to meet Ed downstairs in two minutes. Anh's mascara is running down her cheeks. I send a quick text.

Running late. We'll meet you at the party.

I take the champagne from Anh and set it to the side. "You won't know. But is knowing making you happy?"

Anh sighs. "No."

I go to the little Keurig machine and put in a hot chocolate pod.

"It's a connection, but it's not real." I offer Anh a hand, helping her to her feet. I lead her to the bathroom, wet a washcloth, and wipe off her face where the mascara and eyeliner have run. Anh closes her eyes, and I can see her shoulders relax.

"Plus, who says 'do this life'? You don't need that hippy yolo shit blocking up your feed."

Anh snickers at this. "She did start to get pretty woo-woo toward the end there. Our apartment had so many crystals."

"Hey, don't knock the crystals."

Anh laughs, a real laugh this time. "I forgot you like those, too."

I finish washing Anh's face, and she opens her eyes, looking much calmer than before.

"Now, do you want to do your makeup again, or would you like to get out of this dress and into the fluffy robe behind you?"

"Robe, please."

I nod. "I'll just text Ed and tell him we're not coming."

"No," Anh says, her face stern. "I'm staying. *You* are going."

"If you're not, I'm not. I'll make another mug of hot chocolate, and we can watch whatever housewives you want."

"Look at you in that dress." Anh grabs my hand and twirls me for emphasis. "You can't miss the party. You'll meet all sorts of publishing people and become the famous writer you're destined to be."

She smiles as she slips out of her dress and into the robe. "Look at me talking about destiny. I can be woo-woo too. Please go. I'll be fine." She clicks a few things on her phone and turns it to show me. "See, unfollowed. Already doing better."

"Are you sure?"

"Yes. You look so amazing; you can't waste it. I'm fine. I might even start one of the books for Story Club."

I hug Anh tightly. "If you need me, I will be back in a flash."

"I know, honey. Go have fun."

WINTER SOLSTICE

TEN YEARS AGO

L ight white flakes fall onto the boardwalk, making a sugar-coated dusting. It's beautiful but slick—dangerous. Christmas lights twinkle all around. Wrapped around the lampposts, lining the little coffee kiosk. Even the passing boats are decked out in colorful designs. The large sailboat passing right now has green lights strung back and forth from the mast, making a giant Christmas tree.

Gingerly, I make my way to the bench. The same bench I sat on six months ago when Ed bought me an ice cream. Tonight is definitely not a night for ice cream. It's thirty-two degrees and dropping. Pulling my coat closer around me, I tuck myself into my scarf and tug my hat down around my ears, pushing my hair out of the way. The green streak is gone. It's all my normal chocolate brown. A boy in my Intro to Philosophy course told me I have beautiful hair. He said it like it surprised him that it was coming out of his mouth. He asked me to coffee, but I said no. How could I have coffee with some other guy when my heart belongs to Ed? I've replayed our day together, *that day*, nonstop for the last six months. For me, it feels like it never ended. Like Ed will walk out on these slippery planks and we'll pick up where we left off.

I check my phone—7:13 p.m.

Ed's late.

But that's not too surprising. I walk to the coffee kiosk, and the woman opens a little sliding glass window, just like at a drive-thru.

"What can I get you?"

Scanning the menu, I try to decide. It's too late for coffee for me. I've found it makes me jittery and panicked if I have more than a morning cup. "Peppermint tea, please."

"You got it. Just in time. We're about to close."

"Oh, could I get a hot chocolate too, then?"

This time, I'll buy the treats. Ed will have a warm cup of sugar waiting for him when he arrives. Then we can get in my grandma's car and go somewhere warm. I borrowed it for the night. Too cold and snowy to bike and skate.

Drinks in hand, I head back to the bench and brush off the snow that instantly covered my seat. I set Ed's drink down on the ground. Steam rises out of the hole in the lid of my cup. I'm greedy for the warmth and take a small sip. The tip of my tongue yelps in protest. Too hot.

Wrapping my hands around the cup, I suck in all the warmth I can. I think about pulling out my book, but I don't want the snow falling to wet the pages. So, I just stare out at the dark water.

Thirty minutes go by. My tea is cool enough to drink now, which warms me up a little, but my face is so cold, I can't feel my cheeks. The coffee kiosk is dark, and the woman who was working is long gone. I'm completely alone on this dark, snowy night. The longest night of the year. I check my phone again.

Why didn't we exchange numbers? It was idiotic. What if something happened to him?

What if he just plain forgot?

No, he wouldn't forget. How could a night that's branded in my brain be completely forgettable to him? Something must've happened.

What if he got in a plane crash on his way to Colorado? What if he was in a skateboarding accident? What if he tried to skate here tonight and he slipped and hit his head and he's lying in a ditch somewhere, unconscious? What if he met someone? What if he met someone in

Colorado—another writer, a poet with super long hair like the pink-haired girl from the Polaroid in the tree house—and they fell madly in love and he's with her right now?

The tree house. I check the time again—8:03 p.m. I throw away Ed's full cup of hot chocolate, more like freezing cold chocolate now, and get in my grandma's Honda Civic, cranking the engine to life and turning up the heat to full blast. I'm honestly not sure I can find my way back to his mom's, with the tree house in the back. But I'm going to try.

This can't be how our story ends.

The college radio station plays Beck's "Heart is a Drum." His voice is soft on this album, the guitar ethereal. It's eerie driving with the snowflakes whizzing past the car like stars. I go to the drive-in first. It's dark and shuttered, closed for winter. From there, I follow the exact route we took that night. I'm usually terrible with directions, but I remember every second of that night. Every move, every turn, every touch.

After about thirty minutes of driving up and down streets, the familiar light-blue house with a white picket fence comes into view. I park the car and walk through the snow-covered yard. Before I go to the front door, I peek in the backyard to look at the tree house, to make sure this is the place. The tree is there, but the house is gone. Completely gone. All the blood rushes to my toes in a whoosh, so swift it makes me dizzy. I know this is the house... The roses—thorny bushes at the moment—are still there, the little patio is still there, but no furniture. I look again at the tree. Two rungs of the ladder remain on the trunk, like streamers overlooked after cleaning up a party. They look almost burnt. But it's dark and hard to see.

There's a light on in the living room and a Christmas tree in the window, tossing light into the night with wild abandon. Rolling my shoulders back, I walk up the three little concrete steps to the front door. I've come this far; I might as well see it through. With my heart in my throat, I knock.

A man with gray hair and a Seahawks sweatshirt answers the door.

The strong smell of chili wafts through the cold air. Maybe it's his grandfather, but part of me knows it's not.

"Can I help you?"

"I... Is Ed here?"

A woman comes to join him at the door in a matching Seahawks sweatshirt and blue leggings, her hair in a neat bob. "Who is it?"

"I didn't mean to disturb you; I was just looking for my friend Ed. He used to live here."

"Oh, I think the owner before had a son. Was that him?" the woman asks, but not to me—more to her husband.

The man frowns. "We bought the house in the fall. Short sale on account of the fire."

"Fire? Was everyone okay?"

"As far as I know, it was just some cosmetic damage. But I'm afraid I don't know much about the previous owners."

"Thanks."

They close the door, taking with them the warmth and strong spices.

I trudge back to Grandma's car, turning the heat on full blast again as tears fall unchecked down my cheeks.

Ed didn't come. Not only that, but I have absolutely no way to get ahold of him. He probably doesn't even want me to. If he wanted to see me again, he would've been there.

I drive straight to Robin's house. She calls Anh over for reinforcements and lends me some cozy clothes. We make hot chocolate and put on *Elf*.

"Do you want to talk about it?" Anh asks, her eyes so full of concern, it makes me want to cry all over.

But I swallow back my tears. "No."

"At least tell us his name," Robin pleads. "We might know him; we might know how to get in touch with him."

It's tempting. But I don't want to give up what little I have left of that night. What if he had a girlfriend the whole time? Or what if he's a terrible person and Anh and Robin know that because they know him? But this way, I know Ed. I know the Ed I spent the summer solstice with. And I won't let anyone take that from me.

"If he wanted to be there, he would've been there. He wasn't. Can we not talk about it anymore?"

Robin and Anh nod. I sip my sweet hot chocolate and try to lose myself in the comedic genius of Will Ferrell, but all I can think about is *that day.*

CHAPTER 11
TUESDAY, JULY 2ND

L eaving Anh cuddled up on the couch with her mug of hot chocolate and an Emily Henry book, I check my phone on the way to the lobby. I have three missed texts, all from Ed.

Ed: I can wait if you want.

Then two minutes later.

Ed: Or I can meet you there.

Then five minutes later.

Ed: I'll meet you there.

A Lyft picks me up, my nerves crackling. I open the purse I borrowed from Anh and remove the contents, searching for my lipstick. Why is it that the smaller the purse, the harder it is to find anything? Finally, I find the lipstick and swipe on a fresh coat, but it doesn't have the desired calming effect I was hoping for. I don't need to be so nervous. It's just a book launch party for a famous author, with a bunch of other famous authors and industry professionals. I wipe my hands on the soft fabric of the seat as the car drives up, up, and up.

I'm equal parts dreading and hopeful that we can find a moment alone so Ed can explain why he stood me up ten years ago. I'd be lying if I said it hadn't been in the back of my mind ever since I saw him standing in the kitchen. Before that, even. But what could he possibly say? My mind runs through the familiar loops on the track of possible reasons Ed couldn't come that day. He had an accident. He was sick, so sick he was in the hospital. He was in jail for robbing a convenience store, only he was the getaway driver, and he didn't know his friend was robbing it. But they all got busted. He had a terrible head injury that caused amnesia. Or he didn't and just forgot.

What if his reason is stupid and I can't forgive him?

The Pittock Mansion comes into view. It's massive, almost more a castle than a house, gray stone with two spires on either side. There is a balcony that wraps around the bottom, littered with men in tuxedos and women in flowing chiffon and shimmering silk, all chattering with drinks in hand. I exit the car and make my way down the winding path, through a luscious green yard, the scent of roses wafting through the air. I keep my eyes peeled for Ed.

As I walk through the entryway, a server hands me a glass of champagne. An enormous marble staircase with more fancy people takes up the entire entryway. But still no Ed. I continue wading through the sea of people up the stairs. I go to pull out my phone from my purse and send a quick text.

Me: I'm here. Where are you?

To the left of the stairs is a stunning library, all dark wood, row after row of leather-bound books, a crystal chandelier and a large carved wood and stone fireplace. They set up a bar in the corner, and that's where I spot Ed. He's leaning one elbow on the bar, the other holding a crystal tumbler of whiskey.

Ed's brow is puckered, his mouth a stern line. As he sees me, his forehead relaxes, and his ears rise with his smile. He crosses the room in a black tuxedo with a green satin bow tie that makes his eyes leap from his face. He's smiling, looking me up and down and sending tingles down my legs.

"You clean up nice," I say with a smile.

He lets out a breath, like he'd been holding it, and rubs a hand over the back of his neck. "You look… Wow."

I smile, butterflies fluttering erratically in my chest.

Ed grabs my hand. "Let's go meet some people."

He leads me through the mansion. We explore the rooms, much of them with placards explaining what's original to the house. Along the way, we meet two agents, three editors, and four authors. One agent asks about my book, and I tell her the basic premise. She leans in as I tell her and gives me her email, saying she'd love to read it when it's finished. My smile is so big it hurts.

By the time we make it to one of the bedrooms, I feel a little dizzy. The room has a tiny bed, so small it almost looks like it's for a child.

Ed moves through into the attached bathroom. "Whoa, look at this!"

I go in. There is a walk-in shower with a crazy number of pipes. It looks more like a torture device than a shower. "That's intense."

Leaning in to get a closer look at the contraption, I can feel Ed's eyes on me. He reaches out and touches the soft fabric of my skirt. "That's an awful lot of fabric for a very revealing dress."

I gasp. "Is it too skimpy?"

"No," he says quickly as he moves his hand to my waist and pulls me into him. "It's just skimpy enough."

His palms move up my bare back, sending shivers down my spine. He gazes into my eyes.

"Hattie, about December…"

He wants to talk about this now? In the antique bathroom of a mansion at a literary party. With his hands on me and his citrus scent wafting around us like a spell. Whatever the reason, once he tells me…there's no going back.

One kiss. Before we talk, before he explains, I just want one kiss. As I lean in, my mind fills with flashes of *that day*, anticipating the feel of his lips before I press mine to them.

Our lips meet. His kiss is soft. It's different than I recall—*he's* different. I've remembered and re-remembered that day so many times, playing the scene of us together over and over, like rubbing my thumb across a worry stone, softening the sharp details to a smooth vague surface. Polished and safe.

What am I doing? This man is more back and forth than a see-saw. I should push him away, but instead, I push into him. The pressure of my lips increases. I open my mouth, and so does he, his hand still on my bare skin. He runs his fingers up my spine, then through my hair, my scalp tingling at his touch, the sensation traveling down to my thighs. I put my hand on the taut muscles of his back, pulling myself closer to him, our bodies flush against each other, his stiff jacket almost rough against my chest through the flimsy layers of chiffon. At the contact, my body melts into a puddle of lust.

Our kiss ends, but Ed still holds me close. "Hattie…"

My heart tries to leap out of my throat and cover his mouth. What if he says something neither of us can take back? What if he was with another woman and didn't think I deserved an explanation? What if he just forget?

"We should go." I pull away, brushing off my dress. "Let's find somewhere quiet to get a drink."

At the very least, I don't want to cry in front of all these literary professionals.

His eyes sparkle. "Okay. I know a place."

CHAPTER 12

We catch a shuttle downtown, and Ed takes me to a tall stone and stained-glass church, with a looming bell tower.

"You need to confess?" I instantly regret my choice of words.

He shakes his head, smiling. "Come on."

There's a small set of concrete stairs around the back, a slat wooden door at the bottom that looks older than Portland itself. Ed opens it, and the thumping sound of PJ Harvey's "To Give You My Love" pours into the night. The bar is dark, with long wooden tables like something you might see in an episode of *Game of Thrones*, two pool tables, a Medieval Times pinball machine, and a jukebox in the corner. Ed leads me to the bar, and we wait our turn. Ed orders two Pabsts.

I whisper in his ear, "Can I get a wine?"

"Not a good idea here unless you're a fan of Carlo Rossi."

"A whiskey, then."

Ed nods and changes my order.

We take our drinks to the corner of one of the long tables. A small candle in a red glass holder flickers between us, and the question hangs in the air like a thought bubble in a graphic novel. *Where were you that night? Why didn't you meet me?*

Ed takes a swig of his beer, and it feels like he's buying time. I run my thumb over the smooth glass in my hand and don't say anything. I wait. I've waited for ten years to hear this. What's a few more minutes?

"I wanted to be there. I did. It just...wasn't possible. Do you remember that night we were together how my mom was home?"

I nod.

He sighs. "She lost her job. At the time, she said she was laid off. But part of me knew she was lying. My mom has a problem with pills. It wasn't the first job she lost. But this time, she couldn't find another one. While I was at the residency, she accidentally set the house on fire. I'm not even sure what happened. I'm positive she was either drunk or high or both. She says she had a seance with all these candles, and the spirit got out of hand." He runs a hand over his face. "She was already behind on the mortgage. She had to sell the house. Then she met a guy online. He lived in Seattle, and she moved in with him. He was a big drinker. So, they would just get fucked up."

He turns his can on the table; the condensation runs off the aluminum. "Toward the end of the residency, I got a call from the hospital. My mom fell off the railing of her deck trying to hang Christmas lights from the roof while drunk and high. I went to Seattle to take care of her. Moved her out of that place and into a friend's for a bit. She was so pissed at me. We all lived there in this tiny apartment. Broke as fuck. We were in Portland on the day I was supposed to meet you. It was all such a mess. How could I meet you and bring you into that? That day we spent together, we felt so connected. Like you really saw me."

"It felt that way for me too."

He reaches across the table and runs his fingers along mine. "When you're trying to do everything you can to survive, the last thing you need is to be with someone who sees straight to your soul."

My chest feels heavy, my breaths shallow.

He *couldn't* come.

It all makes perfect sense. He needed to be with his mom. Somehow, it feels like there's something missing from this story. I can't put my finger on it. But maybe it's just that I've been waiting so long to hear the reason, built it up in my head, that now that I have it, it doesn't feel like enough. Like the end of *Lost.*

"Did you ever get my message?"

I look up into his face. The light from the candle kisses his cheek, catching his green eyes and making them sparkle like sunlight on a lake. "Message?"

He runs his hand on the back of his neck. "I couldn't help trying to find you online. I sent you a Facebook message and a friend request. When you never responded, I figured you were pissed."

"I'm not on Facebook."

"Now, but I sent this like the day before we were supposed to meet."

My brows knit together. "I was on Facebook in high school, but I deleted it before we even met."

"No, it was you. It had to be. How many Harriet Stevens are there? And the profile picture was a book."

With a swift movement, he whips his phone and scrolls down, down, down. "Here it is. Shit. Now it's blank and just says Facebook user. I swear it said Harriet Stevens and had a picture of a leather-bound copy of *Pride and Prejudice.*"

He hands me the phone. The date says December twentieth. He's not lying... He really did send it before we were supposed to meet. I read the gray bubble.

Hattie. I think this is you. I hope this is you. I know we said no texting, and I get it. But I wish we had exchanged numbers just in case. I can't be there tomorrow. I wish I could. Please know that I truly, deeply wish I could. But it's just not possible. My life is a mess. I wish I could explain more, but it's not completely my story to tell—or maybe it is and I'm not ready to tell it. Please know I've thought about you every second of every day since we met. I wish I was going to be there tomorrow, but I just can't. Text me.

His number is in a separate bubble. I can't stop staring at the screen, too bright in this dark bar. Our lives would be so different if this had been me.

Ed breaks into my thoughts. "I was sure you read it and ghosted me."

He moves his hand from mine, running it over scratches in the table. "Do you think you can forgive me?"

I can hold on to this hurt over him not being there that day, like I have for nearly a decade, or I can let it go like a balloon floating up into the atmosphere. I can feel the string of the balloon slipping through my fingers, but at the last moment, I yank it back down to earth.

"What about the signing? I even gave you my name. You had no idea who I was."

Ed lets out a long breath. "That whole tour was a shit show. I can't believe I didn't recognize you, though."

I reach up to tuck my hair behind my ear. "My hair was short and blonde that day."

Ed raises his eyebrows. "Blonde, huh?"

I nod. "It was my breakup hair. I was very into the movie *Sliding Doors* at that time, and I took a picture of Gwyneth Paltrow from that movie into the salon."

"Never seen it. I'm sure it looked amazing. I wish I could remember. I was behind on my second book. Then my mom went off with some other guy. She moved to New Mexico. I wanted to cancel the rest of the tour, but they wouldn't let me."

"Sleep Walkin" by Modest Mouse comes on. Ed fiddles with the tab on top of his beer.

"How's your mom doing?"

Ed shrugs. "We don't talk anymore, but she and my buddy we lived with stay in touch. He says she's doing alright. Off the pills. Working at some bar near Roswell."

I want to ask more when he says, "Tell me about this breakup that had you hacking all your hair off…"

I take a tiny sip of the whiskey. A nearby table filled with dudes in flannels and girls in black tank tops erupts into laughter. We are definitely overdressed for this bar, but no one seems to care. When the noise dies down, I say, "His name was Chad."

Ed makes a disgusted bleh noise.

"Yeah. It wasn't just a breakup. It was a divorce."

There's a hefty pause before Ed says, "I'm sorry. I didn't know. We don't have to talk about—"

"It's okay. I thought we were going to have kids, be together forever. He was also a teacher, so we both had summers off. I had this whole vision for our lives together. Traveling in the summers. Camping trips with the eventual children. But he was cheating on me. With one of his co-workers."

"No."

"It was a long time ago." Even as I say it, talking about him brings back the old feelings. Not the love that was the first to fade into oblivion, but the sting of betrayal.

"What a dick."

There's a long pause where neither of us speaks.

Ed finally breaks the silence. "Hattie, can you forgive me for not recognizing you when you were impersonating Gwyneth Paltrow?"

I laugh, and he reaches for my hand across the table again. His skin is warm, his fingers catching the light of the candle, all except the inky black letters of his tattoo.

"Seriously, can you forgive me for not showing up that day in December?"

I inhale deeply, the stale beer scent catching in my throat, but underneath it is him, his citrus clove musk the same from our day so long ago. I let the balloon go and watch it float into the atmosphere, feeling as light as it. "Yes. I forgive you."

Ed's rugged jaw cracks into a wide smile. He finishes his beer and looks at me. "Want another drink?"

I shake my head. "Let's get out of here."

His smile is so bright, it lights up the room. He takes my hand and leads me out the door. Night has settled, but the air is still muggy. My skirt billows around my legs as we walk down the sidewalk.

We stop at a crosswalk, and I turn to him, putting my arms around his neck. He leans down, and I meet him halfway, reaching my lips up to meet him. Our kiss feels inevitable. Like we were always meant to be here on this street corner, on this muggy night. He runs his hands over the soft fabric of my dress, and my body immediately responds, goose bumps covering my arms.

The chirp of the crosswalk chimes, and we part. Ed takes my hand as we walk down the street. "What do you want to do?"

I look him square in the eye, my voice unwavering. "You."

He swallows hard, a nearly cartoon gesture. When we get across the street, he pulls me close and kisses me deeply; the city falls away —his lips, his scent, his body the only things that exist. He whispers in my ears, his lips brushing my earlobe, "The hotel is just a couple blocks this way."

CHAPTER 13

We race like children on the playground, past food carts and people out smoking in front of bars, until we finally make it to the hotel. I lean against the wall of the elevator, trying to catch my breath, but Ed takes my face in his hands and kisses me softly, seizing what little breath I had left. Time slows.

The elevator dings open. Ed intertwines his fingers with mine as we walk down the long hallway, the anticipation between us so thick, you could snatch it right out of the air and take a bite. Ed takes his keycard out of his pocket, and the beep sends a pulse straight to my thighs.

He holds the door open for me as I enter the room that is identical to ours. I head straight for the bedroom, stepping out of my shoes along the way. Ed follows at a measured pace, his hands in his pockets. I can feel his eyes on me.

In front of the bed, I move one of my straps off my shoulder, then the other, feeling the cool air conditioning on my bare breasts. I let the whole dress fall to the floor in a pool of fabric at my feet, wearing nothing but a light-blue thong. I look over my shoulder.

Ed's hooded and hungry eyes are fixed on me. He comes up behind me, putting his hands on my breasts, his palms cold and his grip firm. His lips make a trail from behind my ear to my collarbone.

"I've thought about this for so long," he whispers, his voice thick. "I've wanted you for years."

It's all I've ever longed to hear. I turn to face him, taking his jacket off, lifting his shirt up over his head. Unbuckling his belt and letting his pants fall to the floor. Our skin presses together.

He lays me down on the bed, starting where he left off, kissing my collarbone then moving down to my breast, taking my nipple into his mouth. He sucks harder, and I cry out with pleasure. Want pulses from deep inside me. I take his hand and move it between my legs, showing him exactly what I want. He moves rhythmically as pressure builds up, starting at my thighs, moving to my chest.

I whisper in his ear, "Do you have a condom?"

My skin feels cold as he moves away momentarily, running to the bathroom. The condom is on before he's even back in bed. I laugh.

"That was fast."

He licks at my neck. "Don't worry. The rest won't be."

He moves his mouth to my ear, taking the soft lobe in his mouth and nibbling while he moves his other hand down my body, squeezing my breast on the way down, running his hand across my stomach, then finding my most sensitive spot and swirling.

I reach for his length, taking him in my hand, and he gasps at my touch. Running my hand up and down before I line us up, I say, "I need you."

His pupils flare as he moves slower than I think he ever has in his entire life as he pushes inside, filling me inch by inch as he watches my face.

I lean my head back, moaning as he pulls out and does it again, this time going even deeper.

"Is that too much?"

"No. I want more." I breathe out, my thighs shaking.

He thrusts deeper, picking up the pace, and I arch into him, increasing the pressure.

"I could watch you like this all night."

His words make me clench harder, and an animal noise escapes him. He pulls out and enters me again slowly, but I can't take it anymore. I need more; I need him faster, harder.

Rolling on top of him, I settle myself down on the length of him as his hands grip my hips then my ass.

I brace myself with my palms on his chest, his tattooed skin underneath my fingers. He moves one hand to my breast, half sitting up to take it into his mouth. It's too much and not enough. My whole body convulses as he sucks strongly on my nipple, and I come down harder on his erection.

I freeze, stars filling my vision, my body taken by wave after wave. I feel Ed clench and swell, and then he stills as well. When I open my eyes, he's watching me, his jaw slack, his eyes smoldering.

"You are so beautiful."

I flop down on the bed, and he lies next to me, running his hand on my arm. I roll into him, his arms around me, my head on his chest.

We melt into each other as the night stretches in front of us.

***

MORNING COMES FASTER than seems decent. I don't even know what time I eventually fell asleep last night, tucked in the crook of Ed's arms, the small spoon to his big spoon. The light outside is pearly pink. Quietly, I move out from our cozy nook to go check on Anh. I put my dress back on, wishing I had something else to wear, but I just have to go down the hall, one door over in fact.

Shoes in hand, I go barefoot, the *Shining* carpet in the hallway soft under my feet. I open the door and head straight to the bedroom. Anh is still sleeping in the king-sized bed, a red satin sleeping mask snug on her face. Relief washes over me. I should've checked on her last night, but I was too swept up in the moment.

I'm about to head back to Ed's room, snuggle back into the warmth of his body, but I realize I don't have a key to get back in. Instead, I grab some cozy clothes out of my luggage—a threadbare T-shirt with Queen of Mystery printed on it and a pair of sweat shorts—and take them into the bathroom. I stand for a long time under the warm water of the shower, replaying last night's events in my head. Ed's lips on my neck, on my stomach, on my…

Anh rushes into the bathroom, interrupting my thoughts. I peek out of the shower curtain; she's hunched in front of the toilet, retching. Hopping out, I wrap a towel around myself quickly and hold her hair back.

After a few minutes, she presses the handle and sits on the cold tile floor. I move my hand to her back, rubbing slow circles.

Anh wipes her mouth. "I should not have finished that champagne."

"Oh, honey. Come on. Let's get you into bed."

I help her back to the king-sized bed, and we find a trashy reality TV show marathon on the hotel's cable. We look at the room service menu, but Anh throws it across the room. "It all sounds disgusting."

"You have to eat something. I can go find you Saltines."

She nods then winces. "And some club soda?"

I smile while I transfer my stuff from Anh's fancy purse to my mini leather backpack. "Yes, and club soda. Any other requests?"

"Tylenol."

"You got it."

"Thanks, Hattie. Hey, are we going back today? If we are, we might need to bring a bag for the car."

"A bag?"

She mimes yakking, and I understand what she's saying. "Got it. I'll talk to Ed. Maybe we can stay one more night."

I head back to Ed's room and knock lightly on the door. A few minutes with no answer. Should I knock again or just leave? But then Ed opens the door, a towel wrapped around his waist, water trickling down his chest, his face in a sleepy smile. "There you are."

He wraps his hands around my waist, pulling me inside. Our lips meet as the door clicks, the taste of mint from his toothpaste bright on my tongue. He backs me against the door, running his hands down my spine and lifting me up, cupping my ass in his hands. He moves his mouth to my neck, and a moan falls from my lips. The towel from Ed's hips hits the floor.

Then I remember my mission.

"Ed, I have to go."

He mumbles into my neck.

"Anh's not feeling well."

"Bummer." He sets me down softly. "She's sick?"

"Hungover. She needs crackers."

"Okay. I can come too. Just give me a minute." He gestures to the fact that he has no clothes on. I follow him as he moves toward his luggage, admiring his ass, desire building in my chest. I grab his hand as he reaches for some boxers.

"Maybe we could be quick?"

His smile overtakes his face. He reaches for a condom instead with a small eyebrow raise at me. I nod and quickly shimmy out of my shorts. Ed helps bring the shirt up over my head then picks me up again, this time leaning me against the massive window.

"Ed, someone will see."

"There's no way. We're too high up."

I'm not sure he's right, but I want him too much to worry about it. "Okay," I say in a breathy voice.

The glass is cool against my back, while Ed is hot against my chest. Running his mouth along my shoulder, he thrusts inside me. I clench around him with each of his movements then sigh and relax as I let him in deeper and deeper. His arms are shaking, either from exertion or pleasure, I'm not sure. I get down, turning toward the window, and guide him inside me again from behind. He groans out my name, sending fresh tingles on my skin.

Ed puts his hands on top of mine on the glass then runs them down my arms to my breasts, cupping them in his massive hands and pinching my nipples between his fingers. I cry out with the over-whelming pleasure from it. He squeezes harder, and I arch farther into him. My entire body is on fire as a massive pulse shoots through me. I can feel him release as well, every muscle tight. We're both left panting and wet-noodle relaxed.

He pulls out and turns me around, wrapping me in his arms.

"Holy shit."

I sigh. "You can say that again."

He laughs and yells, "Holy shit! Why haven't we been doing that all summer?"

I kiss his cheek lightly. "We can make up for lost time. But first, Anh needs crackers."

AFTER A QUICK CLEANUP and getting our clothes on, we head out in search of a convenience store, stopping by the front desk on the way out to book an additional night. We'll leave tomorrow, and no one will vomit in the car.

Down the street, there's a Plaid Pantry. I get Anh a club soda, Saltines, her favorite peanut M&M's, and two kombuchas—ginger for her, spirulina for me. Looking at the fashion magazines, I'm trying to decide which to pick, when Ed pops up from the other side of the aisle wearing ridiculous pink rhinestone heart-shaped glasses.

"Are they me?"

The pink actually looks good with his mussed-up hair and dark stubble. "I think you might need them for your next author photo."

He laughs, pushing them up on his head like a headband. "My publisher would *love* that."

His smile vanishes, and he wanders off.

We head back to the hotel and split up when we get to our rooms. Anh is asleep, the television still on the reality TV that was playing when I left. I take my kombucha, the breakfast bar I bought, and my notebook and head to the balcony. It's a gorgeous clear morning, not a cloud in the light-blue sky.

I check my email and find an interview request for the middle school position in New Haven. After a few clicks, I select one for first thing Tuesday morning after the holiday. I never pictured myself living there full-time, but it would be nice to be close to Grandma.

Setting my phone down, I open my journal and make a quick to-do list, update my calendar, and then tuck into my story. It's a tricky scene; my protagonist finds out the man in the book can't leave the bookstore.

"What are you writing?"

Anh startles me. I didn't even hear the sliding glass door open. Her hair is wet, her face clean, and she looks a little less green than when I saw her last.

"It's nothing."

She sits in the chair and cracks open her club soda. "So…"

I put down my notebook. "So?"

"Where were you last night?"

So, she hadn't been asleep the whole time. I smile, unable not to. "I was with Ed."

She swats at me. "I knew it! Details. I need all the gross heteronormative details."

I laugh. "You know what's really crazy about the whole thing? Do you remember when I told you about that guy I worked at the bookstore with for one day?"

Anh nods. "The perfect day."

"That's the one." I take a sip of kombucha, biding my time and trying to decide if I should tell her. I swallow and go for it. "It's him."

Anh freezes mid swig. She coughs, sputtering on the soda. I pat her back. "Are you okay?"

She slowly gets ahold of her cough. "It's him, like actually him? I thought you were going to say he reminded you of that guy. But he is *that guy*? From *that day*?"

"Yep."

I tell her about our night but don't go into excessive detail. I know she's hurting, and I don't want to rub my happiness in her face.

Anh sits back in her chair. "That's nuts."

"It really is."

Standing, she puts a hand to her head. "Be careful. He broke your heart once already. Don't let him do it again."

I'm about to defend Ed, to explain that he was with his mom that day in December, but I don't. Part of me knows she's right. He could very well destroy me again. Anh heads back inside. I open my notebook again and lose myself in my story, where the only people getting hurt are fictional and it's all my doing.

I'm not sure how long I sit there before there is a small knock on the sliding glass. I turn to see Ed's face smashed against the slider, his arms spread out wide.

He opens the door. "Want to go see a movie?"

"Sure."

I go inside, where Anh is lying on the couch reading. "Anh, do you want to go see a movie with us?"

"No," she says without looking up from her book.

"Okay, we'll be back later." I slip on my sandals, grab my backpack, and kiss the top of her head.

She whispers to me, "Remember what I said. You only have one heart."

CHAPTER 14
WEDNESDAY, JULY 3RD

The early afternoon is already sweltering. Despite the heat, Ed takes my hand in his. My heart soars at his touch. I feel free, like the first day of summer vacation when I was a kid and the days stretched out long with no responsibilities but to be back at Grandma's by dinner.

I laugh.

He turns his playful eyes on me. "What is it?"

"I just realized I never even asked what we are going to see." It's so unlike me. Usually, I have everything planned. Even on my carefree summer days, Anh and Robin can attest, I was always making lists of things we should do. Goals for the summer.

"There's a little theater on 21st playing some new movies and some second run. I thought we could get there and decide." He has mischief in his face, like he has a secret.

"Okay."

Downtown is a mix of old brick buildings, concrete ones from the seventies, and newer glass skyscrapers. After about twenty minutes, we walk through a luscious green park. A carved wood sign in a bed of flowers catches my eye. I read it aloud. "Couch Park."

I pronounce it how it's spelled like a couch that you sit on.

Ed laughs. "Don't spend much time in Portland, huh?"

"This is my second visit."

"I hate to break it to you, but it's pronounced Cooch."

"Cooch? No, it's not. That's ridiculous."

Ed laughs and holds up his hand. "I didn't name it, but that is how you say it. I swear."

"You are trouble. If I get a job teaching here, some student is going to come to me for directions, and I'm going to tell them to take a left on Cooch and get fired. Ha, ha, very funny."

Ed stops a woman walking a stroller. "Excuse me, miss. My girl-friend and I…"

My ears roar, and it's hard for me to follow what else he's saying. His *girlfriend*? I'm sure he said it to put the other woman at ease. A shorthand to explain who I am. He couldn't very well say this girl I slept with a decade ago and have now reunited with and am currently sleeping with.

They're both looking at me. The woman smiles and says like she's repeating herself, "It's pronounced cooch. Unfortunate but true."

I give a halfhearted smile. "Thanks."

Ed's face is pinched in concern. "Now you know."

"Now I know."

"Do you think you'll end up moving here?"

I shrug. "I applied for a job in SE, but I haven't heard back yet. Lots of people take time off in the summer, so I might still hear from them. We'll see."

Ed is nodding. "It's a fun place to live."

"I did get an interview today in New Haven."

"Whoa. Like you'd live there."

I laugh. "Sadly, most teaching jobs are in person."

"Right. Do you *want* to live there?"

I bite my lip. The honest answer is that I don't know. It could be good. "I'm not sure."

"I'm never moving back. It was not for me."

"Why?"

"Too small, not enough to do."

I nod and wonder if he's right. Would I be bored there? My

hobbies are running, reading, and writing—I can do that anywhere and be happy. I'd be close to Grandma.

He reaches out and grabs my hand as we round the corner to the little theater with a large awning over it, *Cinema* spelled out in red neon cursive. There's a line of gold frames on the brick wall of the building, each with a different movie poster. There's one blockbuster, one art house film, and I do a double take at the last poster. Staring at me with the exact haircut I sported post breakup is Gwyneth Paltrow starring in *Sliding Doors*.

I cover my mouth, my eyes wide, and point to it.

Ed laughs. "It starts in ten minutes if you want to see it."

"I can't believe *you* want to see it."

Ed shrugs. "Let's get some popcorn."

He buys us tickets, a large popcorn, a large drink, and Reese's Pieces. The auditorium is dark, ads flashing on the screen, and the theater is half empty. We find two seats toward the back and settle in.

"How did you find this?" I ask.

Ed chews the popcorn in his mouth. "I was Googling *Sliding Doors* and saw it was playing here."

"You were Googling it?"

"I wanted to see the haircut. I still can't believe I didn't recognize you that day."

I put my hand in his. "It was a rough tour."

The theater gets a notch darker. Nineties pop music blares out, telling us to have fun living in the city, with bright cityscapes to match on the screen.

As I reach for some popcorn, Ed puts a hand on my leg. I haven't seen this movie in quite a few years, but I watched it so many times the summer Chad left, I practically have every line memorized. I felt so seen by Gwyneth catching her boyfriend cheating on her. I didn't catch Chad, but I sometimes wish I had. Would I have been as dry and funny as Gwyneth? Probably not.

Ed opens the candy mid movie and places them one by one on my leg, each time brushing my bare thigh, sending goose bumps all the way up my legs.

Once there's a row of five, I whisper, "What are you doing?"

"Eating snacks and watching the movie." He puts his finger to his lips. "Shhh."

I roll my eyes. He places a few more, going higher and higher on my thigh each time. Ed casually eats the candy off my leg one at a time. Each skim of his fingers sending shivers down my spine. Once he gets to the last piece, he turns his face to mine. I put my hand where his jaw meets his neck and pull him into a soft kiss. His lips are sweet and a little salty from the popcorn. Our kiss is light and playful, a perfect matinee movie kiss, but it quickly turns more passionate.

His lips find the spot right behind my ear he knows I like.

"You're making me wet," I breathe out without thinking.

He sits back in his chair, his hand still on my thigh. "Can I?" he asks as his hand moves inch by inch up my denim skirt.

My breath catches in my throat. I sit back in my seat, placing a hand on either arm rest, looking around. There are two other couples both closer to the screen, and no one is paying attention to us. I nod, biting my lip as his hand moves up.

He moves my panties to the side and runs the long finger of his hand lightly along my wetness.

"Fuck," he groans, hardly audible over the movie.

As his finger moves lightly, I try to keep my breaths even so anyone looking over couldn't tell. He increases the pressure, and I hold tighter to the seat, feeling like if I let go, I may float away.

Ed leans in, placing his finger at my center and slowly entering, "Is this okay?"

"Yes," I breathe out.

He moves back and forth as my breasts swell, my nipples hard as diamonds.

Ed adds another finger, and I kiss him to keep from crying out. He eases up on the pressure, but I need it—more, harder, deeper. I put my hand over his, placing his fingers back inside, clenching around him as all the nerve endings in my body ignite in a fiery blast.

I relax, sitting back in my chair breathless.

Ed moves his hand slowly, whispering, "You are so fucking beautiful."

The rest of the movie, his fingers trace mine then lazily move up my arm and down again. He's still always moving.

After the movie is over, we go get a slice of pizza at Take Another Little Pizza My Heart. It has scuffed-up hardwood floors, pinball in the corner, and "War of Pigs" blaring over the stereo. Each of us orders our slices, along with a beer for Ed and a can of red wine for me. We sit at a booth near the window. I'm careful to find a spot to sit on the bench where the red vinyl seat isn't ripped and scratchy.

"What did you think of the movie?"

He chews the massive bite of sausage pizza he just took, smiling. "It was very satisfying. Didn't you find it satisfying? One might even say orgasmic."

"Very." I laugh.

"It was better than I thought it would be. I liked the end."

"You did?"

"Yeah. It's like no matter what choices we make, fate is still fate. We have no real control over the events of our lives. The thought is freeing." He takes another bite of pizza.

I run my palm over the scratched Formica. "Do you believe that, though? That no matter what we choose, things will turn out the way they turn out?"

Ed looks toward the spitball-covered ceiling. "I'm not sure."

"Isn't that the complete opposite of your book, where every choice the dude made had dire consequences?"

He laughs. "Yeah, that's true. But it's comforting to think that none of it matters because some unseen force is orchestrating the whole thing. What do you think? Do you believe in fate?"

I take a sip of my canned wine, considering the question. Do I believe in fate? How can I not? Robin and I reading the exact same book at the exact same time, and both of us lugging them to swim class on a sunny day when we were kids had to be fate. *Anne of Green Gables* wasn't exactly a popular book for kids our age at the time. Plus, what are the odds of Ed and I coming together again, and again, and again over the years? It has to be fate.

"I do, I think."

We finish our slices and our drinks and head back into the balmy evening, sun dappling through the tree-lined street. The light seizes Ed's green eyes, making them glow like enchanted jewels. He catches me staring and wipes his face. "What is it? Do I have cheese on my face?"

I shake my head. "You're pretty."

Pulling me into him, he says, "You're prettier."

He leans down, and our lips meet. Our kiss is bottomless, endless, timeless. The city street falls away beneath my feet. Everything feels *more*, the light breeze on my bare legs, the bra strap across my collarbone, the soft fabric of my tank top, Ed's hand on my back.

When we finally pull away, he says, "Should we get out of here? I know a place."

I laugh. "Your hotel room?"

"It has a big bed. Really big."

"And a large window too." I smile as flashes of us flit through my mind. Then stop abruptly as it occurs to me—why are we staying at a hotel, anyway? "Don't you live in Portland?"

Maybe he doesn't have room for guests.

Ed turns towards the sidewalk, his hand finding mine as we walk back toward the hotel. "I'm between places."

I wait for him to say more, but he doesn't. Ed always seems to share just a glimpse of what's going on in his life, not the whole picture. But maybe I'm just being paranoid. Since my parents told me they'd been living a lie for years, and Chad was lying to me for months, I sometimes struggle with trust.

We fall into Ed's room, a tangle of limbs and lips. Ed moves away, pulling his shirt off. "I'm all sweaty from the walk. I'm going to shower."

I'm breathless. "Oh."

"Wanna come?"

"More than you know."

He laughs, and we strip like it's a race then *literally* race to the shower. It's a massive walk-in with an overhead rain showerhead. The water is cool and refreshing. I get my hair wet and push it back from my face.

Ed looks me up and down. He puts his mouth to my breast, cupping it around my nipple, already hard from the cold water. He flicks his tongue against it then bites a little, the sensation of his teeth on my sensitive skin making me cry out. He continues his descent, finding my more sensitive skin, flicking and sucking until my legs are shaking with pleasure. I call out his name as stars erupt in front of my eyes, my voice echoing against the tile.

Ed picks me up and carries me to the bed, laying me down gently. He grabs a condom but can't open it with his wet hands. I take it from him, open it with my teeth, and roll it on the length of him, taking my time as his eyelids flutter.

I climb on top of him and slowly lower myself down, both of us crying out as, inch by inch, he fills me up. He grabs my hips, but I don't want his help. This is my show now. I move them to my breasts, and he groans as I rock slowly, then faster and faster, until Ed is calling out my name and every muscle in his body goes tense.

We fall into a sweaty heap side by side on the bed, Ed stroking my hair. Our eyes connect.

Ed's voice is raspy. "Whether it's fate or not, I don't know. But I'm glad I met you ten years ago, and I'm glad we're here now. I wish now, right now, could last forever."

CHAPTER 15
THURSDAY, JULY 4TH

The drive back to Fortune Falls is quick. Anh is feeling better and chatters on. She finished the Emily Henry book last night and has wanted to discuss it the whole way back.

"I forgot how good it feels to finish a book. You know? It's like a vacation for your brain. I forgot how much I love that."

"Yeah, I know what you mean."

"I can't believe I let myself go so long without reading."

Ed shrugs while maneuvering around one of the many twists on the road. "You were just in a different season."

"Season?"

"Yeah, like that old song, you know. 'Turn! Turn! Turn!' There's a season for everything. It just wasn't your time to read, and now it is again."

"Hmm, maybe. What season are you in?"

Ed catches my eye in the rearview mirror and pauses a beat. My heart flutters. "Hopefully it's a time to create, because I have a ton of deadlines fast approaching."

My heart sinks a little bit. I was hoping he'd say a time for love. But that would be sappy—and completely insensitive to say to Anh who just broke up with her partner. Maybe he was saying it to me with his look.

"You two should make it a race. Competition always motivates me," Anh says.

"A race?" I ask.

Anh turns around, her smile wide and devilish. "Yeah. The first to finish their book wins."

"What do we win?" Ed says.

Anh shrugs. "I can't think of everything."

Ed's eyes are focused on the road, his finger tapping against the steering wheel, but I can see the gears spinning. "A race. Hmm."

———

WHEN WE GET BACK, Nathan and Robin are in the kitchen prepping food. Robin is cutting a watermelon, and Nathan is pouring vodka into a pitcher of lemonade. As we walk in, Robin sets down her knife and wipes her hands on a tea towel with an illustrated map of Fortune Falls on it, walking directly to Anh and pulling her into a big hug. She motions for me to come over, and we envelope Anh in a group hug.

"You guys." She squirms in the middle. "You're going to crush me."

Planting a kiss on her cheek, I move away. Robin kisses her other cheek and goes back to chopping watermelon. "We're going to start the grill in an hour or so, and then as soon as it gets dark, we'll start a fire on the beach. Nathan thinks we should be able to see the fireworks from here."

"Nice," Anh says.

I take my bag upstairs, not sure where Ed disappeared to. He's perched on the edge of his bed as I pass his door, tapping furiously at his phone, his brow deeply creased.

"Hey."

He puts the phone underneath him on the bed, a move I recognize from when Chad and I were together. Ice fills my veins. Is he hiding something?

"Everything good?" I ask, trying to keep the tremor out of my voice. I don't want him to think I'm paranoid and insecure, even though I clearly am if after one whole day of hooking up, I'm already sure he's hiding something from me.

He nods. "You know, I'm pretty beat from the drive. I think I'm going to take a little nap."

"Want company?"

He walks over to me, leaving his phone on the bed, puts his strong arms around my waist, and brings his lips to my ear. "If you keep me company, I definitely won't sleep."

He gives me a soft kiss and pulls away with his hand on the door.

"Okay. Come find me when you wake up. Hey, what do you think of Anh's suggestion?"

Ed yawns. "Which one?"

"About racing with our books?"

He shrugs. "We can think about it."

After he closes the door, I pick up my notebook, trying to write some more and shake off the antsy feeling I have about our interaction. He's just tired. But who was he texting that he didn't want me to see? Maybe it's a habit to not show his phone to anyone. Everyone is like that, right? After changing into cut-off shorts and a bright-blue tank top, I make my way to the porch. Robin and Anh are sipping drinks, and Nathan is grilling burgers.

Robin smiles when she sees me. "There you are! Where's Ed? We thought you two may have snuck off together."

"He's napping."

Nathan is nodding. "Yeah, dude is a pill when he's tired."

My heart lifts. See, he was just tired and cranky. He's like that with everyone. My whole body feels lighter.

Robin stands, grabbing a glass. "Drink?"

"Yes, please."

Anh shifts in her seat. "When are we going to have our book club meeting?"

Robin laughs. "Um, when you actually finish one of the books."

Anh's mouth is hanging open. She looks at me. "You told her."

"I didn't."

Anh looks back at Robin. "How did you know?"

Robin hands me my drink, and we all sit together at the table on the porch. "Because when you used to actually read the books, you had a lot more to say about them, your thoughts on them didn't sound like CliffsNotes, and—this is the one that really did it—you were always so agreeable. I would say I think Poppy is a little selfish, and you would say totally. If you had actually read the book, you would never agree, at least not so fast."

Anh sighs. "You're right. But I really did read one of the books this time. I read the whole thing on our little trip while Hattie was..." Anh arches an eyebrow and hides behind her drink.

Robin claps. "I knew you two would get along."

Anh swats at my shoulder lightly. "Tell her the crazy part."

Robin sets down her drink and rubs her hands together. "Oooh, there's a crazy part?"

I take a sip, suddenly feeling very on the spot. "So, you remember that guy I met at the bookstore?"

"The guy from the perfect day?"

"Yeah." I take another sip, buying time. "It's Ed. Ed's the guy."

Robin's mouth is hanging open. "No."

I nod. "Yes."

"You've got to be joking."

"I'm not."

"Nathan, why didn't you tell me Ed worked at Neighborhood Books?"

Nathan doesn't respond, and I notice he has ear pods in. Robin gets up, takes one out, and repeats her question.

Nathan looks at her with a lot of love and a lot of confusion. "I didn't know. We lost touch when we were in high school. I moved to Portland. We just reconnected since we've lived there. You know that, babe."

"Right." She gives him a kiss on the cheek and puts his ear bud back in. Then she makes her way back to the table and takes a long swig of spiked lemonade. "That's crazy. Why didn't he show up six months later like he said he would?"

"He had to be with his mom." I don't want to say more.

"Okay... This is so nuts. And now you two are an item?"

"Uh..."

Anh jumps in. "Stop giving her the third degree. You'd think you were the lawyer."

We all eat burgers—veggie for me, beef for them—and drink more of the delicious lemonade. It is so sweet and tart, you can hardly taste the bite of alcohol, but my cheeks are warm, and my worries are pleasantly blurred.

I check my email idly as the others chit chat around me. Right there at the top is one from Chad. Quickly reading, I stand.

"Oh my God. You guys! We sold the house."

Everyone cheers and pours more drinks, and for the first time in a long time, my shoulders relax.

As the sun starts to wane, we make our way down to the beach. Nathan rolls a large cooler, Anh has a blanket in her hands, and Robin is carrying a bag of snacks. Ed still hasn't emerged from his room, but I'm not as worried as before the three spiked lemonades.

Kyle is a little ways up the beach with a big group. He waves, and I wave back.

After setting everything up, Anh, Robin, and I take off our shoes and run to the water. The icy froth of waves licks my toes like an overexcited puppy. It's exhilarating.

It may have something to do with the lemonades, or the house sale, or Ed, but my heart is full, and this place feels so right. "I love it here."

Robin smiles, lacing her fingers with mine. "I do too."

Anh just nods, holding Robin's other hand.

We break apart, and I wade into the water up to my calves. It's amazing, given how hot the summer has been, how cold this water stays. It must be because of its magnitude. I look out to the horizon, and the water has no end. The sheer size of it overwhelms me. I stare out at the rhythmic crash after crash of waves and get lost in thoughts of my book.

I hardly notice when Anh and Robin make their way back to the blanket. When I can't feel my toes anymore and the next two chapters are plotted in my head, I head back, the sand sticking to my wet feet.

Ed is walking down the beach as I am walking up. He smiles, and my insides melt like a forgotten popsicle in the sun. I don't think. I just run, the sand kicking up onto my calves in prickly bursts. He catches me when I get to him, lifting me up, and I wrap my legs around his waist, planting a big kiss on his mouth. I can hear whistles from our friends over on the blanket, but I don't care.

When our kiss ends, Ed puts me down. "Whoa. I feel like I should've been carded for that kiss."

I shrug. "The lemonade is a pinch strong."

"Apparently." He grabs my hand, and we find a spot on the blanket. He sits down first, and I sit in front of him, leaning back like he's my chair. The sexiest chair. He drapes his hands around me, and it feels like we've been a couple for years instead of days. The sunset is brilliant, shades of deep pink and swaths of gold. We all sit, watching it in silence for a while.

"So, Ed," Robin says, lying on the blanket and propping herself up with one elbow. "You are the man from the perfect day."

Ed's cheeks turn a shade of pink deeper than the sunset. "Uh…"

"Robin." I give her my *don't do it* eyes, but she ignores me.

"Hattie has talked about that day for years. About how you two shared this connection."

Ed moves away on the blanket then stands to get a beer from the cooler. I've switched to water, my head still swimming from the lemonades. "Yeah. It was pretty magical."

Anh sits up, getting involved now. "So, why weren't you there six months later?"

My stomach roils, like I'm on a rollercoaster after eating too much fried food. I may actually be sick. They're looking out for me, and in their drunky drunk way, they think this is a good idea.

"I…I couldn't get away. I'm going to check out the water." Ed walks off toward the shoreline without even a glance my way. No invite. No, would you like to come?

I throw a chip at Robin then Anh. "Why do you two hate me?"

Anh frowns. "We love you. That's why he needs to answer for where he was."

Robin is pointing at Anh and nodding.

"Babe," Nathan says but quickly stops when Robin shoots him a glare.

"We're just looking out for you," Robin says.

"Please don't. I can take care of myself."

Robin holds up both hands, one still holding a mango White Claw. "Okay. I'm sorry, honey."

Anh sighs. "We worry about you. We just don't want to see you get hurt again."

I soften, the fire in my argument snuffed out by the genuine concern in her eyes. "Thank you. But please don't mama bear this, okay? He explained it to me."

They both nod as I stand, a little unsteady on my feet, and go after Ed.

I catch up to him walking along the edge of the water. "They're a little protective."

Ed laughs. "You could say that again."

"I told them to ease up."

Ed runs a hand through his hair. "I'm happy you have people that have your back. It's just a trip, you know. I don't like talking about my mom's problems. Honestly, I've kicked myself for ten years for not being there that day. It's hard to have other people do it too."

I hold his hand in mine.

He lets out a quick breath. "And what was it all for anyway? She's still out there getting fucked up—maybe not with pills, but how long is that going to last? She hates me for trying to help."

"Hey. It's okay. I get it. My dad and I don't talk. It's hard."

He takes a beat, his face turned toward the ocean. When he speaks again, his words are careful. "It's not the same. You can text him anytime you want, and he'll respond."

"Yeah, maybe in five to ten business days."

"My mom..." He shakes his head. "It's different."

He's right. We may both have strained relationships with our parents, but I have no idea what it's like to have a mom battling addiction. "I talked to Robin and Anh. They're going to back off."

He takes my hand, rubbing the back of it with his thumb. We walk hand in hand down the beach until the stars come out one by one. As we head back, fireworks explode in the sky. We stop, and Ed puts his arms around me from behind. Without the sun, the sand is cold in between my toes, but Ed's arms are warm around my body. We watch the light show in each other's arms.

CHAPTER 16
FRIDAY, JULY 5TH

I wake up in Ed's arms, pearly gray light drifting in through the open window along with a sea breeze. My eyes are crusty, and my head is foggy. I shouldn't have drunk so much last night. Those lemonades were sweet and tasty but lethal. I get out of bed, but Ed grabs me back.

"It's too early."

He's right. But my internal alarm clock will not be silenced. "I know. You can sleep. I need a run to clear my head."

"You really don't mind if I sleep more? I'm exhausted." He gives me a meaningful look through half-opened eyes. "For some reason."

I smile, remembering us falling into bed together, making fireworks of our own after watching the ones on the beach.

"I don't know what you're referring to, sir." After throwing on my running clothes, I give him a kiss on the head. "It's totally fine. I'll bring you coffee."

"You're a goddess."

The beach and the trail are both quiet this morning. It seems everyone can sleep in but me. It's good to feel the sweat prickle the back of my neck and the blood pump through my heart. I run up through the dirt trails, thinking about all the times Ed and I have run these trails together in our short time here. Sparklers ignite in my heart when I think about all the things we have in common—writing, running, and other unmentionable preferences. We definitely have a lot of differences, too. Like Ed can't sit still to save his life, and on occasion I have been known to binge watch an entire season of *Murder, She Wrote*, hardly moving a muscle all day, except to get snacks. Ed's also wildly successful, and while I was nominated for teacher of the year in 2022, I don't think anyone would call me a success without some serious prompting. Ed also… Honestly…there's still so much I have to learn about him and him about me.

Back at the house, Anh is sitting straight as an arrow on a yoga mat on the deck, her eyes open but unfocused, her hands on either knee.

When I walk up the stairs, she looks my way and smiles. "Want to join me? I saw another mat in the mudroom."

It's been years since I've done yoga, probably since we stayed at that resort in Puerto Rico and Anh dragged us there every morning. I'm never good at stretching before and after running like I should.

"Sure." I go inside and kick off my shoes, grabbing the light-gray mat and rolling it out next to Anh.

Anh leads us through some sun salutations and warriors. I feel so much better than when I woke up.

Robin finds us. "You two are yoga-ing without me?"

She runs back inside, coming out after about ten minutes in yoga pants and a sports bra, with a pale-pink mat tucked under her arm, rolling it out next to mine.

We flow together, Anh giving instructions. She's so much softer when she leads yoga. They don't feel like orders, more suggestions. She used to teach at a studio when she was an undergraduate at UCLA. She guides us into a hand-balancing pose, where we squat and tilt forward, placing palms on the floor, balancing our knees on our elbows and lifting our bodies off the ground. I wobble and fall on my face. We all laugh, and it feels like I'm nine years old again. I try again and again—we crack up as I tip too far forward each time.

I sit on my mat. "My arms aren't strong enough for crow pose."

Anh shakes her head. "Bullshit."

I laugh.

But Anh continues, "You're looking back, when you need to look out. My yoga teacher always told me to *look toward the future*."

She points to a spot beyond my mat. I gaze at it, getting into position again. Gently, I lift one leg, then the other, and suddenly I'm doing it. My feet are off the ground, my arms supporting my body.

I set my feet back down softly, smiling. "I did it."

"You did it!" Robin cheers.

As we move through the rest of our flow, I wonder how many other times I've fallen flat on my face because I was too concerned with muscling my way through the task at hand, too focused on where I could fall instead of looking out to what could be possible. The future. What do I want for my future? I want love—unending, all-encompassing love. I want to get married and start a family. I haven't admitted that to myself since Chad left, but it's true. Could I have that with Ed? I want one of my books to be published, to stop holding myself back and believe in my writing, in my book, in myself enough to actually give one of my novels to an agent. I've been so afraid of rejection and then of the reception once it is published. People tearing my books to shreds for likes on TikTok or one-star reviews on Goodreads. But what if someone loves it? What if it's someone's favorite book? I just need to finish it.

And if I'm being completely honest with myself, I want to open my own bookstore.

I don't want to go back into the classroom.

Anh leads us into savasana. My arms splay out to either side. I grab Robin's hand on one side and Anh's on the other. We lie there for a few long deep breaths, holding hands, listening to the ocean waves, and my heart is full.

"Thank you, Anh," I say as I roll up the mat.

"Of course. It's been a minute since I led a class. I missed it."

Robin puts a hand on her shoulder.

"We should have our book club meeting today," Anh says. "I have to leave Sunday."

"What?" I say. "But you just got here."

Anh sighs. "I know. I have to go back to work. But I'll come back again for a whole week at the end of August."

"I have some things going today." Robin smiles brightly and links arms with both of us. "Let's have our meeting tomorrow."

We all agree. I grab two cups of coffee and bring them to my room. Ed is sitting up, typing on his phone, still shirtless and still in bed. He puts his phone on the bedside table when I come in. I hand him the coffee, and he smiles. "Thanks."

I wriggle off my sweaty clothes and get under the covers in my underwear.

"I think we should do it."

He sets his mug on the bedside table. "You don't have to ask me twice."

He throws an arm around me and pulls me down farther on the bed. I laugh, holding my coffee up, so it won't spill on the white comforter. "No! I mean—*yes*, but I was talking about the race. We should race with our drafts. I really believe in this book; I know it's corny, but it feels like the book of my heart. I just need a deadline."

Ed sits back up. "You could give yourself a deadline."

"But a race would be more fun."

"I can't race."

"Why not? Are you afraid I'll win?" I tease.

Ed gets his mug, taking a sip of coffee. "I can't race because I got another extension. My agent let me know this morning."

"Extension?" I lean back against the pillows, my muscles suddenly feeling tired.

"Yeah I have too many other deadlines right now. I asked last week."

"Last week?" What other deadlines does he have, I wonder, but feel like I'm already asking enough.

"Yeah she just emailed me back before the trip."

"You didn't tell me about it."

Ed shrugs and stands stretching. "I know you were still busy working on yours. I didn't want to distract you. It's not important anyway."

All his words make perfect sense, but I can't help feeling left out. He grabs his phone in one hand and coffee in the other. "I'm going to hop into the shower."

I try to smile, but the corners of my mouth refuse to obey.

"You alright?" Ed asks.

"Yeah. Fine." I swing my legs off the bed, sitting on the edge. I should be happy for him. Why do I feel like this?

"You can still set a deadline, and either make a reward or a consequence if you don't make it. Do you prefer treats or punishment?"

"Who doesn't prefer treats?"

Ed shrugs. "When do you want to finish by?"

"A month," I say without thinking, but when it comes out, it feels right. A month to finish up the first draft will give me time to clean it up then get some opinions and start sending it out by my birthday in October. That feels right.

"Okay. If you finish your draft by August fifth, I'll buy you ice cream."

I frown.

Ed laughs. "Not good enough. I'll…" Ed leans down and whispers naughty nothings in my ear.

My cheeks are warm, and the sensation spreads down my neck, through my stomach, to my thighs.

I look up to meet his green eyes, on fire from the morning sun. "That and an ice cream."

Ed smiles, slow as honey. "Deal."

He puts down his coffee and his phone.

"I thought you were going to shower."

"Hmm, I think we should get dirty first."

He pulls my sports bra off then bends down to kneel in front of me, grabbing one side of my underwear then the other. I move a bit to help him take them off, a pulse of want spreading through me. He moves one of my legs open, so slowly I can feel every fiber of the smooth cotton sheet underneath my skin, and then he does the same to the other leg. He just looks for a long slow beat with one hand on each leg. My breath seizes. He moves his focus to my eyes.

"Do you want me to touch you?"

"Yes."

"Where?"

My heart is racing. "There."

"Show me how."

I move my fingers over the sensitive swollen skin, my nipples hardening with every circle. Ed watches me, and then he leans in and licks softly. He moves my fingers and replaces them with his, mimicking my circles. I lean back, the sensation overwhelming. He moves one finger inside softly then a second. I cry out as I clench around him. I try to pull him up toward me, but he keeps the steady rhythm of his movements. The motion makes my hips buck toward him. He puts his mouth back on me, his soft lips causing tingles to shoot through me.

Stars erupt, and all my muscles tighten. I pull on Ed's hair as I come.

He climbs onto the bed and holds me, the big spoon to my little spoon. My heart is still beating fast.

I turn to him. As we kiss, I move my hands down his body, but he stops me. "I'm going to get in the shower now."

"What about you?" I look down to emphasize my point.

He plants a small kiss on my head. "This morning was just for you. A preview of the prize waiting for you at the end of your novel."

He kisses me again then walks out the door. It's sweet, really. But I can't help but feel cold and alone. I didn't want this morning to be just for me. I wanted it to be for us.

I throw on a robe, then, grabbing my laptop, I get to work, trying to shove words into the hole left by Ed's absence. I'm being dramatic. He's just in the shower, but it's an occupational hazard.

As I write more, I realize maybe I don't need Ed's prize at the end of this draft. It will be nice, sure, but I can get there on my own. What lies before me is murky and uncertain. So much of life and love is out of my hands, but this is not. My book is in my control. I can finish my novel when I want and how I want then show it to who I want. And so too can Ed.

CHAPTER 17
SATURDAY, JULY 6TH

Our book club meeting is tonight. Nathan and Ed are going to stay out of our hair. We are out getting all the supplies, wine, snacks, and a new journal for each of us. It's our tradition. Well, when we started the club, it was Kool-Aid, snacks, and sticker books. Robin is getting the snacks, Anh is getting the wine, and I'm in charge of the journals. There is no bookstore in Fortune Falls, so I drive down the coast to Seaside.

Beach Reads is not open yet. I'm here a little too early—story of my life. I decide to get an oat milk latte at the coffee shop next door. Checking the email on my phone, I see I have another interview request, this time from the private school in Portland. I select one of the times provided, a tight knot forming in my chest. This is great. Right?

A deep voice startles me. "Hattie?"

I turn and see Superman with brown eyes, Kyle, holding a ceramic mug in his hand.

"Are you following me?"

"No." I laugh. "I'm just killing time until the bookstore opens."

"Ah. Care to join me?"

His laptop is open on the table by the window. "Oh no, that's okay. You look busy."

"I'm not." He hands his ceramic mug to the barista, and they fill it back up with black drip coffee.

I grab my latte and sit with him as he closes his laptop and puts it in his bag on the floor. It's a nice leather bag and compliments the white button-up shirt and blue slacks he has on this morning.

"What are you working on?"

"Listings."

"What are you listing?" eBay comes to mind. Maybe he's a hobby seller. He probably has a baseball card habit.

"Properties. I'm a real estate agent when I'm not pulling beers."

"Oh." There goes the eBay theory, and now I feel like a dick.

"You seem surprised."

I shrug. I honestly hadn't thought much about Kyle, but him selling real estate does surprise me. "I guess I am a little. I just didn't know."

"I got into it a few years ago. Not that I don't like The Vern. It's fun for the most part, and sometimes I get to meet interesting and very beautiful people."

My cheeks warm. Is he talking about me?

He laughs. "Real estate pays better. It didn't at first, but it does now. And I like helping people find their homes. It's fun to see them imagine their future in a place, you know. Christmases, birthdays, anniversaries. It's like selling memories before they happen."

I smile, intrigued by this way of looking at it. "So, you deal in dreams?"

He returns my smile. It's warm and a little lopsided...and undeniably charming. "Basically. Why are you banging down the door of the bookstore on a Saturday morning? Is there a book you just have to read today?"

"No—well, yes. There's always a book I'm dying to read, but I'm in the market for some journals this morning." I explain to him about our book club and our tradition with the journals. "I forgot I was on journal duty this year. Last year, Robin had monogrammed leather-bound beautiful books sent to our houses. I'm hoping I can at least find their favorite colors."

I check the time. "It's getting late. I should go."

"Mind if I tag along? My showing doesn't start for a bit, and I could use a new book."

"Sure," I say before truly considering it.

As we walk next door together, guilt creeps up my spine like a snake slithering through the long yellow grass. It's fine. We're just hanging out; it's not like this was planned. If he were a woman, I wouldn't feel weird about it. But he's not. He's a very tall, incredibly handsome man, and if the roles were reversed and Ed went shopping with a cute girl, I would be jealous. But that's silly, isn't it?

The bells jingle as we open the door, and the woman behind the counter greets us.

Kyle waves. "Hey Nancy."

He knows everyone, it seems. He must notice the look on my face, because he lowers his voice and says, "Helped her buy a new place after her divorce."

Stopping at the center table, he picks up a book with a gray and silver cover. "Any recommendations?" he asks me with a hint of mischief in his warm brown eyes.

"What do you like to read?"

"I'm open. What do you write?"

I swallow hard. "I haven't published anything."

He looks at me with warm eyes. "Not yet."

There's a long beat where it feels like he really sees me. Then he smiles. "What do you like to read?"

"Mysteries."

We wander to that section.

"Any favorite authors?"

"I love Tana French."

Kyle runs his finger along the spines of the books and stops on one. When he pulls it out, the cover is as familiar as looking in the mirror. Stark white with black tree limbs. The title is written in bold black: *In the Woods*.

I take it from his hands. "This one is great. It's the first in the series, so if you haven't read any, it's a good place to start." I reach past him and pull another book off the shelf. "This one is my favorite, though."

I hand him a copy of *The Likeness*.

"Sold." Kyle takes the other from my hand, tucking both under his arm. "We should look for your journals."

We wander over to the leather-bound notebooks. I pick a black one for Anh, a rose petal pink one for Robin, and a sky blue one for me. I also grab some beautiful matte finish Japanese pens, one for each of us in as close to the journal colors as I can get. Anh's was easy, but Robin's is more of a hot pink than pastel, and I get a brown one to go with my blue journal.

We walk to the counter; Kyle puts his books on the down and motions for me to do the same.

I shake my head. "Oh no. I can get it."

"Please, it's my treat."

I hesitate. I don't want to send the wrong message. Hanging out is one thing. Accepting gifts is another. I realize he's already handed over his card. He buys two Beach Reads bookstore tote bags too, and Nancy splits up our purchases for us while they chat about her condo.

She hands me the tote with the journals and Kyle the other one. We thank her and walk out together.

"I'll pay you back."

He waves me away. "Buy me a beer sometime."

I bite my lip, wondering if I should ask, and then decide to go for it. What harm could there be in asking? "Hey, do you know what the story is with the bookstore in Fortune Falls?"

"That blue house down the road from The Vern?"

I nod.

"The owner passed away...gosh, must be about ten years ago now. I think the family debated for a long time what to do. None of them live here or anywhere close. They're all out on the East Coast. But they put it up for sale a couple of years ago."

"Ahh."

Kyle's eyes spark. "Why do you ask?"

"I don't know. Do you know how much it's listed for?"

"No, but I can find out; my buddy is the agent on that one. I can probably get the keys. We could look around."

Kyle checks his phone. "Oh, it's later than I realized. I have to run. Maybe I'll see you at the bar? I'll be there tomorrow—and all the other days except Saturday. It's my day off."

I smile. "Your day off to go work."

He laughs. "Exactly. Do you want me to get the keys to the bookstore?"

"Yeah, actually. If it's not too much trouble, I'd love to take a look." There's no harm in looking.

"No trouble at all. Here, give me your number. I'll text you."

He hands me his phone, and I enter my number, feeling incredibly guilty as I do. But I shouldn't. It's not like we're going on a date. As I hand the phone back, our fingers brush for a brief moment.

There is a heavy pause where I think he may lean in, but it's over before I know it.

"See you later." Kyle walks away extremely fast down the street.

I call after him, "Thank you!"

He waves over his shoulder.

I GO FOR A LITTLE WALK, finishing what's left of my latte, window shopping and trying to escape the feeling that's lingering from my run-in with Kyle like perfume hanging in the air. I should've mentioned Ed while we were hanging out. But how? Just say, "Oh hey, remember that guy I insisted I wasn't dating? Turns out I'm dating him now…I think. Just so you know, FYI and all that."

He would've looked at me like I was insane. Completely uncalled-for information. It's fine. Kyle and I are just friends. Friends buy friends journals all the time. I just bought these journals for my friends, in fact. Technically, Kyle did. I finish off my oat milk latte and throw the empty cup in a nearby trash can.

When I get back to the house, the deck is set up with a cheese board to rival all other cheese boards. It has all varieties of olives—

green, Kalamata, an oily mix of chopped ones. There are five different cheeses, three kinds of crackers, and little pickles that are so cute, I nearly clap when I see them. A bowl of cashews, one of rosemary roasted almonds, and another of walnuts mixed with dried cherries dot the spread. Fresh raspberries are interspersed throughout the board at the same time, separating sections and tying it all together. I reach out for one and pop it into my mouth, the mix of sweet and tart hitting me right in the back of the jaw.

"Hey, no pilfering the snacks. Wait until it starts." Robin wags her finger at me, a bottle of white wine in her other hand. She dunks it in the waiting ice bucket.

"I couldn't help it."

Anh comes out with three stemless wineglasses. "I bought red too. Should I bring it out now?"

Robin purses her lips to the side, eyes searching the clouds before declaring, "We'll start with the white. Are we all ready?"

"Let me just use the bathroom, and then I'm all set."

Robin and Anh both flit around the table, fixing little things, making it perfect. It fills my heart with so much joy. Giving them both a kiss on the cheek, I head inside and run up the stairs, feeling like a kid before a birthday party.

I use the bathroom quickly, wondering if I should've wrapped the journals. I take my tote bag to my room, thinking maybe I can find some ribbon or string to at least tie the pen to the journal, but I stop dead in my tracks. Ed is in his room, door open, audiobook blaring out impossibly fast words. He's packing.

"Oh, hey." Ed catches me watching him. "Getting ready for book club?"

I nod. "Are you and Nathan going somewhere?" I motion to the small rolling suitcase open and half full on his bed.

He runs a hand over his hair. It's the exact same gesture he used to do when he had a shaved head. I wonder if that's when the habit started. I wonder if he expects to feel the soft yet prickly hairs under his hand instead of his longer hair he has now. It's like my brain is trying to distract me from what's happening. "I have to go."

"Go?"

He clears his throat. "Yeah, my trip to LA. My agent sold the film rights to *Vex*, and there's a director attached—a big one. He wants to meet me. Didn't I tell you all this?"

"No." All the blood rushes from my face. "Ed, that's great."

Ed keeps packing while he talks. "He wants to meet me—him and the producer. They want me to write the screenplay. There's a party at his house in LA tomorrow."

"Tomorrow?"

Ed stops and looks me in the eye. "Yeah, my flight's in a couple of hours."

"Oh." This can't be happening. How could I forget about his trip? We just started getting closer, finally after all these years, and he's leaving. For how long?

"In Portland."

"Oh." It hits me how little time he actually has. Portland is a two-hour drive at least, on a good day. On a Saturday, I'm not even sure. "Shit. You have to go now."

Ed nods and throws a few more things into his suitcase. "I really do."

"When will you be back?"

"A couple weeks. I'm not exactly sure."

He zips up his suitcase and heaves it on the floor. He grabs me by the waist and kisses me, his lips soft but insistent. It's a kiss that has an end right from the beginning.

It's a goodbye kiss.

We part, and he says, "I'll text you as soon as I know more."

"Okay." I hate how small my voice sounds, how meek. I should be happy for him. I *am* happy for him. But this feels an awful lot like a goodbye we shared once before, and then I didn't see him for a decade.

He lugs his suitcase down the stairs and out the door without a look back in my direction.

CHAPTER 18
MONDAY, JULY 8TH

My overnight bag is packed and in the back of the car. Since my interview is in New Haven tomorrow morning at eight, I'm driving to Grandma's to stay the night so I don't have to roll into the interview after a two-hour drive. The sun is low in the sky, too low for the visor to be much help.

Ed left Saturday. Anh left Sunday. For two days in a row, I got to say goodbye to people I love. *No.* People I care about. I mean, I love Anh, but it's very new with Ed. New and old. I've been pining for him for a decade, and here I am, doing it again. I crank up my audiobook and try to lose myself in the story, instead of the pity party I was about to throw.

When I get to Grandma's, the overwhelming smell of falafel fills my nose as soon as I open the squeaky screen door. Clanks from the kitchen let me know exactly where to go, if the smell hadn't.

Grandma's taking a tray of perfectly browned falafel from the oven, her massive oven mitt in the shape of a chicken on her hand. "Hattie Bear! You're here!"

"Grandma, you didn't have to go through all this trouble."

"When's the last time you stayed the night? Of course I'm making your favorite. You still like falafel, right?"

I smile. "Yes, thank you."

She gestures to a bottle of wine on the counter. "Sit, sit. Have a glass. I'm almost done."

"I'll just put my bag upstairs first."

She nods and grabs a cucumber off the counter.

Each stair squeaks on the way up past framed photos hung on the wall. There's my eighteen-year-old face smiling ear to ear, in a shiny purple cap and gown. Farther up is my cousin, her blonde hair in flowing curls and her husband smashing a piece of cake on her cheek on their wedding day. At the very top of the stairs is a black and white photo, in front of this very house. My grandpa is holding my grandma in his arms. She's in a beautiful calf-length white dress, her leg kicked out toward the sky. It's their wedding day. They're both smiling like they won the lottery.

Muscle memory takes me to the room I spent so many summers and sometimes spring breaks in. The walls are a light pink, a choice made when I was eight that stuck. The twin bed is covered in a white comforter, with a hot-pink crocheted blanket thrown on top.

I set my bag down by the desk, the cork board hanging above it filled so not one speck of the brown cork shows. Magazine photos of Idris Elba from a brief fascination I had in eighth grade with the movie *Obsessed*, ticket stubs, photo booth pictures of Robin, Anh, and me making funny faces.

I run my hand along one strip, faded from the afternoon sun hitting this wall. In the last picture, I'm in the middle, my cheeks smashed on either side by Anh and Robin planting kisses. We must've been seventeen, because Anh had what she liked to call her "fuck-it-all" pixie cut.

Another glossy magazine photo catches my eye, a bookstore in Venice, right next to my dream life list.

Own my own bookstore
Fall madly in love
Get married
Have three kids
Publish a book

A long exhale comes out in a whoosh. When I met Chad and really started to fall for him, I thought I was on my way to checking some of these off. And I did, sort of. We never fell what I'd call madly in love, but there was love. And we got married. That's all gone now. I'm back to square one.

"Dinner's ready!"

I make my way down. The dining room table is set with falafel, soft pita bread, hummus in a crystal bowl, and a colorful array of veggies. Grandma's pouring a glass of red wine and hands it to me.

"This is amazing."

"Cheers, my dear." She clinks her glass with mine. "Hopefully, it tastes as good as it looks."

Grandma tells me about the farm. The chickens got out the other day and got into the raspberries. The neighbor about a mile away had a family of barn swallows trying to nest on their property. They had to shoo them away.

"Why? Why couldn't they let them live there?"

"Oh, Bear, they are so loud, all the time, too. And they poop everywhere!"

When dinner's over, I insist on doing the dishes, but Grandma insists on helping. Together, we get through them quickly and then take our wine to the porch.

It feels wrong to sit in Grandpa's chair but rude not to. When he was alive, I used to love to steal his spot. He'd come out and poke me in the ribs. We thought the whole thing was so funny.

Grandma notices my hesitation. "Sit wherever you feel comfortable, dear."

I give her hand a small squeeze and take my usual perch on the steps.

"So, tell me about this interview?"

"I'd be teaching English still. It's down the hill at Nelson Middle School."

Grandma's lips twitch the smallest bit into a frown. "Middle school?"

"Yep." I run my hand along the edge of the step, the rough texture a nice distraction.

"Hmm. Didn't you say that you'd rather teach preschool than middle school?"

I shrug. "I say a lot of things."

She nods, gazing into the fields surrounding us, the sky dimming to a deep blue.

"I'm surprised you want to live here."

"Not here in this house. I'd find a place in town, maybe somewhere in Old Town."

She purses her lips. "And you'd be happy here? Teaching middle school?"

"It'd be nice to be close to you."

Her eyes close, her frown there in full force now. "I've been thinking about moving, actually."

"Moving?" She's lived here my whole life.

"It's a big job for just me. The neighbor kid comes over to help sometimes, but he's headed off to college in the fall." She sighs. "Honestly, this place was your grandfather's. I lived here because he loved it. Uncle Rob invited me to visit him last spring in Hermosa Beach. It was so nice. Warm, less rain, no snow. If I sell this place, I could get a condo near the beach. There're a few places available by Rob. You know, he swims in the ocean every day."

I set my wine down, struggling to keep up. "You're going to swim in the ocean?"

She laughs. "Probably not, but it would be nice to have the option."

"You could swim here—drive out to the bay."

"Too cold."

"It's probably cold there, too."

She lets out a sigh. "This house is so empty without him."

Her words permeate my skin with the chilling night air.

"Grandma..."

She waves a hand at me. "I'm lucky. We had so many years together. I'm not set on this idea—just thoughts." She rises from her chair and comes to sit next to me on the stairs with the smallest hint of a wince. "What I'm trying to say is I don't want you to move here for me. You should move someplace that gets you excited. You should look for a job that makes those baby blues of yours light up with life. Don't settle. You're too young."

I open my mouth to protest, but what would I say? She's right, as usual. I don't want to teach middle school. I don't want to move to New Haven.

She puts a hand on my shoulder as she stands. "You've had enough of my sage advice. I'm going to bed."

"Maybe it would feel better, more like home, if I lived close?"

Her eyes flash, like a wave of sadness washes over them. "Maybe. Goodnight, Hattie Bear."

THE NEXT MORNING, I go for a run, one of my old routes through the fields, mulling over what Grandma said the night before. I thought about texting Ed last night, but I wasn't sure what to say.

Once I'm showered and dressed in a white shirt, light-blue sweater, and denim skirt, I head out to the interview. After a quick drive, I'm at the school. The yellow concrete walls are in need of a fresh coat of paint. On my walk to the office, I pass a massive field torn up with muddy tire tracks, and a queasiness settles in my gut. I should've canceled. This is not the place for me.

The office is stuffy, despite the cooler morning. The woman who greets me has long blonde hair, signs me in, and shows me where I can sit while I wait. It's just the two of us in the office, listening as the radio plays country music. My appointment was for eight a.m. I got here at 7:56, and it's now 8:19.

I pull out my phone and scroll to my kindle app. As I'm reading, a text notification from Ed appears. My stomach flutters as I imagine what the text could be. Maybe a good luck or an I miss you.

As I click, the screen comes to life with a soft-lit photo of Ed's washboard stomach, his black and gray–striped boxers barely concealing a substantial bulge.

My cheeks flame.

"Ms. Stevens."

I'm so startled, I drop my phone.

A man in a blue polo shirt with the school logo on the chest is smiling, reaching down to help pick up my phone.

"No!" I dive and grab it right before he does. Standing, I shoved the phone into my purse and then pull down my skirt a little. "I mean, yes. That's me."

The man's eyes narrow. "Right this way. Sorry I was late. Had to call maintenance. Someone did donuts all over the field last night," he says with a chuckle.

I smile, my cheeks still warm from my potential new employer seeing my boyfriend's morning wood. If he's even my boyfriend.

The interview is quick and to the point. Despite not being all that excited for the position itself, my overachieving, people-pleasing nature kicks in, and I walk back to my car nearly an hour later, confident I just aced an interview for a job I don't want.

I start the car, plug in my phone, and turn on my audiobook to drown out my own thoughts. A text comes in, and I have Siri read it to me as I head back to Grandma's.

"Kyle says: Hey, got the keys to the bookstore. Any chance you're free today? It'd have to be before my shift starts at two p.m."

My heart sparkles like someone just dusted it with glitter. I check the time. It's nearly eleven now. If I grab my stuff from Grandma's quickly, I could be back in Fortune Falls a little after one p.m.

I hit *Reply*. "Does one p.m. work?"

The car asks if I want to change or send, and impatiently I hit the button for it to send now.

The response comes back almost instantly.

"Kyle says: Works for me. See you then."

———

AFTER I LOAD my bag in the back of the car, Grandma squeezes me in her thin arms. "You sure you have to rush off?"

"Yeah, I have a thing."

"A date?" she asks with a devilish grin. I didn't tell her about Ed while I was here. I wasn't really sure what to say.

"No—more of an appointment."

"Hmm, very mysterious."

I smile and figure if I'm going to tell anyone, it might as well be Grandma. "I'm looking at a bookstore for sale."

Her eyes light up. "You are?"

"Yes, but don't get too excited. I'm just looking. I have no idea how much they want for it. It could be millions of dollars."

"Pssh. Millions. I doubt it." Grandma waves her hand as if dispelling a bad smell. "You know, Grandad left me a bit of money, and I've been thinking of investing."

"I haven't even seen it yet."

She holds up both hands. "Keep it in mind."

"I will. And I'll come visit soon."

———

THE DRIVE IS long and hot, and despite breaking the speed limit on several occasions, I'm late. I park by the bookstore instead of walking to save a few minutes. Kyle is waiting at the bottom of the porch steps in an olive green T-shirt and dark jeans, his jaw smooth from what looked like a fresh shave.

"Hey!" he calls as I get out of the car and cross the street, a light dusting of sand blown from the beach crunching under my feet.

"Sorry I'm late."

"No worries." He swings the keys around on his finger. "Ready to go inside?"

The blue Victorian lit by the afternoon sun has to be the most beautiful bookshop I've ever seen. Even prettier than the one in the magazine hanging on my cork board at Grandma's. Walking up the steps, I picture covering them in a fresh coat of white paint, or maybe I can paint the risers like bookshelves, with colorful spines and all my favorite titles. People can sit on them and take selfies. *Oh shit*. I'm going to have to get an Instagram.

Kyle opens the red door, pulling me out of my spiral. The floors are black and white—right now they're more dirt colored, but they will be black and white when I'm done with them. That is, if I decide to really do this.

Most of the room is exactly what I spied from the window, a massive chandelier, peeling wallpaper that would be charming if it was all in one piece, shelves still filled with books. I take one down, flipping through the pages—it still smells like a new book. No mold spots or musty scent. I lean in and take a big whiff, like I'm smelling a fragrant flower.

Kyle laughs. I didn't realize he was watching me. My cheeks are warm as I put the book back on the shelf. "Pretty good stuff, huh? Nothing quite like a brand-new book. The asking price includes the stock as well."

I keep walking into the space, too nervous to ask about the price yet. In the far corner of the shop is a counter with a silver La Marzocco Espresso machine, it's small but has two spouts and two steam wands. Underneath is a small fridge on one side and a cupboard on the other.

In the cupboard underneath an ancient-looking cash register are mismatched porcelain teacups, saucers, and mugs with sayings like *Life's a Beach* and *Sorry I'm Booked*, with a painted hardback on it. Smiling, I hold it up to show Kyle. "I didn't even know there was a little coffee shop in here."

"Yeah, my mom used to love their lavender lattes."

I look around, taking it all in. "It's amazing."

"Wait till you see upstairs."

My chest warms with excitement. I sort of figured upstairs would be storage, or maybe an office. I follow Kyle as he opens the door, picturing boxes and boxes of back stock, but it's better—so much better.

The entire second story is an apartment. There is a small entryway with a built-in bench. I resist the urge to kick off my shoes. The floors are a light hardwood, and I don't want to scuff them. When I live here, I'll be a *no shoes in the house* kind of girl. *If.* If I live here.

There is a small sitting room and kitchen all in one space, filled with light from the massive windows. In the corner is a breakfast nook, and one whole wall of the sitting room is a built-in bookshelf. To the opposite side of the kitchen is a small hallway with two doors. I open the one to the bathroom first. It has teal blue tile and a massive claw-foot tub. The shower head is the only thing that looks updated. I'm excited and a little nervous to see what the water pressure is like, but it feels like an overstep to turn on the tap.

Across the hall is the bedroom. It has a large window with no curtains at the moment. And the view is amazing. It looks right out onto the beach and the ocean. I run my hand along the windowsill. A writing desk would fit perfectly right here.

Kyle clears his throat, announcing his presence in the room.

I swallow hard, nervous to ask, but I have to know. If it's out of my price range, I can move on, but it'll be hard to put this place out of my mind. "How much do they want?"

His smile is wide, and the number he says freezes me to my spot.

"Really?"

He nods. "Not sure what your price range is, but the family is very motivated to sell. It's been on the market for a quite a few years already."

My lips feel numb. I could do this. Once the house money comes in and with maybe a small loan, I could live here. Fix it up. Run the shop. My smile grows as it dawns on me exactly what I'll name it. If I decide to do this.

My watch alerts me to a text, and my stomach drops. Shit. I never texted Ed back after he sent that photo this morning. I pull out my phone.

Kyle says, "I have to get going. My shift starts soon at the bar."

"Right. Right." I shove my phone into my back pocket. "Thank you for taking the time to show me this place."

"Sure. No trouble." He hands me a business card. "This is my buddy handling the sale."

"Great."

Then he hands me another card. "This is the contact info for the FFBIF—the Fortune Falls Business Improvement Foundation. They're a group that helps mentor local business owners. They set up a table every Wednesday at the library. Might help if you have questions."

I look down at the card, running my fingers over the thick cardstock. "This is amazing. Thanks."

Walking out, I soak in every detail I can about the place, mentally making notes. On the sidewalk, I pull out my phone and take another picture.

Kyle's watching me. "Are you seriously thinking of putting in an offer?"

I purse my lips to the side. Am I? It feels right. It's been my dream to own my own bookstore since I was a kid. But what would pursuing it cost me? Ed doesn't want to live here, that's for sure. We're not really at the stage of talking about our future together—but where does that leave me? I need to make some crucial decisions about my life with or without his input.

I sigh. "I'm not sure yet."

CHAPTER 19
FRIDAY, JULY 12TH

All week, I've been trying, without much success, to write. Today is no different. This morning and afternoon, I've toiled away, butt in chair, and I have only a handful of words to show for it.

It's been more of a distraction than anything else. My brain feels heavy with thoughts of Ed and the bookstore. I pick up my phone to look up a better word to use but find myself on Instagram once again, looking at Ed's feed. I joined Monday night, thinking if I do I open my own bookstore, it's going to need an online presence. It seems that I'm always on it now. The last picture Ed posted was on Sunday of a fancy schmancy party at an even fancier schmancier house with a massive aquamarine pool with a waterfall. A goddamn waterfall. Is it a party at the Playboy mansion or something? Or maybe all the pools in LA look like that. How would I know?

I texted him back as soon as I left the meeting with Kyle. When he didn't text back right away, I lay on my bed and Googled "How to open a bookstore."

The first thing I need, according to the internet, is money. Thanks to the complete and utter destruction of my previous dream life, I'll have that soon. I'm not quite sure it's sufficient, though. I need the down payment and enough for the mortgage each month. I'll also need some new inventory and to fix the place up. Definitely paint the porch. The house itself should be fine for a couple more years.

I made a list of all the things I need and researched a ballpark figure of the expenses involved. Then on Wednesday, I spoke with one of the very helpful people from the FFBIF. While I can wrap my head around the actual steps involved in making this dream a reality, I can't quite come to terms with the magnitude of the decision yet.

Ed's texted a few more times over the week, but honestly, it all felt removed. He's supposed to FaceTime me tonight at 5:30, which at the moment feels like centuries away. I throw my phone at the bed and turn back to my laptop.

Come on. I can do this. If I write a novel that's a success, I can do it anywhere and not be tied down to one place. But wouldn't it be nice to be a part of the community? To have a business I'm proud of? To have a home?

I can have a home and write my own best-selling literary fucking masterpiece that will sell a million copies. The film rights will sell. Greta Gerwig will direct, and we'll write the screenplay together and also become best friends. Ooh, she'll join our book club, but none of this can happen without the damn book.

Sam looks at June like the first sunny day after endless clouds, like a soft bed after a hard day's work, like a Big Mac after a green juice cleanse.

A Big Mac? I close my laptop with a little more force than necessary. *Garbage.* Greta won't direct a Big Mac–loving hero trapped in a book. Plus, Sam wouldn't even know about Big Macs or juice cleanses. Food. Maybe I just need some food. I must be hungry if I'm waxing poetic about Mickey D's.

I grab my bag and head for the bar. After being cooped up in the house all week, I deserve a treat. It's already happy hour, so the hummus plate will be half off. I venture past the office downstairs to see if Robin wants to come, but the door is shut and I can hear voices beyond it—hers and tinny ones coming from Zoom.

It's beautiful outside, sunny but breezy. Not too hot. I contemplate sitting outside, but not for long. I go on autopilot to my usual spot in the corner at the bar. Kyle isn't here, but I order my hummus plate and an iced tea from Darla. Pulling out my phone, I scroll to Instagram again, going immediately to Ed's profile. Nothing new. But this time I keep scrolling down, back in time. Lots of books. Bookstores, Ed hiding behind the cover of friends' novels, book signings. As I go further back, scrolling through the years, there's more skateboarding, still a ton of books, and then I stop. A side shot of Ed. He's in profile because his face is directed at the blonde girl next to him. Her smile is taking over the frame, big soft pink lips, pearly white teeth, mouth wide open as Ed's nose presses into the side of her face.

A book slides across the bar, and I practically drop my phone. It's *In the Woods*.

"I loved it."

My mouth drops. "You already read it? The whole thing?"

"Yeah. It's great. I'm on to the second one."

Kyle's pulled away by another customer. He pours them a beer then comes back.

"What's your book about?"

I shrug.

"Is it like this one?"

"No one writes like that except Tana French. She's the best." I finish my iced tea, and Kyle makes eyes at it, silently asking if I want another. "Actually, I'd love a glass of red wine."

Smiling, he picks up one of the bottles that is way too expensive, especially if I really want to sink all my money into the store. I quickly add, "House red is good."

He shrugs. "This one's already open. On me. So, what's your new book about?"

"Love and time."

He leans on the bar, his brown eyes sparking. "Tell me more."

And I do. I tell him all about June and Sam. He asks me my thoughts on the bookstore, but I swiftly change the subject because the truth is I have no idea what to do. We talk and talk until the bar is too busy for Kyle to chat with me anymore. He keeps getting pulled away to pour beers or bring people food. I close my tab with Darla.

Before I leave, Kyle yells out, "Wait."

I check my phone. Shit. It's 5:36, and I have one missed call from Ed.

There's a big line at the bar. I wave. "I have to go."

Out the door and down the lane, I run to the house. I try to call Ed back, but my FaceTime won't connect. My flip-flops smack on the asphalt. Once I'm in the house and my phone links to the Wi-Fi, I try again.

The screen comes to life, the phone ringing and showing me my own face as I wait. Cheeks flushed from the run and the wine, my blue eyes bright, and my hair looks like it was styled by the wind of a convertible. It's so frizzy from the humid bar and my run down the road. I try to smooth it down a bit, when Ed answers.

"Hey, there you are," he says, and I wonder if he's annoyed I didn't pick up on the first ring.

"It's nice to see your face." And it is. He looks handsome, with just a light dusting of dark stubble on his square jaw. His green eyes are covered in sunglasses, and the jostle of the phone tells me he's walking. "I can't talk long. I'm headed to drinks with the director and the actor he's thinking of for the main part."

"Oooh, who is it?"

"Technically, I'm not supposed to say, but he played Elvis and his name rhymes with cutler."

"No, Austin Butler. Wow. That's very cool. How's it been?"

"Amazing. It's fast. Everything in publishing moves so slow, but this has been like bam-bam-bam. Lots of meetings."

I want to know when he'll be back, but I don't want to be the one to ask.

"What have you been up to?"

I shrug and think about telling him about the bookstore or the interviews I've had recently. The one for the private school in Portland was yesterday over Zoom. But I don't. It feels like opening up a bigger conversation about the future that I'm not ready to talk about. Or, more accurately, I don't think he's ready to. "Writing, running, reading. Same ol', same ol'."

There's a beat of silence that stretches on and on. Ed stops and pushes his sunglasses up. His green eyes catch the light. Sometimes he's so beautiful, it hurts a little to look at him. Or maybe it hurts because he's so far away. He sighs, like he's getting ready to say something. But then he waves.

"Shit, I'm here and they spotted me. I have to go. Can I call you later?"

"Yeah. I'll be here." Because honestly, where else would I be?

He smiles at me. "Talk soon."

And then he's gone. My screen shows me my face again, lips turned down, eyes sad. I plug in my phone. It doesn't really need to charge, but I'm sick of the sight of it.

Leaving it in the room, I go out onto the deck, where Robin and Nathan are sitting at the table having a drink.

"Hey," Robin says softly, almost too softly.

I tousle my hair and try to make my face not look like a sad doll in a Mark Ryden painting. "Hey!" I say with a false brightness that I definitely don't feel.

"Did you talk to Ed?" Robin pours me a glass of wine.

"Yeah, you're never going to believe this… Austin Butler might be in the movie. Isn't that wild?"

Robin nods.

Nathan says, "He was so cool in *Dune*. Bummer he won't be back this summer though."

For a minute, I think he's talking about Austin Butler. I raise my glass to my lips then lower it without taking a drink as it dawns on me. He means Ed.

"Huh?"

"Yeah. He texted me earlier. He has to stay out there. They want him to be available while he writes the script. He already found a long-term Airbnb. Dude forgot his running shoes under the bed. I had to mail them earlier today. I told him it'd probably be easier to buy new ones, but he said they don't make that kind anymore."

Robin is studying my face like there's going to be a test later. I don't want them to know he didn't tell me. I don't want Robin to be mad at Ed. I don't want them to feel any worse for me than they probably already do. So, I smile and nod. "Yeah, it's such an adventure for him, though. An amazing opportunity."

I try to smile and make chit chat, but I am lost in my thoughts. That must've been what he was going to tell me when he had to run. I wish he would've just taken two extra minutes to let me know. Maybe he wasn't sure how I'd take it. How *am* I taking it? It's probably what he wants to talk about later. After I finish my glass of wine, I stand. "I'm going to get back to writing."

Robin's face pinches. "We're going to grill. Do you want us to throw something on for you?"

Food sounds terrible. "I'll just grab a sandwich later. I'm at the seventy-five percent mark, and I can't wait to see how it ends."

"You don't already know?" Robin asks. She knows I'm usually a meticulous plotter.

I shake my head. "Nope."

Propping myself on the bed, I open my laptop and throw myself into the story. I give my happy couple a problem in the form of a Henry Cavill look alike. Now June has to choose between the man in the book and a real live man, one who doesn't live most of his days in a fictional world. I work past the sun setting outside my window. I'm still typing as the first stars come out. I'd like to say I don't notice at all that Ed never calls, but that would be a lie.

CHAPTER 20
SATURDAY, JULY 13TH

U sually, I listen to an audiobook or a podcast on my run, but this morning I left my phone at home. I'm tired of checking it every two minutes. When I get back, I see the missed call from Ed and throw the phone on the bed to take a long shower.

After I've dried off, I put on makeup, my mascara gliding over my lashes. If he's going to tell me he's not coming back, I'm going to look really good while he does it. I pour a cup of coffee in the kitchen then get myself situated in my little window seat.

My put-together face stares back at me on the screen, and I give myself a nod before I hit the button to call him back.

Ed answers on the third ring. His green eyes are bright but rimmed in dark circles, like he didn't get much sleep. "Hey."

His smile is warm.

"Hey yourself. How'd it go last night?"

"Great. Austin is super cool."

"That's awesome." I don't know what else to say. So, I just wait.

"Guy, the director, asked me if I'd be willing to write the screenplay down here so we can collaborate." There is a pause that I fear may swallow me whole. Ed clears his throat. "I'm not coming back to the house this summer."

He goes into more detail about the script, him and the director's plan, their process. I just listen. I don't react. I knew this is what he was going to say. It feels an awful lot like when he said he had to go to a writing retreat in Colorado.

"But I still would love to go to the Oregon Book Awards with you."

I nod. I've always wanted to go to that dinner, and of course I want to see Ed again. But it's more than a month away. I can't believe this is happening again. I try to smile. "I'd love that."

"Hattie—" There's a knock at his door. "Room service. It's my last morning at the hotel. Got to soak it in."

I try to smile, but my lips feel heavy.

"I'll text you later."

"Sounds good." No, it doesn't. Seeing him in person, kissing him, sounds good. Texting for the next month sounds dumb.

He makes a little kissy face, and then he's gone. And now I have a ton of questions. When he comes back, and he's in Portland and I'm in Portland, are we going to keep dating? Are we still dating now? Are we a couple? Are we exclusive? Am I even going to be in Portland? What if I stay here? Or move to New Haven? What then?

The sound of the front door opening pulls me out of my sandstorm of questions. "Honey! I'm home!"

It's Anh. I run to the stairs, and she has a massive suitcase. "What are you doing here?"

Sprinting down the stairs, I wrap her in a hug before she can answer.

"I guess you missed me." She squeezes me back, and that's when the tears come.

Anh pulls back. "Honey. What is it?"

I close my eyes, feeling so dumb. It's not like Ed broke up with me. I wipe away my tears. "It's fine. Ed's gone, again. But it's fine. I'm just being silly."

"Don't do that. Don't diminish your feelings." She takes a big breath. "Come on. Let's get some coffee."

We take two mugs onto the porch, and I unload. About feeling left behind—not just in the relationship, but in life. "Here I am, not even able to publish a book, no job, not even sure what I want to be when I grow up, and Ed is meeting with A-list actors and sampling hors devours at fancy pool parties. And what am I going to do? Just live my small life, teaching kids and writing my little stories that no one ever reads."

Anh shakes her head. "No life is small."

I stare into my mug. Then I tell her about the bookstore. Her face is calm, but there's a spark in her eyes.

"What's stopping you?"

I'm unsure how to answer that—really, the only thing holding me back is the dream of Ed and me. Then I realize Anh never said why she was here. "I thought you couldn't get more time off until the end of summer?"

Anh sits back and takes a deep inhale, the smile on her face wide and bright. "I quit."

I nearly drop my mug. "You what?"

"Oh man. Your face." Anh laughs. "I quit. I work all the time. I literally eat, sleep, work, and sometimes not even the first two. Then I came out here and saw the ocean and read a book and led you two in yoga on the porch. I had an epiphany. I want more of that. More living. So, I quit."

"Wow." I'm stunned. "What are you going to do?"

Her smile gets even wider. "I'm so glad you asked. I'm moving to Orcas Island."

"What?"

"Remember when I did my yoga teacher training in New York? My mentor put out a post on our Facebook group looking for a guide for the resort she's partnered with. I texted her, and that's that. I'm going to teach yoga at a resort and spa near Cascade Lake."

I set my coffee down. "Holy shit. When did this all happen?"

She sets her coffee down, gesturing wide with her arms. "It's nuts. I saw the Facebook post on the fourth, and then I messaged her at the airport on my way back home—which isn't home anymore. By the time my flight had landed, I had an offer for the position in my inbox."

"I can't believe you let me blather on about my stuff when you're moving to an island!"

She shrugs. "I wasn't the one crying."

I sip my coffee, still trying to wrap my head around it.

Anh sits up. "You should go to LA."

"What?"

Anh's eyes are bright. "Just for like a weekend or something. You two need to talk, really talk."

"Oh...I don't know... He's so busy..." *And he didn't invite me.* "Plus, it'd be so expensive."

Anh waves a hand. "I have so many miles from work trips." She scrolls her phone and taps the screen. "There's a flight that leaves in a couple hours. You could be in Ed's arms by tonight."

My whole body reacts to that thought, a whoosh of excitement thrumming through my body, but it's short lived. The tension knots in my muscles, replacing it. "I'm not sure. I should call him."

"Do you have the address where he's staying?"

"Nathan does."

"Surprise him."

Yes. It'll be romantic, impulsive, adventurous. Excitement bubbles up in my chest. "Okay."

Anh beams and taps the screen on her phone. "Done. The tickets should be in your inbox."

I hop up. "Eee! Wait, when do you have to leave for Orcas Island?"

"Not for a week. Your return ticket is for Tuesday."

"I have to pack; I have to go." I run to the house but quickly turn back and throw my arms around Anh. "Thank you."

She squeezes me back then turns me around, giving me a little push. "You're welcome. Go."

It's late afternoon and sweltering while I wait for my Lyft outside LAX. The drive from Portland, the plane ride... Everything has gone so smooth, it's like I'm always jet setting about. I'm waiting for a white sedan—me and about fifty other people at the taxi station—reading each license plate as it comes until finally there's my white Prius.

Throwing my small carry-on in the back, I get in. The inside of the car is freezing, the air conditioning cranked all the way up. Goose bumps instantly cover my legs, exposed in my cut-off shorts. I pull out a cardigan from my bag and wrap it around my torso. The driver is already driving toward our destination, Top 40 pop blaring from the stereo.

"There are waters back there. Help yourself."

I grab a small bottle and can't quite twist the cap off. Wrapping my sweater around it, I really crank it, right as we swerve around a car stopped in the middle of the road with their flashers on. The water spills all over my white shirt, not only soaking it, but also making it completely see-through. I let out a small, shocked scream.

So much for being a put-together jet setter.

He lets me out on the corner of a cute white stucco house with a rounded blue front door. I double check the address. I don't know why I was expecting an apartment, but this is adorable.

It's so hot, I want to take my sweater off, but I'm also soaked, and my pale-blue bra is on full display through my wet shirt, so I keep it on. I take a deep breath and knock on the door. Nothing. I give it a few minutes and then knock again. There's no answer. Shit. He's not home.

I walk back to the sidewalk. Should I wait? Should I text him? No, I've come this far. I want to surprise him face to face. I pull up the map on my phone. There's a coffee shop about half a mile from here. I'll get a coffee, sit in the sun and dry off, then try again.

The walk is nice, the neighborhood darling. When I pictured LA before, I thought about mostly palm trees, which there are, but I pictured big buildings, high-rise apartments, not these cute houses, with terracotta tile roofs and colorful gardens.

The coffee shop is just as cute as the neighborhood, with big windows and lots of plants. I order an iced oat milk latte and a brownie.

I'm just waiting for my drink when I spot Ed sitting in the corner.

There's an iced coffee in front of him, and he's sitting with a man in thick, black-rimmed glasses, salt and pepper hair, and a huge beard that's more salt than pepper. Next to them is... I do a double take.

Chloe Kramer, one of the hottest young actresses in Hollywood right now. She's in practically everything—that new sci-fi movie, that new tennis movie, even the latest biopic about Diana Ross, surely cast not only for her amazing acting talents but also because she's a dead ringer.

I look down at my still-soaked shirt. Can I sneak out without them seeing me? As I'm planning my escape, the barista calls out, "Hattie."

Ed looks up from the table, and we lock eyes. The expression on his face makes my stomach plummet. I may actually be sick. It's not one of joy, that's for sure. Shock. It's pure shock. I give a half wave. When he waves back, both the bearded man and Chloe look over. There's whispering at the table, and the bearded man laughs.

I grab my iced latte, leave the brownie, thrust my shoulders back, and am going to walk over when Ed pushes back from the table. He makes it over to me in four long strides.

"Hattie. What are you doing here?"

"I...uh..."

What am I doing here? I can't believe I let Anh talk me into this. Honestly, I didn't think he'd be working on a Saturday. I thought he'd be excited to see me.

"Surprise."

He laughs, but it's not a full body expression of joy. It's an uncomfortable sound. "Yeah, you can say that again. What happened?"

I nearly forgot my soaking wet, transparent shirt. "It's a long story. I didn't know you'd be here."

His eyes are huge. "You didn't know I'd be here?"

"I mean at this coffee shop. Obviously, I knew you'd be in LA, I came to see you... Anh quit, and it sounded like a good idea..." I trail off.

Ed fishes his keys out of his pocket and hands them to me. "We still have some things to go over. Just go to my place, and we can talk about it later."

I feel like a child being sent to their room, but it's not even my room. I want to hand the keys back. I want to say don't bother, but I can't. Despite this being one of the most uncomfortable situations ever, I still want to talk to him. I take the keys and avoid any further eye contact. I don't look at the table of shiny, fancy famous people as I take my iced latte, hold my head as high as possible in my grubby cut-off shorts and wet shirt, and strut out the door.

CHAPTER 21

The last thing I want is to be impressed by the house, but as I turn the key in the blue door, open it, and step inside, it is genuinely impressive. Light-gray hardwood floors brighten up the sitting room as well as the huge windows and so many houseplants, it's a little like stepping into a garden store.

I set my bag down and go over to the kitchen sink, splashing some cold water on my face, trying to wash away some of my humiliation. At least I don't have to worry about getting my clothes wet. He didn't even introduce me. I peel my shirt away from my skin and see why he didn't, but it doesn't make it feel any better.

The rest of the house is LA chic for sure. There is one bedroom with a huge king-sized bed half covered in a white fluffy comforter, all bunched up and tangled. Ed never made his bed at the beach house either. It's good to see that's still the same here. He hasn't come to LA and suddenly become a different person.

I continue wandering to the back, where there is another sitting room with French doors that open out to a beautiful kidney-shaped pool sparkling in the late-afternoon sun. It's completely fenced in with a tall hedge. I step outside, shrug off my sweater, peel off my wet shirt, shimmy out of my cut-off jean shorts, and jump in without a second thought. I haven't thought through anything this whole trip. Why start now? I hold my breath and sink to the bottom feeling like Dustin Hoffman in *The Graduate* or Bill Murray in *Rushmore*. They were right. There's no better place to be when you're feeling sorry for yourself than the bottom of the pool.

When I surface, I take a huge breath.

What was I thinking, coming here without even texting him first? He probably thinks I'm clingy, desperate, unhinged. I swim around casually at first, but the more my thoughts spiral, the more deliberate my strokes become. My breaths more measured. Back and forth, back and forth, back and forth—until I'm too exhausted to be embarrassed anymore. Water runs down my body as I get out. I grab one of the towels on a shelf near the pool chairs, wrap it around myself, and sit, letting the sun warm my face. I shouldn't have come here. I should've asked him when a good time would be to visit or if he even wanted me to be here. And what am I supposed to do now? Stay until Tuesday, while he meets with famous people and acts half annoyed that I'm here?

Nope.

Not going to happen. I grab my phone from my heap of clothes, pulling it out of the back pocket of my jean shorts. A few quick taps and a twenty-five-dollar fee later, my plane leaves first thing in the morning. I schedule a Lyft to pick me up at five a.m. Then I drag myself to the shower, throwing on the wrinkled blue sundress from my bag, putting on mascara, pinching my cheeks, and feeling like the capable woman I am again.

I keep expecting to hear the door, but there's nothing. Silence echoes through the house.

Ed's still busy.

I get out my notebook and try writing some of the scene I was working on before I left, but the words won't come. So instead, I start scribbling something else. A business plan. I pull up the template I got from the nice people at the FFBIF and start filling it in.

At around six, there is a soft knock at the door. Ed's standing there with a bag of takeout and a bottle of wine. He looks handsome but also utterly exhausted. His shoulders sag like his head is heavy.

"I thought you might be hungry."

"Starving." Taking the bag to the kitchen, I get plates out. I open the plastic clamshell containers; one is tofu pad Thai, and the other is cashew chicken. I scoop some of each onto two separate plates as Ed opens the wine.

"Should we eat outside?"

I nod.

Ed flips a switch and turns on the string of Edison bulb lights. They twinkle on the water of the pool as stars start to appear in the dusky sky.

We both have a seat at the small glass table. Ed takes a big gulp of wine then sighs. "I'm sorry about the coffee shop. You surprised me."

"That was kind of the point."

"I was working."

My shoulders slump. "I didn't know. And I had no idea you'd be at *that* coffee shop. I just wanted a latte. I tried to surprise you at the house, but you weren't here, and then I'd come all this way, it seemed silly to text when the whole point was to surprise you face to face. It was supposed to be nice."

Ed smiles, but it's strained. "It was. It is. I'm thrilled you're here. Really. I'm also just swamped. I have to meet with Guy again tomorrow to go over the outline for the script."

I set my fork down and pick up my wine. "Don't worry. I'll be gone. My flight leaves early."

"You're leaving already?"

Heat rises through my arms, settling at my shoulders, hiking them up. "Yes, Ed, I'm leaving. You clearly don't want me here, so I changed my flight. I can book a hotel room and go right now. Leave you to your work."

Exchanging my wine for my phone, I pull up Booking.

"Don't get a hotel." Ed stands and comes over, kneeling in front of me on the concrete. "I'm being a dick."

I frown. "Yeah, you are."

He turns my chair to face him and grabs my hands. His eyes are so intense, they practically glow in the reflection of the lights. "I'm out of my depth here. These people. Guy, he's intense. What if I'm not good enough? What if he sees right through me and finds out that I'm just some punk who fucks around with a laptop every now and then? He's going to fire me. He—"

My heart sinks for him. I cup his face in my hands. "Ed, it's your story. Who better to write it than you? You're good enough."

He freezes but doesn't respond. I say it again. "Edgar Allen DeArmas, you are good enough."

A smile cracks his serious face. "Still not my middle name."

He leans his head into my hand then turns his face toward it, kissing my palm.

My thighs are jelly.

When he turns his face back to me, I lean down and kiss him, his lips soft and a little sweet from the wine. His jaw is strong and prickly with stubble under my fingers. We pull apart, and he helps me to my feet then picks me up in one fell swoop.

He carries me inside to the bedroom.

We explore each other in a slow, unhurried way like we have all the time in the world, when both of us know that's absolutely not the case.

Afterwards, the summer night breeze drifts in through the window, skimming my skin. I lie awake for a long time, too wired to sleep.

How is this ever going to work? Does Ed even want it to? Or is this just another summer distraction, to be forgotten in a few years' time?

I must eventually drift off, because I'm awoken in the middle of the night by Ed reaching for me, planting a soft, warm kiss on my lips. It's sweet and a little sleepy, almost like a dream. He runs his hand down the length of my body. We make love in a dream-like haze. After we both come, me more than once, he holds me, and we stay like that for a while. Him the big spoon to my little spoon.

After a few minutes, I take his hand in mine but don't turn around. "I've had some interviews recently."

"Anything promising?"

I trace each tattooed letter on his fingers. "Yeah, maybe. I think that middle school in New Haven might offer me the position. And there's a private school in Portland."

He plants little kisses on the back of my neck. "You'd like Portland."

"It seems cool. There's also... Well, this idea is a little crazy, but there's that bookstore for sale in Fortune Falls."

"Right," he says, his voice hesitant.

"I went and checked it out. It's beautiful, and it has an apartment above it so I wouldn't have to worry about getting a place on top of buying the shop. I even talked to some people about a business plan."

"Wow. You're serious?"

I roll over on my back to see his face. His brow is furrowed.

"It could be really amazing."

He runs a hand over his mouth, sitting up. "You've been busy."

"What do you think I should do?"

He rolls off the bed, stepping into his boxers long ago discarded on the floor. "Whatever makes you happy?"

I swallow hard and then go for it. "What about us? If I was in Portland, it would be easier, right?"

He shrugs. "I don't know. I'm not sure that I'm going to live there much longer. But I might. I'm not sure. Right now, I just need to focus on this film, you know."

I sit up, wrapping the blanket around myself. "Yeah."

He heads into the bathroom, and I hear the tap running.

When he gets back, he wraps me in his arms again. His breaths are rhythmic and heavy almost instantly, but I'm left awake, staring at the plant in the corner of the room. What if I take the job at the school in Portland, and he moves?

In the dark morning, our bodies find each other again. It's passionate, and as he kisses me over and over, I can't help but think it feels a little like it might be the last time.

With the minutes ticking by before my scheduled ride, I pack quickly and shower even quicker.

Ed is in the kitchen in his boxers, making coffee. "Do you want some?"

I check my phone. My driver is on the way. "I'll get some at the airport."

He nods. "Look, I—"

I stop him. "Ed, I get it. This whole Hollywood thing is intense."

He puts his hand on my hips and pulls me close. "*This* is intense."

I smile. He's not wrong. It is. But is it enough?

"I'll miss you." I kiss his neck.

He groans. "How am I going to survive without being able to touch you?" He runs his hands down my back. "I don't know how I'm going to concentrate today. I'm just going to be replaying last night," he whispers in my ear, sending shivers down my spine.

But a thought tingles in my head stronger than that. "I have an idea."

His eyes light up. "Ooh, do you think we have enough time?"

I laugh. "No. And that's not what I meant. Are you still going to the Oregon Book Awards at the end of the summer?"

"*We* are, I was hoping."

"Perfect. I don't think we should talk until then."

His hands fall away. "What?"

"The dinner is in four weeks. You need to write your script; I need to finish my book and make some big decisions. We'll have a month to work on our projects without distractions. Then we'll meet and can focus on each other."

"No FaceTime?"

I shake my head.

"No pics."

Another shake.

"No texts."

"Nope. We'll meet at the dinner."

He rubs his hand on the back of his neck. "I do need to concentrate."

"You'll be able to." And I won't be checking my phone every other minute for a text. I smile, but it feels fake. Too bright.

"I don't know." He sighs, his brow pinched. "We tried this once before, and we lost each other for a whole decade."

I take my finger and smooth out the wrinkle between his brows. "We'll do better."

I don't point out that it would've only been seven years if he'd been paying attention at that signing.

He looks at me. "I'll do better."

We kiss, and this time it really is a goodbye—not forever, but for now. My watch buzzes with a notification. My driver is here.

Ed takes my face in his hands, his fingers moving all the way back to my hair. "Thank you."

I'm not sure what exactly he's thanking me for... For my time here or the gift of our time apart. My driver honks. I grab my bag and head out the door into the inky blue pre-sunrise morning.

"YOU WHAT?" Anh is staring at me, jaw hanging open.

"We agreed to meet in four weeks."

"And have no contact until then?"

"Yes."

"No texts?"

I shake my head.

Anh sits up, her wineglass perched on her knee. We're having a drink on the deck. My flight that was supposed to leave first thing in the morning was delayed, then delayed again, then canceled. The traffic to the coast made the drive take twice as long. I kept running circles in my head the entire time. Is not talking for a month practical, mature, maybe romantic, even? Or just completely idiotic.

It'll definitely show him I'm not a crazed, clingy, lovesick girl-friend. But I'm not even his girlfriend. We never had that conversation. We've never even talked about being exclusive. And he's in Los Angeles, the land of beautiful people.

By the time I finally arrived back, I was dizzy and nearly in tears. Anh took one look at me, sat me down on the deck, and grabbed a bottle of wine and two glasses.

"So," Anh says. "Let me get this straight. You are crazy about this guy and have been for literally years. You two finally found each other, you're both single, you're both into each other, and instead of putting yourself out there and maybe telling him how you feel, *you* suggest not having any contact for the rest of the summer. Longer, I might add, than the total time you two have spent together."

"That about sums it up." I take a long sip of my wine. "But aren't you the one who told me to protect myself? He can't break my heart if he can't even text me."

Anh's eyes are soft. "Can I be honest?"

I sigh. "I kind of wish you wouldn't."

She sets her glass down. "What were you thinking?"

"I wasn't, okay? I just completely humiliated myself by showing up there unannounced. I wanted to show him I didn't need him. That I saw how hard he was working and that I had shit to do too. It'll be fine. We can pick up where we left off in a month."

Robin is running toward us from the beach. Not walking, not a casual jog… It is a full-on run. Robin doesn't run. She cycles or takes the odd hip hop class. Robin does Pilates like it's her religion, but she doesn't run. Nathan is close at her heels. My pulse spikes. I stand. "What's wrong?"

Anh stands too. Robin stops and puts her hand on her knees, catching her breath. "Nothing's wrong."

She holds up her left hand, and there on her ring finger is a round-cut diamond engagement ring. It momentarily catches the sun, putting a white sunspot in my eye.

"We're engaged."

Anh flinches next to me. It's tiny, minuscule, and she catches herself quickly, pasting a huge smile on her face, but I saw it. "Whoa."

"And we're moving here! We're going to buy this house from Nathan's grandparents."

"Oh awesome! Congratulations," I say, and I mean it, but part of me—a small part, the tiny angry spinster that lives in the corner of my brain—feels left behind.

Anh's moving to Orcas Island, starting a new life, Robin's getting married, Ed is making a movie, and here I am. Still trying to write a book good enough to be published, going to teach a bunch of high schoolers in the fall, again.

Unless I don't.

I don't have to teach. I can buy the bookshop, fix it up, and live my dream. Maybe Ed will come around on the idea of small towns.

Anh runs inside and grabs two more glasses, pouring Robin and Nathan each some wine. She holds up her glass. "To Robin and Nathan."

Nathan smiles, his eyes melting as he wraps a hand around Robin's waist. "To love."

We all echo her words.

CHAPTER 22
FRIDAY, AUGUST 9TH

I write like my life depends on it. Some days it feels like it does. If I'm writing, I'm not thinking about texting Ed. When I suggested we not text or talk or see each other, I really didn't think it would be as hard as it's been. So, I write. I finished a draft last week and sent it off to two of my critique partners. I also finished a draft of my business plan and sent it to Anh. I'm now anxiously awaiting their feedback.

It's a beautiful sunny day, so I decide I'll wait with a glass of wine and a hummus plate. There is a sandcastle festival this weekend, so The Vern is more crowded than I've ever seen it. I have to push through people to even get through the door. My usual spot is taken— well, not exactly. There's an open space at the bar but no stool. Kyle is pouring two pints, chatting with a woman waiting. His eyes meet mine across the crowd, and he smiles. He hands off the two beers then pulls a stool out from behind the bar, putting it in the available space.

"My lady." He motions to it like a prince showing me to my carriage.

I laugh. "Thank you, sir. How'd you know I'd come?"

While I'm here a lot, it's not every day.

He shrugs as he grabs a glass and pours me some red wine. "I didn't. Just hoped."

He hands me the drink, and our fingers graze for just a moment. Kyle has asked me out a few times, but I've declined, saying I'm focusing on my book and trying to plan my life, which is true. I haven't explained about Ed, mostly because I don't know how.

"I was thinking of going for a walk to look at all the sandcastles after my shift. Care to join me?"

It sounds like fun and not too date like. "Sure. When are you off?"

"Midnight."

There's no way around it. A midnight walk on the beach is a date, a very romantic one at that. Ed and I never said we were exclusive, but I know how I would feel if he did the same thing. "I think that's a little past my bedtime."

Kyle pushes his lips out in an adorable pout. Then he makes his eyes look twice the size. I laugh.

"I have work to do. I can't stay up all hours of the night."

"I'll be out there. If you change your mind. Oh, hey, my buddy said someone else called, asking about that bookstore."

An icy pang of fear stabs my heart. I haven't decided what to do yet. I received an offer for both the job in Portland and the one in New Haven. I asked them both for some time to think about it. I should take one of them. It would be the smart, sensible thing to do, and if I take the one in Portland, Ed may move back there. We could try to be a couple for real. But I can't stop thinking about the bookstore.

"Did they put in an offer?"

He dries a glass as he answers, "I don't think so. Said they seemed really interested, though."

Shit. I take my new journal from book club out of my bag and make a list of all the things I need to do. Each stroke of the pen calms me down and cements my decision.

I finish my glass of wine and my hummus plate, while Kyle runs back and forth behind the bar, keeping up with the constant swarm of people. There're so many couples. A young couple, her in a white sundress and him in nice jeans, sharing French fries. An older couple sitting at the bar, her with a clear cocktail and him with an amber one, both with matching white hair. Big couples, small couples, short couples, tall couples. It's like I've wandered into a romantic Dr Seuss book. I need to leave.

The walk home is quick, and I go straight to my room. I was going to work on my book some more, but I can't look at another couple right now, not even the one I made up.

I call the Fortune Falls Business Improvement Foundation and make another appointment with a consultant. Then I call Anh, and we talk over my plans. I haven't heard her so excited in a long time, and it makes me feel once again like this is right. She's on board, ready and willing to help with whatever I may need. I assure her the only thing I need from her is her encouragement and maybe a little help with paperwork. With the sale of the house and with the expertise from the FFBIF, I should be able to set up a small business SBA-backed line of credit.

After we hang up, I pull up my text thread with Ed. I'd like to talk to him one more time before I make this giant leap. One text wouldn't hurt right? I type:

> How's it going?

And delete.
I try again:

> So, about that bookstore?

Delete.

> I miss you.

Delete. Delete. Delete. I can't be the one to text first. I'm the one who went to LA, and look how well that went. Stick to the plan. We'll meet in Portland for the awards dinner. He'll be in a tux; I'll wear the same dress I wore to the book launch. It's stunning, though, so I'll look gorgeous. I'll put my hair up so he can take it down later. That'll be hot.

My fingers tap on the phone, but my mind is lost in my fantasies.

When my eyes focus on the screen, I'm scrolling on his Instagram page, *again*.

There's nothing new, really. But then it occurs to me, I've never looked at his tagged photos. The screen fills with copies of *Vex* in all sorts of staged pictures. A carefully manicured hand, nails the same color as the cover, holding it up next to a full bookshelf. The top of a stack of other books, including Kafka, Salinger, and Hemingway. Open and next to a cup of coffee with a little latte heart on top. It goes on and on.

But the photo that catches my attention is right at the top. It's Ed and Chloe, her in light-denim cut-off shorts and a white tank top, him in dark pants and one of his band tees. He has her swooped up in his arms, his biceps flexed, even though she must weigh practically nothing. Her long leg is kicked out, and she is whispering something in Ed's ear. His smile is devilish.

How many times has he swooped me up like that? All of them usually end with him throwing me on the bed.

I click on it, a glutton for punishment. It takes me to another account, ChloeKramerOfficial. The caption reads: *Valet Service.*

Valet Service? What does that even mean? How long did he carry her? Did he carry her to her house? To his? Did they fall into bed, tangled in the same sheets we made love in?

I put the phone down and pick it up again over and over. There's no mistaking it. Ed's into her. He has to be. Even if this is just friends messing around, look at her. She's gorgeous. She's an actress, a starlet.

Fuck.

Without thinking, I dial. I want an explanation, and the only person that can give it to me is Ed. I want him to explain it all away. The phone rings and rings. I don't leave a voicemail.

Trying to sleep, I toss and turn. I keep checking my phone to see if Ed's called. Eventually I turn the ringer on so I won't miss it. When I check my phone again for the two-hundredth time, I notice the time. 12:11 a.m. Kyle will be out on the beach.

I throw my cut-off shorts back on, feeling a lot less sexy in them after seeing how Chloe looks in hers, put a bra on under my tank top, and head out into the night. The air has cooled off. It's that nice kind of chilly where you know it won't last. When the sun comes up, it will be scorching again, but for now, the nip in the breeze sends goose bumps up my calves.

Kyle is easy to spot. The beach is deserted except for him, his Converse sneakers in his hands, the water reaching toward his feet. I run past a massive sea turtle made of sand then a mermaid riding a dolphin.

"Kyle!"

He turns, and I can see his smile even in the moonlight. When I reach him, he surprises me by wrapping me in a big hug, his long arms lifting me off the ground and spinning me around. "You came!"

When he puts me down, I nod. "I came."

I feel like I could throw up. What am I doing here? Ed hurt my feelings, so I run off to another man. Is this who I am? But Ed and I aren't exclusive, obviously. And he's probably going to break up with me once he finds out I'm not leaving Fortune Falls. Why shouldn't I explore my options?

We walk along the beach looking at the elaborate sand sculptures, the moonlight shimmering on the black waves.

"This is incredible."

Kyle nods. "It's always been my favorite time of year since I was a kid. My mom used to compete."

"Really?"

"Every summer. She won once when I was nine. She built a VW bug, and it took the prize. I was so proud. Wouldn't shut up about it my entire fourth-grade year."

"Does she still compete?"

"She died a couple years later, when I was thirteen."

"Oh, I'm so sorry."

"How would you know? It's been over twenty years, so I've had time to get used to it. But some days…" He trails off, swallowing hard. "Anyway, I like to come here at night, when there's no tourists. I feel close to her."

We weave our way through the sculptures, surprisingly only a couple of actual castles at this sandcastle festival. There's a giant two-foot-tall octopus with intricate suckers carved onto each tentacle, a massive crocodile with a clock between his teeth, and a giant book with its pages open. I get closer to look at the pages. In front of the book is a sculpture of a man on one knee, holding out a ring to a woman in a dress, all made out of sand. Carved into the pages of the book, it says, "Elizabeth, will you marry me?"

"Whoa, that's a proposal."

Kyle looks at me, his gaze intense. "Is that the kind of proposal you're looking for?"

My heart stops. "No. I'm not sure I ever want to get married again."

Even as I say it, I know it's a lie. I do want to get married and have a family, and hopefully it'll turn out better than it did for Chad and me and for my parents. "I don't really know anymore, honestly. I was really against it for years, but now...I can see the appeal."

Kyle steps closer to me, And I realize that he might've just taken what I said the wrong way. Like I could see the appeal because of him, which is not what I meant. I was just rambling. He brushes a lock of hair behind my ear, his hand lingers on my cheek. He leans down, and time slows. He brings his lips to mine. Is this happening? Should I let this happen?

My heart is about to beat out of my chest, but more from anxiety than excitement. Kyle's lips are soft, not like the pillow soft of Ed's kiss though. He takes his other hand on my lower back, pulling me closer. Mechanically, Kyle is doing everything right, and with the sand sculptures, the moonlight, and the sea, it should be a perfect moment. Except it feels all wrong. My phone is burning a hole in my pocket, and I want to check to see if Ed has called back, but of course he hasn't. It's the middle of the night.

I pull away, putting my hand to my lips.

Kyle seems stunned. "Was that too much? We can take it slow. I just got carried away." He takes my hand. "I've wanted to do that since you walked into the bar that day at the beginning of summer."

I smile. "Kyle, that's so sweet. But..."

But what? But I'm with someone that I'm not speaking to. To be fair, that whole *not speaking* thing was my idea. I'm dating someone who I met a decade ago, who stood me up, didn't remember me three years ago, and who's holding Hollywood "it girl" Chloe Kramer in his arms, probably even as we speak. I sigh, not knowing what to say. "It's complicated."

He lets my hand go. "Oh."

"You remember that other guy? I'm sort of dating him."

Kyle's frown expands. "Oh."

"I should've told you before. It's just, I didn't know what to say, because…" I take a deep breath. "I wasn't sure you liked me in that way. And things with Ed are tricky at the moment."

"It's okay. You don't have to explain." He looks at his watch. "It's getting pretty late. I should walk you back."

We stroll back silently. My mind spins, looking for something, anything, I could throw out as chit chat, but there's nothing.

When we get to the house, Kyle takes my hand again. "Hattie, if you're ever free, I'd love to make you dinner."

I open my mouth, but he holds up a hand.

"I know you're seeing that other guy and it's complicated. But love doesn't have to be. Relationships don't have to be. I like you. I'd like to spend more time with you. It's simple. My offer stands, no expiration date. You just give me the word."

I smile, even though I want to cry. Kyle is saying all the right words, and for a moment I can picture it, our life together. An engagement party at The Vern, our wedding on the beach, a little house in town, him holding our baby, cradling her tiny head in his large hands. Could this be my fate? Could Kyle be my forever? Am I making a huge mistake by holding out for Ed?

"Goodnight, Hattie."

"Goodnight, Kyle."

He walks out into the night. I could break it off with Ed and date Kyle. He's handsome and funny, and he wants me.

But Ed is…something else. When I'm with him, it feels like my veins are filled with glitter. Possibilities are endless. It also feels fragile, though, like a temperamental house plant that will die without just the right mix of water, sunlight, and expensive, hard-to-find soil enhancer. It feels hard. And part of what Kyle said about it not needing to be struck a chord with me.

I feel genuinely lost.

CHAPTER 23
SATURDAY, AUGUST 10TH

In the morning, I go for a run. The rhythm of my feet that usually calms me does nothing to quell the relentless wave of thoughts. This is quite possibly the biggest decision I'll ever make.

After showering, grabbing a cup of coffee roughly the size of my head, and checking Instagram a billion times, I dig out the card Kyle gave me.

The agent answers on the first ring. "This is Rick with Beachside Properties."

"Um, yes." What am I doing? "My name is Hattie Stevens. I'm interested in one of your properties."

"Ahh, Hattie. Kyle's friend, right?"

My stomach drops, remembering last night, but I say, "Yep. That's me."

We make an appointment to meet at 1:30 at the bookstore. I walk there, savoring the light breeze billowing the skirt of my sundress.

The blue Victorian building is just as beautiful as before. The Books sign is swinging lightly in the breeze. Rick is waiting for me at the top of the steps. It's as perfect as I remember—well, not perfect, exactly. It would need a lot of work. After taking another tour, lingering again to look at the view in the bedroom, I'm still not sure what to do. Rick hands me his card after he locks the red door. "I have another interested party, so let me know if you want to put in an offer."

My mind is spinning in so many different directions, I don't know which way is up.

The walk back feels heavy, my limbs, my heart, my head. I'd like to stop at The Vern for a glass of wine, but I'm not ready to see Kyle.

Instead, I stop by the little general store on the way home and grab some Cabernet Sauvignon, olives, crackers, and cheese. I take it all out onto the porch and check my phone again. Ed still hasn't called me back from last night. But I do have an email from my critique partners.

Pouring myself a generous glass of wine, I read through their comments. Definitely some things to fix, but so far, nothing too major.

That is until I get to the end. Both of them don't feel the ending is right. June has to choose between the man in the book and the real man that she could have a life with. She chooses the real man. Even though her feelings for the man in the book are stronger, what they have could never be more than fleeting moments. You can't marry a book, much to my dismay.

But both my critique partners think the man in the book is who she should end up with.

An idea begins to form, so quickly I pull up my notes app to jot it down before I lose it. I write an alternate ending, one where June and the man in the book end up with their happily ever after. I'm not sure which is better, which I like more. I'm too close to it and can't tell anymore which is the right answer.

I need to give it some space.

Sighing, I set down my phone and look out at the ocean. I think about making another list, but how has that really helped me so far? Can I find the answers in the waves? Then a thought occurs to me. I pick back up my phone and download a magic eight ball app. Let the ball decide.

In order for the app to work, you have to shake your phone.

I close my eyes, take a deep breath, and jiggle softly.

Should I put an offer on the bookstore?

Bright-green letters appear, saying, *"It is decidedly so."*

I close my eyes again.

Are Ed and I going to end up together?

"Ask again later."

I let out a frustrated huff. After a sip of wine, I shake more vigorously and ask again.

Are Ed and I going to end up together, even if I buy the bookstore?

"Very Doubtful."

I jerk the phone up and down.

Are Ed and I going to end up together if I move to Portland?

Robin startles me mid shake. "What are you doing?"

I let out a long breath and look at the screen.

"Reply hazy. Try again."

I toss the phone at a nearby pillow.

"Honey, are you okay?" Robin asks, her voice soft.

As I consider how to answer, I gaze out at the ocean, the sun on my face bright and warm.

"Honey?"

"I'm fine." I hold up my glass. "Do you want some wine?"

I check my phone again. Nothing. Ed hasn't called. Hasn't texted.

"We're going to explore the sandcastles then go to dinner. Do you want to come?"

"No."

"Whoa… You hate sand art?"

"I want to work on my book." Which is a lie. I want this magic eight ball app to tell me what I want to hear.

"Okay, maybe later we can all get a drink at The Vern?"

The wine turns sour on my tongue. That sounds terrible, too. "Maybe."

"What's going on? Are you upset that I've been spending so much time with Nathan?"

"What? No."

Am I? Maybe a little at first, but since then I'd been too caught up in my own stuff to really notice.

Robin still looks concerned. "Are you sure? We can go to the castle thing another day. You and I can do something."

"No. Really. I'm not upset about you and Nathan."

"But you are upset."

I sigh and tell Robin all about Ed. How it was a disaster when I went there, and in order to save face, I suggested we not have any contact for the rest of the summer. Then about when I was trying not to text him, finding the picture on Instagram. I tell her about Kyle and how we've been hanging out a bit and how we kissed last night.

"Kyle's nice, handsome, and he likes me. He's been so up front with wanting to spend time with me."

Robin is nodding, her pink lips pulled into a straight line, not quite a frown. It's her thinking face. I've seen it many times. "Kyle's super cool. But Hattie, I've seen how you and Ed look at each other. *You* suggested not talking for the rest of the summer. You can't be pissed that he's respecting your wishes."

"But what about the photo?"

"I think you should talk to him about it. Maybe it was just friends goofing around. We don't know. What are the odds that you two would find each other again after all this time? Stick to the plan. Ask him about it when you see him. When are you supposed to meet?"

"In a week."

"There you go! You can talk about it then. What made you finally join Instagram?"

"Well, there's this bookstore…"

I describe the shop to Robin. I can tell she's trying very hard to be neutral, but the smile playing at the corner of her mouth gives her away.

"That all sounds amazing! So, what's stopping you?"

The question gets under my skin.

"Ed. What if he doesn't want to live here?"

She frowns. "He may not. But what if he moves to LA? Do you want to live there?"

I think about the cute cafe, the house with a pool, Ed. Would it really be that bad?

"I don't know."

Nathan calls out from the house. "The castles are waiting."

Robin smiles at the sound of his voice. "I'll tell him we're not going. Let's eat ice cream and watch *Gilmore Girls.*"

I'm not going to ruin the day they had planned, and I need to get things in order. "I really do want to work on my book. Thanks for listening."

We both stand and share a big hug.

"Anytime. Hattie, I was wondering, will you be my maid of honor?"

I nearly fall back on my chair. I thought for sure she would ask Anh. But with Anh's engagement broken off, maybe it would be too painful. "Of course."

She smiles. "When I leave, are you going to get back on Instagram?"

I shake my head.

"Are you going to keep asking that magic eight ball questions?"

I sigh. "No."

"If Ed wasn't a factor, would you buy the bookstore?"

"Yes. In a heartbeat."

And as soon as it's out of my mouth, I know it's true.

She shrugs. "You'll figure it out. If this is what you want and you and Ed are meant to be, then you can figure it out together."

We hug again, and she heads off with Nathan.

I turn my phone over in my hand, take a shaky breath, and check my bank account. Still not looking great.

But as soon as the money is there, I'll make an offer on the bookstore.

CHAPTER 24
FRIDAY, AUGUST 16TH

There's a tiny knot of anticipation that has wedged itself in my throat, and no amount of runs, or yoga on the porch, glasses of wine, or episodes of *Gilmore Girls* will dissipate it. Today is the day I'm going to see Ed after our month of no talking.

The weather has been windy and gray. Robin stands with her arms crossed, in flip-flops, sundress, and oversized cardigan while I put my bag in the car. It's adorable. She insisted on seeing me off.

"This summer has gone by so fast; I can't believe it's already mid-August."

I smile. It has and it hasn't. Some days have felt like a year with no end, and some have gone by in a blink of an eye. But I just say, "It has."

We hug, her fuzzy sweater soft on my cheek. "Call me and let me know how it goes."

"I will."

The sun is just starting to shine through the cloudy day as I drive away from Fortune Falls, the white caps of the ocean bobbing in my rearview mirror. In the short amount of time I've been here, the trails, the wind-whipped sand, the ocean, Main Street… It's all started to feel like home. Maybe it will be.

Turning on my new audiobook—I bought the latest Annabelle

Monaghan as a treat for the drive—I lose myself in the story as the miles pass. Before I know it, I'm pulling up to the hotel I booked in NE Portland, right off Flanders. After I find parking, I check my phone. Sitting right at the top of my email is an offer letter from the private school in Portland. My heart races, and I shove my phone into my bag, uncertain of how to reply or what to do.

Despite the name being the Gold Pony Hotel, the sign for it is bright red. When I booked the room, I chose this place because it was one of the more affordable. The lobby carpet is brown with yellow swirls covering it. Maybe they're supposed to be gold. I check in and make my way to my room on the second floor. The room itself is clean but smells like this was once the smoking wing of the hotel. I toss my bag down, hang up my dress, and throw myself on the bed, the soft cushion of the comforter billowing around me as I do.

It's about ten degrees hotter here than it was on the coast. I'd be lying if I said I didn't miss the ocean breeze. I cross the room to the window, opening the thick red curtains. My room looks over the pool, aquamarine water sparkling in the sun. My mind flashes to my visit to LA. To him kissing me next to the pool, so soft and hungry.

My watch alerts me to a phone call, pulling me out of my thoughts. It's Chad. My breath catches in my throat. He must have news.

I answer. "Hello."

"Hattie. Are you sitting down?"

Blood rushes to my face. We haven't spoken in over a year, and the first thing he does is tell me what to do. Fuck that. "What is it, Chad?"

"It's the house."

I continue to stand, staring out the window at the chlorinated water as Chad explains the sale fell through. The foundation is cracked, and it needs a new roof. There's no money coming anytime soon.

My knees wobble, which is probably why he suggested I sit. He is still talking, but there's a roar in my ears. Like the ocean.

He's saying things like hiring contractors and re-listing. But it's all useless words. The bookstore is perfect, and there's no way I can buy it.

After we hang up, I go back and lie down on the bed.

The clock on the nightstand changes to five before I know it. If I don't get ready now, I'll be late to meet Ed. If he's still meeting me. He never returned my call.

I want to take my time getting ready so I look my best, but I spent too long wallowing and don't have the luxury of slow, methodical movements.

Once my makeup is done and my hair is up the way I planned, I put on my light-blue dress, slip on my silver sandals, and call a Lyft.

The ride to the museum where the awards are being held takes longer than I expect. Traffic is bad, and my hotel is farther away than I realized. My nerves crackle as I get out of the car and walk through the sculpture park to the museum's main entrance. Women in long dresses and men in tuxes are milling about, some on their way in, some with drinks in hand, admiring the sculptures. I'm drawn in by one of a horse that appears to be made out of driftwood. Running my hand over it, I realize it's metal. The patina is so realistic, the color just like the dried pieces of wood lying all over the beach at Fortune Falls.

"I'm afraid you can't touch the art."

I pull my hand away, my heart in my throat as I turn to apologize.

It's Ed, his green eyes full of mischief, his head shaved again, just like that first time I met him. He's smiling ear to ear and looking very dapper in a black tux, with a Breeders T-shirt instead of a typical collared shirt. I want to think of something clever to say, but my mind is blank, all the blood pumping wildly through my heart, none left for word play.

"Hey."

We close the distance. He puts his arms around me, and our lips meet. It's a soft kiss. A kiss very appropriate for the public space we are in. But I'd be lying if I said I didn't want more. I want him to lean me against this driftwood horse and run his hands down my body. Audience and art be damned.

He pulls back first. "Ready to meet some people?"

I'm not. I can't even remember why this party felt so important to me at the beginning of summer. I can find an agent on my own. It doesn't even seem as important anymore. Now that the bookstore isn't possible, it's all I want in the world. Ed grabs my hand and squeezes. The motion goes straight to my heart. Maybe not the only thing I want.

I want to take Ed to my funky hotel and have him lay me down on the bed. I want to hear all about his time in LA. I want to ask him about Chloe and why he didn't call me back.

It'll all have to wait. I smile and nod. "Let's do it."

Ed introduces me to his agent and his current editor. He introduces me to the vice president of one of the big five publishers, as well as a whole list of some of my literary heroes, all before we've even made it to the bar for a drink. There's a long line, and Ed runs his hand along my back. "I'll get us something while you mingle. Red wine?"

The museum is stuffy. "White please."

"You got it."

Wandering, I take in the art. There is a stunning Frida Kahlo exhibit. I stop to look at one of my favorite paintings of hers, *What the Water Gave Me.* It's an intricate painting of her feet in the bathtub, the reflection of the water making two sets of toes on either side. The bath is filled with scenes—two women on a bed, two men in suits behind some ferns, a volcano with a skyscraper erupting from it. Her legs are just visible in the water underneath all of it. It's so funny, because it's so fantastical and mundane at the same time. What is it about staring at your feet in the tub that opens up a window to your soul?

A tap on my shoulder startles me, and I turn around, expecting to see Ed, but find a very tall, very blonde woman. "Have you seen Ed?"

"Uh, he went to the bar to get us some drinks."

Her hot-pink lips turn up in a small smile. "Will you tell him to find Megan? I want to say goodbye before he moves."

The blood rushes from my head to my toes in one fell swoop. He's moving? Robin mentioned something about him moving to LA. I thought she was just throwing out wild possibilities, but what if she knew something? What if he told Nathan?

I'm nauseated and my cheeks are burning. I make my way through the sea of tuxedos and gowns, the smell of cologne and perfumes overpowering in the warm room. When I get outside, I gulp in the fresh air like surfacing from underwater. I have a seat on an open bench, the metal cold through the thin layers of my dress. My heart rate starts to slow, my cheeks feel less flushed.

After a while, Ed comes out the front door with two drinks in his hands, looking back and forth, his eyes lingering by the horse where he found me before. Then he spots me, his face breaking into a smile.

He strides over. "There you are."

"I needed some air."

He hands me my drink. "Yeah, it's really crowded this year."

"I ran into Megan."

His eyes widen for a fraction of a second. "Oh yeah? I didn't see her in there."

I take a sip of my wine. "She wants to talk to you."

"Yeah, I'll catch up with her later. I want to spend time with you."

Here goes. I watch his face closely for any reaction as I say, "She mentioned you're moving."

He sighs, rubbing his hand on his head to the back of his neck. "I wanted to talk to you about that."

"Where?"

"To LA. But it might not be a permanent thing."

"Are you seeing Chloe Kramer?"

There is a minuscule flinch. "Chloe?"

"I saw the Instagram post."

Ed blows out a long breath. Then takes an even longer sip of his beer, his Adam's apple bobbing with the motion. Each second that goes by is torture. When he brings his beer down to his leg, his green eyes look deep into mine. I want him to tell me I'm wrong.

"Hattie. I've been hanging out with Chloe."

My heart plummets, free falls into the pit of my stomach.

"But nothing has happened. We're just friends."

"Friends?"

He nods.

"Do you have feelings for her?"

"Chloe?"

I laugh at his absolutely ridiculous question. "Yes, Chloe."

"No."

"Is that even true?"

"Yes."

"How can I know that? Why didn't you ever return my call?"

"What call?"

"A couple weeks ago, I called when I found the post so we could talk about it, but you never called me back."

Ed sighs again. He looks so beat. Dark circles under his eyes, his shoulders slumped like the weight of his head is too much. Like his bones are too heavy. "I blocked your number."

"You what?" The noise of the party falls away.

Ed closes his eyes. "It was too hard not to text you, so I just took away the temptation and blocked your number. This whole not talking thing was your idea, remember?"

"Because you were hardly texting me anyway. I was tired of waiting for it."

"Was that the real reason? Or was it because you were off with that bartender?"

I sit back and feel like he slapped me. "What?"

"You think I didn't notice you two flirting all summer?"

I laugh. "All summer? You weren't even there all summer. You left, *again*."

"I had to. You wouldn't understand."

My pulse ratchets on the side of my throat. "I wouldn't understand, because I'm not a big fancy author?"

"That's not what I meant. Look, I can't deal with this right now."

"What? Me? You can't deal with me right now?"

Ed looks at the ground. "I've hardly been sleeping—I've just been tinkering with the script night and day. I don't want to fuck it up. This film stuff could lead to something big."

I nod, feeling the truth of what he's saying wash over me like a summer rain. What he's working on is incredible, life-changing stuff. But I thought what we had might be too. "I know. It is. It seems like with you, there's always an amazing opportunity."

Ed shakes his head. "Hattie."

"You know what?" I stand. "That bartender does like me. He even kissed me."

The shock and hurt on Ed's face is exactly why I said it, but now that I'm seeing it, I instantly regret my words. "I didn't kiss him back. I turned him down because I have stupid feelings for you. And the bookstore."

"Are you really going to buy the bookstore?"

"No, I'm not. I can't. I wanted to talk to you about it though, about us—our future. But it's clear that something else will always come first."

I walk away, my light-blue skirt billowing behind me, expecting Ed to come after me or call out my name, but he just lets me go.

CHAPTER 25
SUNDAY, AUGUST 17TH

The sound is turned up on my phone. Text notifications too. I even turned on social media alerts. That's how crazy I've become. So that I won't miss a message from Ed. But it has been radio silence.

This morning, I have a tiny hangover, but I'm pretty sure it's more emotional than alcohol related. Could be both, though.

Ten years, three separate times, he's entered my world, the best sex of my entire life, and now he's just gone. Like a tornado moving on to the next town. Or maybe I'm just being crazy.

I came to the hotel last night, crawled into bed with a glass of wine and a chocolate bar, both of which I purchased on my long, long walk here. My feet are killing me today; my silver sandals aren't really the best walk-clear-across-town shoes. It's days like this I wish I could sleep in. The world might look a lot friendlier after a couple more hours of sleep.

Childishly, I used the kiss with Kyle like a weapon. I shouldn't have told Ed about it like that. I should've told him sooner and been gentler. I knew that it might hurt him, and so I did. I wanted him to feel something, anything, for me. Honestly, I wanted him to fight for me. For us. For what could be. But he let me walk away.

The plastic crinkles in my hand as I unwrap the cup on the dresser and try to figure out the little coffee machine, my audiobook playing on the Bluetooth speaker I packed. I'll be fine. I can accept the job at that private school and move to Portland. There's lots of fun things to do here. I'll meet some nice people. I have my book—which, last night when I got back to the hotel, I sent to the agent I met at the Pittock Mansion. After my second paper cup of wine, I sent her the version where June chooses the real, live, emotionally available man. Why wouldn't she? She wants a future with someone, a family and a stable relationship. How can she have that with someone who keeps jumping back into a book?

A shrill ring comes through the Bluetooth speaker, and my heart jumps into my throat. *Shit.* It's Ed. It has to be. Who else would call me? I walk over to my phone and take a deep breath. When I reach for the phone, I see it's not Ed. It's my mom.

My mom never calls me. I always have to call her first. She says she doesn't want to get my voicemail or bother me, but I think it's really because she's so busy.

"Hey, Mom." I put her on speaker and continue fiddling with the coffeemaker, placing the mini filter in the top, pouring the packet of grounds, and placing the cup underneath.

She sniffles and swallows before speaking. Maybe she has a cold. I grab the freshly poured coffee, holding the warm cup in my hand. "Mom, are you okay?"

"Baby…"

My stomach muscles clench as if preparing for a blow. Mom never calls me baby—not since I was seven and told her resolutely that I was not a baby anymore.

"It's your grandma, sweetie."

The cup slips from my hand, hitting the brown carpet and spilling into a steaming puddle at my feet.

I'M PACKED before I'm even off the phone with my mom. Wheeling my case through the lobby, I freeze in my tracks as the man at the counter turns.

It's Ed.

"Hattie."

I keep walking out the door, heading to my car.

"Hattie, wait."

"I can't."

Opening the back of my Subaru, I throw my suitcase inside. Ed puts a hand on my back, and I wheel around. "I don't have time for this. It's my grandma."

A sob wrenches out of me.

Ed's face turns hard. "I'll drive."

"No." I sniff back tears. "I'm sure you have meetings to get to."

"They'll keep."

"What about your car?" I look around for it in the lot but don't see it.

"Wouldn't start. I took a Lyft."

Tears are still streaming down my face.

"Hattie. You're in no state to drive. Hand me the keys."

I hand them over and get in the passenger seat. "She's at New Haven General."

It's a five-hour drive. Ed doesn't try to talk, which I appreciate. My mind is mush, and my nerves are frayed. Cranking up my audiobook, I try to lose myself in the story, as the yellow line swooshes by, miles and miles to go.

Panic washes over me in a wave. It starts slow and then crashes, pulling me under with it. My breathing turns ragged.

"Are you okay?"

I can't even answer, and Ed takes the next exit. He parks at a Shell station as I heave out breath after breath, feeling like I might not be able to take another. Like my heart might stop.

"What can I do?"

I can't do anything but breathe.

"Are you having a panic attack?"

"Mm-hmm."

"Okay. Where are you?"

"What?"

"Where are you? Just trust me. This helps."

I look into his warm eyes. "In the car."

"What can you feel?"

"The seat heater is warm on my back, but the rest of the leather is cool on the back of my thighs."

"What can you see?"

I gaze out the windshield. "A girl is walking out of the gas station in white shorts and a pink tank top, sipping on a bucket of soda."

"What can you hear?"

I close my eyes. My heart rate slows. My breathing feels steady. "The whoosh of cars on the highway."

"What can you smell?"

I inhale deeply his clove and orange scent, locking eyes with him again. "You."

The air between us feels thick and charged like right before a thunderstorm.

"Are you feeling better?"

"Yeah." It's not the first time I've had a panic attack. But it's the first in a long time. This week has just been too much.

"Do you want to talk about us?"

I shake my head. "Not yet. Is that okay?"

"I've got all the time in the world."

It's an outright lie but a nice sentiment.

He pulls the car back onto the road, turning on the radio. We listen to old time hits the rest of the way to the hospital, until he drops me off at the front and goes to find a spot in visitor parking. I promise to find him in the waiting room, and then I run in and approach the welcome desk.

"Hello. My grandmother is here. Lilian Foster."

The nurse directs me to where I can find her. I get in the crowded elevator, which smells human compared to the antiseptic lobby. Floral perfumes and musty sweaters. I almost wish I could stay a little longer. The chemical smell of the rest of the hospital stings my nose. The third-floor dings, and I step out, looking for room ten.

The cloudy day is casting a blue-gray light through the window and onto my grandmother's face, leaned back on pillows. *When Harry Met Sally* is playing softly on the television, and the remote is nestled securely in my grandmother's sleeping hand. I sit in the chair next to her bed and breathe a small sigh of relief. I made it. I'm here.

Billy Crystal is running down the New York City street while Meg Ryan looks bored at a party. I love this movie. I lean back, ready to watch Billy's big speech.

"Hattie Bear."

"Grandma. You're awake."

"You didn't have to come all this way."

I grab her hand, placing a soft kiss on her thin skin. "Yes, I did. How are you doing?"

Grandma tries to adjust her position slightly, pillows under her knees, but winces and lies back again. "I've been better. Take it from me, never break a hip."

I smile. "I'll try not to. What happened?"

Grandma sighs. "Those barn swallows were nesting in the barn, and it was spooking the chickens. There weren't any babies in there yet. So, I got out the ladder—"

"Grandma. Wasn't Chris available next door?"

"They were on vacation, and the nest had just started. I wanted to get it before it became a real home. Anyway, I fell off and landed on my hip."

The doctor comes in, her black hair tied back in a tight bun and her bright-teal glasses perched on her nose. She explains the surgery is scheduled for this afternoon, in just a couple hours. I get out my journal and take notes about the aftercare procedures, even though the doctor assures me I'll get printed-out instructions. It all seems straightforward. There will be an eight-to-ten-week recovery period, but the full rehab will be closer to a year. My mind is spinning in circles.

"Sorry, could you repeat that last part?"

The doctor puts a hand on my shoulder. "It's going to be okay. Your grandmother is a strong woman. But she needs to stay off the ladders."

Grandma laughs. "I hear you. I hear you."

The doctor leaves. Maybe the job in New Haven is still open. A quick Google search later, I find the position still posted on their website. I can work at the middle school and move in with Grandma to take care of her. My notes feel heavy in my hands. My fingers go cold. It all falls to the floor, and tears well up in the corner of my eyes.

"Hattie Bear. What is it?"

I screw on an *all is right with the world* smile that I definitely don't feel. "I'm fine. I'm just going to find some food." I'm about to ask if I can get her anything, when I remember she can't eat until after the surgery in the morning.

I pick up my things, shove them in my bag, and head to the cafeteria, not ready to face Ed again. The floors squeak under my pink Birkenstocks. What am I going to do? Obviously, I'll move in with my grandma to take care of her.

In the cafeteria, I wander the cases of thick juice bottles and prepackaged sandwiches, looking for something that might be appetizing. A yellow container catches my eye as my heart catches in my throat. A Lunchable.

Unable to hold it in any longer, tears flow in a steady stream down my cheeks. I leave the cafeteria and find the doors to a little courtyard setup with tables for people to eat at. Taking a seat at the farthest one, I wipe the tears that keep falling.

The most infuriatingly stupid thing is, no matter what I do, what I choose, I don't see a way for Ed and me to be together.

I should go find him. I think of all our talks on our runs, sitting in front of the fire, or outside of that glass-blowing place that feels so long ago now. He might know what to do or what to say. He might have an idea I haven't thought of or make me laugh.

I search the lobby with no luck. I go back to the cafeteria, thinking maybe I missed him. Nope. I head out the front doors, looking at the benches sitting in front of the hospital, but he's not there either.

Pulling out my phone to text him, my insides vibrate, and a soft wind blows over my legs. As if reading my mind, a text appears from him.

Had to take care of something. Be back soon.

CHAPTER 26

M y grandma is in surgery. It feels like she's already been there for hours, but the clock says it's only been twenty minutes. I keep checking and rechecking my phone. Waiting to hear from Ed. Even checking my email.

The Drew Barrymore Show is playing softly on the little television hanging from the ceiling.

Drew is sitting in a beige chair, wearing suede red boots and a houndstooth dress, interviewing Keanu Reeves. It must be a rerun. He looks straight out of *John Wick*. Drew shakes her head. "I'm a lover."

The camera cuts to Keanu. "No, no. Because if you're a lover, you gotta to be a fighter."

"How so?" Drew asks, biting her nail, her fingers covered in jewelry.

"Because if you don't fight for your love, what kind of love do you have?"

And it hits me like a hair getting yanked out at the root. Ed has never fought for me. Not when he was supposed to meet me ten years ago. Certainly not at the book signing when he didn't even recognize me. Not when he saw me in the coffee shop in LA. Not when I suggested we not speak. And not when I walked away last night.

Although he did come back, now he's gone again. Probably having one of those meetings that would "keep."

My phone trills in my hand. It's a number I don't recognize. Could it be Ed?

"Hello," I answer, my neck tense.

"Hello, is this Hattie Stevens?"

"Yes?" I say, not able to help the question in my voice.

"Hey, this is Mandy Blackwell. We met at the party, and you sent your book last night."

I turn off *Drew*, stunned.

"I hope you don't mind me calling. I was just so excited. I love this book! And romantic speculative fiction is hot, hot, hot right now! Literally, I couldn't put it down. I was so invested."

Flutters sparkle up my spine. My heart fills like a child's party balloon. She likes it. She really likes it.

"June is just a spitfire, and the whole triangle between Sam and Kurt is riveting. But I have to say, I'm Team Sam. The ending is all wrong."

The party balloon pops.

"June can't choose the safe, boring guy. She has to choose the man in the book. He gives her the tingles. This is a romance novel. We need her to end up with Sam. It's not a Happily Ever After if it's not with the man she really loves."

"Well, but she loves them both."

"Does she, though?"

There is a beat of silence, and then Mandy goes on. "She may in her head, but her heart belongs to one of them, and it ain't Mr. Boring."

She's right.

"It's your book, sweetie. If you want it to end this way, that's up to you. But if you want her to choose Mr. Boring, we need more extensive rewrites."

"No, you're right. She's in love with the man in the book."

I can practically hear Mandy's smile over the phone. We talk for another half hour on ideas of how that ending could work. She's going to send me her notes, and I'll start on the revisions.

When we end the call, I'm both energized and exhausted. I need coffee, but not the hospital kind. I want an actual Starbucks latte, with my name scrawled on the side and extra foam. I check in with the nurse, and they say there's still a couple of hours until Grandma will be back in the room. I make my way through the lobby and am about to head through the sliding doors, when a man stands in my way. I look up into a chiseled face and fiery green eyes.

"Ed! Where did you go?"

"Hattie, I needed to talk to—"

I hold up my hand. "I get it. A meeting. I need some coffee." I can't believe he took a meeting, now, at the hospital. Although I did just talk to an agent. Holy shit. Did I really just talk to an agent?

"Wait, Hattie."

I would like some time to focus on the bookstore and on editing this book without constantly thinking about Ed.

I'm so tired.

"I'm going to get a Starbucks across the street. You're welcome to come."

He nods. We order our drinks and take them to a small table by the window. We sit in silence. It's not uncomfortable, per se, but it doesn't feel cozy either.

"It wasn't a meeting. My mom texted."

"Oh." My stomach drops. I'm such a dick. Why do I always assume the worst? "That's cool."

He sighs. "Yeah. I had to call her. She just needs money. Same old, same old. When I told her I wasn't sure, she went off on me. Ungrateful. You'd be nothing without me. Same old shit."

I reach across the table, placing my hand on his forearm. "I'm so sorry."

He places his hand over mine, and my heart races. The truth of Mandy's words ring through me. My heart belongs to Ed.

Even if we can never make it work, I love this man.

"Hattie, I'm the one who's sorry. I shouldn't have blocked your number. It was just too hard not to text you. And I shouldn't have let you walk away. Once I got Nathan to tell me where you were staying, I thought about holding a boom box up to your window. But I wasn't sure which room you were in."

I laugh. "I'm sure the staff would've loved that."

"I'm sorry I fucked up."

I purse my lips. "We. *We* fucked it up." My heart beats faster, but I still feel hurt. "Why didn't you tell me you're moving?"

"When? I wasn't supposed to text you. I didn't want to lead with that after not seeing you for a month. When were you going to tell me about the bookstore?"

"I tried calling. And I'm the one who came to visit you. I'm always—"

"We're going in circles." He sighs. "When you came to LA, I was excited to see you. But—all cards on the table—I'm underwater on the screenwriting stuff. Things change and move so quickly. With writing, I much more a *mull things over for a couple weeks* kind of guy. But this movie stuff is lightning speed. I'm struggling to keep up. Maybe it's just the way this director works, but it's terrifying. I'm scared I'm going to fail, in a massive, public way, and that it won't only affect my future career adapting my books but my actual writing career as well. This is all I have. I'm a gutter punk skateboard kid who loves to make up stories. I have no other skills. I can't fuck this up. I was excited to see you but also surprised and over-whelmed.

If I could go back, I would swoop you up in my arms the moment I saw you in the coffee shop. And I wouldn't have agreed to not talking for a month."

"That was stupid of me."

"I get it, though. I understand not wanting to wait for me to text. I remember you had that boyfriend in high school…"

I nod.

"I'm sorry you didn't get your bookstore."

There's more sadness in my heart than joy, but I smile anyway. "It's not mine."

He lets out a long breath. "I wish we would've talked about all this more."

I check the time. "I should get back to my grandma. Maybe we can talk more after her surgery?"

He frowns. "I have to head back. My flight to LA leaves tonight."

"Tonight?" My shoulders slump. If I'd known how little time we had, I would've talked in the car, but I was so worried about Grandma, I wouldn't have been able to focus. "How will you get back?"

He shrugs as we both stand from the table. "I can catch a Greyhound or a train."

Tears prickle the back of my eyes. "Is this goodbye for good, then?"

He wraps me in a tight hug, his lips soft on my ear, his breath hot. "I hope not."

I TAKE my latte back to my grandma's room and wait. Ed said he'd call later.

After another hour, the nurses bring Grandma back. She's groggy from surgery and sleeps through the night. Around seven in the morning, she wakes up and wants some food.

After she's had some eggs and toast, she says, "So, what have I missed?"

I shrug, but my face crumples.

"Hattie Bear, what is going on?"

"I'm in love, but I don't know if he feels the same way."

"Have you told him how you feel?"

I shake my head. I tell her about Ed. The whole story, from when we met until now, leaving out all the saucy bits.

She listens intently, nodding and humming, her brows furrowed. "Have you noticed how many times you are the one to walk away?"

"What?"

"I'm not saying he's not a confusing man. He absolutely needs to explain himself if he wants to continue the relationship. But why do you keep walking away?"

"How am *I* walking away?"

"Suggesting you two don't talk."

"I called him, and he never answered."

"Because you told him you didn't want to talk. He blocked your number so he wouldn't text you. He must have wanted to reach out to you pretty bad if he had to block your number. Then you literally walked away at the party."

I sigh. "But he could've come after me."

There is a beat of silence. Her words sink in. He wanted to talk to me, but he was respecting my wishes. My stupid, save face, *not what I actually wanted at all* wishes. He was probably giving me the space he thought I wanted by walking away. And he did come find me in the morning.

Grandma puts her hand on my arm. "I think when you go home today, you should call and talk to him."

"Go home?" The pain medication must be making her foggy, if she really thinks I'm going to leave her alone. "I'm not even sure where home is. That's beside the point. I'm not leaving until you're better."

"That's sweet. But no."

I shake my head. "I'm staying to take care of you."

"No." Her mouth is a stern frown that I recognize from when I was a kid and got into her sewing stuff without asking. "Absolutely not."

"Grandma, it's already done."

"Well, undo it. You're not invited."

I let out a huff of air. "How are you going to manage the farm-house on your own?"

"I won't be on my own."

"What?"

"Uncle Rob is coming."

"Uncle Rob."

"He's going to get me on my feet then help me list the house." She nods. "I'm moving to Hermosa Beach. It will be warm and wonderful."

Her smile is so bright, my heart fills. As much as I love Grandma, I really didn't want to move to New Haven and work at the middle school. "Grandma, that's great!"

"You are welcome to visit anytime."

CHAPTER 27
MONDAY, AUGUST 19TH

Uncle Rob showed up and took over the way only Uncle Rob can do. I said my goodbyes and got back on the road. My mind plays over and over what I might say to Ed when I call. Should I call or wait for him to call? Should I just text him?

The whole way to Fortune Falls, I think of things I can say or things I can do, but nothing clicks. Once I'm back at the beach house, I shower for a long time, letting the warm water unravel the knots in my shoulders.

After, I go to my phone and see I've missed a call.

Not from Ed, but from Anh.

I call her back, and everything comes spilling out of me at the same rate as the tears falling down my cheeks. First about my grandma, then about Ed. And finally. The bookstore.

"Hattie. I'm so sorry. I can't fix most of that. You and Ed should talk. If there's one thing I regret with Melissa, it's that I kept so much of my feelings bottled up. I didn't want to burden her. But it just drove us further apart. Call him, or if that feels too hard, write."

"I can write." I nod to myself, the tears slowing.

"Yes, you can. And about the bookstore… well, I have an idea. It's actually why I called. And now with the house stuff, it almost feels like destiny."

"Destiny? Who is this? Put Anh back on the phone."

She laughs, and my whole body feels lighter.

"Would you ever consider having a business partner?"

My heart bubbles over like a fizzy glass of champagne. "Are you serious?"

"Aren't I always?"

"No." I can't believe this. Anh and me owning a bookstore together? This could be amazing.

"Well, I am this time."

We talk for an hour, going over all the logistics. Anh doesn't want to run the store, but she'd love to be an investor and help with all the paperwork and the legal side of things. She looked over the business plan and made some notes of things we might want to consider. She's going to send it to me. Once it's in a good place, we'll contact Rick and draw up all the paperwork.

Holy shit! We're buying a bookstore.

I run to my laptop and open my email. On top is one from Anh with a document attached. My heart skips a beat. This is happening. I'm about to click on it and tuck into the work, when another email catches my eye—from Ed.

Message sent: Sunday August 18th 11:18 p.m.

Hattie,

I've been trying to figure out what to say to you and how to say it since we said goodbye at the coffee shop. For two people who seem to be crazy about each other, we sure do say a lot of goodbyes. I know email is not a romantic gesture, but maybe it can be.

Writing is supposed to be what I'm good at—so here I go.

That sunny afternoon, when I saw you at the beach house, I couldn't believe it was you. Like literally, couldn't believe it. When you remembered me from the signing but didn't bring up when we met at the bookstore, I thought maybe it wasn't you.

But as we spent more and more time together, I knew it was. I didn't know how to bring it up at first because I didn't want to ruin our new thing. When I finally did, I was so worried I would fuck

this all up. After fate and the universe decided to give us another chance, I couldn't. But it really feels like I have.

I'd like a do-over. Will you come back to LA?

Let me know what you think.

Love,

Ed

I read and reread it until the screen burns my eyes. *Love, Ed*. He put love at the end. Does he love me, or is that just how he signs his informal emails? And he asked me to come to LA… For how long? Is he asking me to move there too?

Either way, I can't. I won't give up my bookstore, not when it's all coming together. My fingers tap lightly at the keys. Typing, deleting, retyping, deleting. Finally, I hit Send.

Message sent: Monday August 19th 1:13 p.m.

Ed,

Recently, I have discovered that I have a tendency to walk away when things are hard or intense. I take the safe route to protect myself. Like not exchanging numbers when we met a decade ago. I was terrified you'd ghost me. And recently suggesting we not talk. I was trying to save face after going to LA and feeling like you didn't want me there. But instead of running from hard conversations and sharing our feelings, I have gone the *bottle it up, keep it to myself* route, which won't help anyone. So here goes…

Thank you for inviting me. Really, truly, thank you, but I can't go. At least not right now. I'm about to see a man about a bookstore!

I don't know where that leaves us. Hopefully, we can figure out a way for there still to be us.

Owning my own bookstore has been my dream since I was a kid. I only have this one life, and I have to go for it. If anyone can understand that, it's you.

You're welcome to visit me whenever you like. There's plenty of room in my new place. Did I mention the bookstore has an apartment above it? It's gorgeous—hardwood floors, a view of the ocean. Would you like to come see sometime?

Love,

Hattie

Brewing another cup of coffee, I open the email and get to work.

About an hour later, a new email pops up.

Message sent: Tuesday August 19th 2:43 p.m.

That's awesome! Congratulations.

You're busy working on your book and about to start this new endeavor, and you don't need to be checking your phone all the time for texts from me. So, I would like it if we could keep emailing. I don't want to stop talking to you, but I also know we both might need space to focus on our own stuff right now. I know in the past, people haven't shown up for you in long-distance relationships, but I promise you I will.

Let me know what you think.

Love,

Ed

Setting the phone down, I take a hefty sip of coffee then stare out my window at the rolling waves. I *would* like time to focus on the bookstore and on editing my book without constantly thinking about Ed. Email would be a good way to stay in each other's lives without dominating it with a million texts a day.

I take a deep breath and pick my phone back up.

Message sent: Tuesday August 19th 2:57 p.m.

That's a great idea.

It takes a solid week of going back and forth with Anh on edits. Once the business plan is perfect, I make an appointment with the bank. Anh offers to come, but I assure her I can do this on my own. Despite the cool gray day, I am sweating in my sensible blue button-up shirt. The walk to the bank is flat, but the way my heart is hammering in my chest, it feels like I'm running straight uphill. The bank looks like it's straight out of the seventies, with lots of brown. Brown tiles, dark wood, and orange chairs. Pushing my shoulders back, I take a deep breath and head to the counter.

"Hi, my name is Hattie. I have an appointment."

An hour later, I walk outside. The clouds have cleared, and the sunshine warms my face. I dig out my phone. Anh answers on the first ring.

"We have an SBA-backed line of credit, baby!"

The whoop that comes out of Anh is so loud, I have to hold the phone away from my ear.

We email Rick, putting in an official—very official, thanks to Anh—offer on the bookstore.

After an agonizing three-day wait, Rick writes us back that the offer has been accepted. We sign everything that same afternoon, my excitement spiking with each digital yellow tab I initial.

The next morning, I put on my favorite light-blue dress with buttons up the front and my pair of vintage red Mary Janes and head out into the sunshine, a spring in my step.

Rick hands me the keys, and the cold metal on my warm palm feels like an electric shock.

This is happening.

I walk from Rick's office to the bookstore—our bookstore—stopping by one of the shops on the way. Since I got here in June, I've walked down this street countless times, but today feels different. Because as of today, Fortune Falls is my home.

Turning the key in the lock of the red door, I close it softly behind me. There's so much to do, to clean, to sort, to organize, but today is for celebrating.

I take the stairs to my apartment, opening some windows to let in fresh air. The previous owner never used the space, so it's been sitting empty for quite a while. Not anymore. First thing I need to get is a bed and a shower curtain. I picture where my things will go, what furniture I need, making my way back to the bedroom. I pop the cork on the champagne and quickly sip at the foaming bubbles.

I own a bookstore with my best friend. It may have cost me the love of my life, but I followed my gut, no magic eight ball needed. Drinking champagne straight from the bottle, I take a photo of the ocean view from my room then send it to Anh and Robin with the text:

Me: We own a bookstore.

Not even a minute goes by before I get texts back.

Anh: Fuck yeah, we do!

Robin: I'm on my way!

I open my email and think about sending it to Ed. After I attach the photo of my view, I think better of it and take a new one, with me in the picture, champagne held high, in front of my amazing view. I write *My new home. You're welcome anytime.*

I hit Send as I hear the door creak open downstairs.

"Knock, knock."

I run to greet Robin and Nathan, holding another bottle of champagne and glasses.

When I rush to Robin, we hug like we haven't seen each other since last summer, like we used to as kids. I laugh into her hair as she says, "I'm so proud of you."

A tear rolls down my cheek then another. When we part, I'm crying in earnest. She pulls me back in for another hug. "Honey."

I sniffle. "They're happy tears."

And it's mostly true, but there's a small part of me that wonders if I shouldn't have signed the papers and instead gotten on a plane to LA.

I WORK HARDER than I have ever worked in my entire life. And I've taught a room full of fifteen-year-olds, fresh out of sex-ed, *Romeo and Juliet*. I know hard work. But this is another level. The bookstore demands all my time and energy.

The wallpaper is trickier than I originally thought. My initial plan was to peel it all off, but I quickly found out that wasn't going to be possible. I tried a blow dryer, then a heat gun, and then when that didn't work, a chemical stripper that stunk to the whole place up for an entire week. When I finally got one long strip off, it was an even uglier wallpaper underneath. So, the floral yellow stays.

To patch up the holes, I'm having the local artist I hired to paint the steps like a bookshelf add more books inside each gap in the paper.

It'll look like the wallpaper is hiding secret shelves. Hopefully, it will be cute. He's also going to paint the name of the store on the sign too, Story Club Books.

With some help from Robin and Nathan, we should be ready to open on the weekend of Fortune Falls Fall Festival, in two weeks.

This morning, I'm lying in bed a few extra minutes before I continue on the great shelf clean out. I'm going to put a fresh coat of paint on all the shelves, but first I need to box up the books—I've already completed a full inventory and ordered some new stock—and wipe all the shelves down.

Burrowing under my soft comforter to keep my limbs out of the chill in the air, I check my email. There is one at the very top from Ed. Every day when I wake up, there's an email from him. He's a late-night writer. I can picture him lying in his bed, his fingers flying over his phone like they were that day we went to the Hideout. I've told him all about every inch of the bookstore and all my insane tasks to fix it up. He's told me all about the famous people he's met and the fancy parties he's been to.

My favorite emails, though, are the ones where he talks to me about nothing. Like the one he sent me last night.

Message sent: Friday September 20th 1:53 a.m.

If we were spies, what would our code names be?

Love,

Ed

P.S. I miss you.

Peeling myself out of bed, it's too perfect a morning to pass up a run. The shelves will still be there to clean when I get back. Smiling in my kitchen alone, I brew some coffee. Miss doesn't even begin to describe my feelings for him. I'm dressing in my running gear when the answer finally comes to me.

Message sent: Friday September 20th 5:53 a.m.

My code name would be Hush Hush. Yours would be Covert. We would have them embroidered on satin jackets like the pink ladies in _Grease_. The real question is, what or who would we be spying on?

Love,

Hattie

P.S. I miss you too.

Putting in my earbuds, I turn my audiobook up and head out the door on my run. The nip in the air is much fiercer outside than in my drafty apartment, making me glad I chose running tights and not shorts. The leaves are turning from their summer green to vibrant yellows and oranges with the occasional pop of red. The air smells of lit fireplaces, the occasional whiff of coffee and the ocean.

Stopping at a bakery on my way back, I order an egg bagel sandwich. Once I'm home and biting into the savory treat, I open my email again, hoping for the next one from Ed but knowing he's probably not up yet.

Right at the top is an email from Mandy, the agent interested in my book. I sent her my manuscript last week, after I made the suggested edits on my novel, which I finished late at night in my bed as a salve for my anxiety. It was nice to escape into the fictional problems rather than the real-life question of if I made the right decision.

A mix of excitement and dread bubbles up from my toes, settling in my stomach as I open her email.

Message sent: Friday September 20th 6:41 a.m.

I love the changes! Would love to get on a call to discuss working together on this and future projects. When would be a good time?

Mandy

Holy shit. Holy shit. This is happening. My story is on its way to being a real book. I dial without thinking, my face staring back at me as I wait for him to answer.

Ed picks up on the second ring, his eyes sleepy, shirtless in the bed.

"Hattie…" He rubs his eyes. "Is everything okay?"

"Ed, I'm pretty sure I just got a literary agent."

"Hattie! That's amazing news! Although I'm not surprised. Your book is so good." Ed read the latest version right after Mandy. He sits up, the blanket falling, exposing more of his bare chest.

"I know we're not supposed to call. I was just so excited."

"I'm glad you did." His eyes are warm, his face sincere. My heart fills with stars. I don't know what to say, so I'm not thinking when the next thing comes out.

"Do you think you'll be able to make it to the opening?"

I invited Ed to Story Club Books's grand opening in an email last week. He replied *how exciting* but never said if he could come.

He closes his eyes. "I'm not sure."

I smile. "That's okay. I was just curious. I miss you, Edgar Allen DeArmas."

He laughs, opening his eyes. "Still not my middle name."

"I should go."

He nods. "Congratulations, really. You're killing it."

Floating through my day, I have a great time with my bucket of soapy water and my audiobook on full blast. I focus on the fact that I have a literary agent and not on the feelings of guilt over breaking the email rule and asking Ed if he was coming to the opening.

At lunchtime, I open my email, and there is one at the top from Ed.

Message sent: Friday September 20th 10:37 a.m.

We'd spy on each other. Obviously.

Love,

Ed

CHAPTER 28
SATURDAY, OCTOBER 12TH

It's finally here. The grand opening of Story Club Books. I wake up earlier than normal, too excited to sleep. On autopilot, I check my email, but the last one Ed sent was two days ago. I reread it.

We had a crazy day today on set. There's a horse for one of the dream sequences, and he must've gotten into craft services, because the poor buddy had so many farts. We kept having to cut. The smell, you would not believe it.

This is a big week! You are going to do amazing.

Love,

Ed

Can't deny I would've loved to read more I miss yous and less horse farts. I bundle up and go for a run. The clouds are thick and gray, like a worn-in white comforter, and there's a sweet smell in the air, like it might rain later.

The trail is beautiful. Bright-orange leaves rustle in light autumn wind, offset by the evergreen trees and the rolling ocean below. I run back through town, down Main Street, pumpkins in front of nearly every business, and the warm scent of campfires and cinnamon permeate the street.

After a hot shower, I throw on thick brown tights, a soft chocolate turtleneck, and a light-blue corduroy dress over both. When I flick on the light switch, the large crystal chandelier comes on, bathing the room in a warm glow.

Fall-themed romances fill the front table. I straighten *You, Again* and *The Ex-Hex*.

Going over to the small seating area with a pair of pink velvet chairs, I fluff the shaggy alpaca pillows as Robin walks onto the porch, her long blonde hair tied back in a low ponytail. She's carrying a tray of three coffee cups, and I hurry to open the door for her. She hands me the coffee, and the strong scent of pumpkin spice fills my nose.

"You didn't have to do that. I have a coffee machine right here."

"Save it for the paying customers." She sets the tray down on the counter and gets one out. "What can I do? Put me to work."

"Don't you have to work at your actual job today?"

She shakes her head while sipping her latte. "Nope. Took the day off."

The bells I put on the door jingle, and I'm about to run over and let them know we're not open yet, but I stop as soon as I see who's walking through the door.

"Anh!"

She beelines to me, wrapping me in a tight hug.

"I thought you couldn't get out of your classes."

We part, and she gives me a quick kiss on the cheek, her minty lips leaving a gooey spot. "I wouldn't miss this for the world."

Robin comes over, and each of them grab one of my hands. I'm overwhelmed with love for these two women, showing up for me no matter what. I want to bask in it, but there is shit to do!

"Let's get started!"

I go to the counter and light the small vanilla candle. The familiar scent of dusty books, leather, and vanilla fills my senses. I open my planner on the counter, and we divide up the tasks.

Grandma calls around nine, and I give her and Uncle Rob a Face-Time tour. She's still recovering, staying in Hermosa Beach with Uncle Rob. The farmhouse sold last week, and when she's back on her feet, she has her eyes on a condo.

At ten a.m. on the dot, I turn on the neon Open sign and set out the sandwich board on the sidewalk. Anh runs down the street with a bundle of shiny pumpkin balloons billowing behind her. She hands them to me, and I tie them to the sign.

I smile at her. "We did it."

"You did it, babe."

A tear forms in the corner of my eyes. "You know, without you, none of this is possible."

A small tear falls from her cheek too. "Okay, I know."

We both laugh and wrap each other in a tight hug.

Story Club Books is open for business.

It starts out slow but steadily picks up. Nathan mans the espresso station, Anh is at the register, Robin is taking tons of photos and uploading them to Story Club's Instagram—turns out it's pretty handy having a social media genius as a best friend—and I greet the customers, offer recommendations, and restock. Every jingle of the bells, I turn, hoping to see Ed's face.

Around noon, my mom comes in with her boyfriend. They're staying in Seaside at a spa. She wraps me in a tight hug. "Honey, I'm so proud of you."

"Thanks, Mom."

She oohs and ahhs and buys five Nora Roberts books.

I talked to my dad. He can't make it this weekend, but he and his family are planning on visiting during the kids' Christmas break.

A little after three, Anh comes to find me. "Hattie, we're nearly out of ones."

I nod, adrenaline spiking my heart. The bank is still open. This is not a big problem. I can do this. "I'll run to the bank."

The Fall Festival is in full swing. The air smells heavy and sweet with the scent of caramel corn. Outside the antique store, kids are bobbing for apples in vintage metal washtubs, the late-afternoon sun sparkling on the sloshing water.

The yoga studio across the street is offering a free flow. I can't go today, but it occurs to me that Anh might want to.

The toy store has set up two tables on the sidewalk—one with tiny pumpkins, paints, and brushes, the other with larger pumpkins and carving tools. Which reminds me I haven't gotten pumpkins for the store yet. A little girl with big brown eyes and long blonde hair is dipping her brush in the black paint, but instead of daubing it on the pumpkin, she glides it over her eyelid like makeup.

I laugh and think about calling out to the adults nearby who must be her parents, but before I can, I nearly run smack dab into Kyle.

He grabs both my arms to steady me. "Whoa."

Any awkwardness we had after our walk on the beach has dissipated. I've been in The Vern many times since, and we've become friends. "Sorry. On a mad dash for change."

"Congrats on the opening. I'm headed that way."

"Great. I'll see you there in a bit."

On my way back from getting the change, I peer into each face I pass, scanning the crowd and hoping my eyes land on dark tousled hair and moss green eyes. No one fits the bill.

I check my email.

Nothing.

Scrolling over, I go to Instagram and am overwhelmed by the numbers popping up in the corner by the heart. Story Club is tagged over and over. Selfies on the porch steps in front of the faux bookshelf, pictures of beautiful lattes made with Nathan's expert hand, pictures of smiling customers with Story Club Books totes. We have nearly 30,000 views and over 300 hundred likes on the reel Robin posted an hour ago. We're going viral!

When I'm back at Story Club, I take in the beauty of the old blue Victorian house. Three women sit on the steps taking a selfie. People drink their coffees at the cafe tables on the porch. A smile takes over my face.

Ed might not be here, but here—this place—is pretty amazing.

I go in and take over on the register, telling Anh she should check out the free yoga class. She comes back an hour later and shoves me to the side.

After the last customer of the day leaves, I click the door shut, and Nathan falls into one of the pink velvet chairs. Robin falls into his lap with an exaggerated sigh.

"I swear, if you two break my chair..."

Robin sticks her tongue out at me. "You owe us."

I laugh. "It's true." I squeeze Anh next to me. "I couldn't have done this without you all. And we get to do it all again tomorrow!"

"I need food and a drink," Nathan says, standing up with Robin in his arms.

"At yoga, Michelle said there's trivia tonight at The Vern."

"Michelle?" Robin raises her eyebrows as she wiggles out of Nathan's arms.Then turns to me. "Want to come?"

I nod. "I'll meet you there."

They all head out, and I'm left alone in my shop. I inhale deeply and let out a satisfied sigh. I count out the till and put the money away in the safe in the tiny back room.

Hoping to hear from Ed, I check my email, but there's nothing. I hit Compose and start to type.

It's real now. Story Club Books is open. It was a great day, but I'd be lying if I said I wasn't hoping to see you, that I didn't look for your face in every customer who came in.

I know you're busy. I'm not trying to make you feel bad. I'm just trying to be honest.

This whole email was a way for us to stay close, but I've never felt farther away from you.

I'm not sure this is working—

I quickly delete the words all the way up to *it's real*. What am I doing? Do I really want to cut off all communication because he wasn't here today?

Bells jingle.

Shit. I forgot to lock the front door.

I run out. "Sorry, we're closed."

Standing there with a bouquet of marigolds and a leather overnight bag, in black suit pants, a dark jean jacket, and a Veruca Salt T-shirt, is Ed, his green eyes shining in the light of the chandelier.

"Hey."

My heart is in my throat. "Hey yourself."

He crosses the room, closing the space between us. "These are for you."

Setting the flowers down on the counter along with his phone, he fiddles with a few things, and "Just Like Honey" plays. The thumps of the bass mirror the ones of my heart.

He holds out his hand to me. "Can I have this dance?"

Warmth spreads through my body. When I take his hand, he pulls me up into his arms. His jacket is rough under my palms. "Covert" is embroidered in hot pink stitching on the chest. I run my finger along the stitches and laugh as he twirls me around to the music.

"Oh my God. Where did you get this coat?"

"I had it made. There's one in my bag for you, too."

"No."

He nods. "It's not pink satin, but I thought it was a nice compromise."

I lay my head on his shoulder. "I didn't think you were coming."

"For a second, I wasn't sure I could either. Hattie." He takes my face in his hands, planting a soft kiss on my lips. When we part, he says, "I'm an idiot."

I laugh, and he takes my hand, his face serious. "I've been doing some thinking—actually a lot of thinking. I've always been a one-foot-out-the-door kind of person. In all my relationships, but especially my romantic ones."

"Okay…"

"If I'm not all in, I can't get hurt or hurt as bad. I've thought I could just enjoy the time we have together and focus on my own shit, and whatever happens, happens. But that's not going to work."

"It's not," I agree, remembering the email I was just about to send.

"If I missed this, it would've been just like the boardwalk that day in December. Or just like how I made you feel all alone in LA. I don't want you to feel alone. And I don't want to miss this. I'm missing major moments of our lives together because I'm too scared to go all in. And that's just fucking dumb. Do you know how you get fucked up skateboarding?"

I half smile but shake my head.

"You don't commit. If you're doing a trick and get too in your head, if you aren't fully in the movement, you're doomed from the start. That's what I've done to us. I'm getting right to the rail and jumping off the board."

"You lost me."

"I've had a mental block. Getting close and opening up, really being there and showing up for us, has been too scary, so I've been bailing. But not anymore. I'm so sorry I left you on the boardwalk that day. I'm so sorry I made you feel all alone in LA. And I'm sorry I've not been fully in this with you. Can you forgive me?"

I smile, my heart swelling so much, my chest can hardly contain it. "Yes."

"I'll never leave you alone like that again. I know what we have is complicated, but I want to figure it out. I want more than just emails. I want you in person, all of you. I love you."

My cheeks ache from how wide my smile is. He's here. Ed is here, and he wants me. He wants a real life together. "I love you."

He leans in, and we kiss. His lips are soft and warm. The music drifts on the air around us. *Just Like Honey.* We spin around, and the lights from the chandelier swirl in my vision.

"Want to see upstairs?" I breathe into Ed's ear.

He takes my hand in his, and we walk toward the stairs, up to my place, off toward our future together.

EPILOGUE

TWO YEARS LATER

The bookstore is too hot and crowded, despite the cool October weather. I can't believe they're all here for me. My book came out last week, and so far, the reception has been wonderful. Lots of tags on social media, lots of positive reviews, a starred review from *Publishers Weekly*. But this is my first event, and I couldn't ask for a better venue—my very own bookstore.

I've set up pink chairs and a vanity-like table with a lace cloth with a ruffle in the back. It's whimsical and delightful. Robin, despite being nearly nine months pregnant, offered—more like insisted—on MCing the event.

"Please welcome the co-owner of Story Club and the author of *My Book Boyfriend*, Hattie Stevens."

Applause erupts from the audience, along with hollers from the back coming from Anh, Michelle, and Nathan. The whole back row is filled with faces I know and love. My mom, grandma, Uncle Rob, a few local friends.

"Thank you all so much for coming." I clear my throat and begin to read.

The air in the room shifts as he walks in, but I keep reading. It's hard to pick a favorite scene. I've spent so much loving time on them all. But if I was forced to choose, this one where the man in the book appears is it. I finish the scene with June stumbling into his arms but accidentally closing the book in the process, making him disappear and her hit the floor with a massive thud, right as her co-worker walks in.

"Thank you."

The applause is almost as startling as June's trip. Ed, tall as an oak, in a Velvet Underground shirt, suit jacket, and ripped jeans is clapping in the back. I catch his eye, and he gives me a wink, sending electric pulses to my toes. We continued long distance while he finished up work on the movie, but with texts and phone calls and frequent visits. He decided the movie biz was not for him and instead went back to focusing on his novels.

When he moved into my place, I was worried that some of the spark might go out. It'd happened to my parents, and it definitely happened with Chad, but so far, the zing between Ed and me has only intensified.

For the next hour, I sign book after book and smile for selfie after selfie. When the line dies down, Robin thanks everyone for coming. Locking the door behind the last customer, I heave a sigh of relief. Ed comes up to the table, his green eyes sparkling with mischief.

"Hey, you. Where'd the others go?"

"We're going to meet them at The Vern."

I smile. "Perfect." I'm about to stand, when Ed puts another book on my table. But it's not mine. This book has a shiny black cover. Mine is bubblegum pink.

"Mind signing one more?"

I run my hand over the cover, an interesting mix of smooth and matte. "Is this an arc of your new book?"

Ed nods. "I thought you might be interested in seeing the dedication."

I open the hardback, and on the front page in beautiful italics, it reads:

Hattie,

First of all, without you, this book would not exist in this form. My book is infinitely better for having met you, and so is my life. Thank you for

moving my plot forward, for giving my life momentum and purpose. I love
you always and forever.

Will you marry me?

Ed

I read and reread the last line, tears forming in the corners of my
eyes. Ed's face is beaming.

He walks around to the other side of the table and kneels in front
of me, a gorgeous antique ring in his hand.

"Hattie. Will you marry me?"

I'm nodding, but words won't come. Of all the things I expected
from today, this was not one of them.

Ed slips the ring on my finger, and I find my voice. "Yes!"

He stands and pulls me up with him. We kiss, my first kiss with
my fiancé.

"Come on." He takes my hand.

I grab my bag, and we run through the streets of Fortune Falls like
the kids we were so many years ago. Passing couples holding hands, a
man walking a dog, a woman with a stroller, so many pumpkins with
carved faces lighting our way. We run right into the bar to the back
patio, where our family and friends are gathered, hummus plates and
several bottles of red wine open on the table.

Ed pulls me close. Fiddling with the ring on my finger, he whispers
in my ear, "We can put this away. We don't have to tell them today."

I kiss him on the mouth to some whoops and whistles from our
friends. When we break away, I say softly, "Fuck that."

I hold up my hand like it's a prize trophy. "We're engaged!"

Ed clasps my hand, beaming. "She said yes!"

The crowd bursts into cheers. Ed squeezes my hand, and I feel it
all. Warmth, love, safety, lust—all pulsing from the warm palm of his
hand.

Ed is my person, and soon he'll be my husband. We pass the
night drinking with friends, celebrating my book and our
engagement.

After the stars have come out and the night has chilled, Ed and I
walk home hand in hand, a rosy glow on his cheeks. The orange

leaves blow down the street, pumpkins flash, and the air smells of campfires, orange, and clove.

"When did you have to turn in that dedication?"

Ed smiles. "In June."

"June? You've known you were going to propose for months?"

Ed stops and takes my face gently in his hands. "Hattie, I should've never let you go the first time, and I won't ever make that mistake again."

We kiss, and the street falls away behind us. All that exists is Ed, me, and this moment. The now in our forever love story.

The End

ACKNOWLEDGMENTS

Thank you so much, dear reader, for immersing yourself in the world of Fortune Falls and spending your precious time with Hattie and Ed. There are two more romances coming this year set in Fortune Falls, so stay tuned.

Thank you to my sister, my first critique partner and my first champion. It has been so fun sharing this passion with you.

Thank you to my daughter for inspiring me to actually write a book and to be brave enough to share it.

Thank you to my husband for encouraging me and always bringing me new ideas for murder mysteries.

Thank you to my parents for always telling me I can be anything I want to be.

Thank you to my mother-in-law Billie for your encouragement and my sister-in-law Lisa for reading my books.

Thank you Nettie for listening to all my crazy ideas for hours.

Thank you to Lindsay Barrett for encouraging me to take my publishing journey in my own hands. This book would not be what it is without you. To my OG crit coven, Mary Fraser and Frances Hope. You elevated my writing so much. I hear your voices in my head when I'm editing. I'm so lucky to have been paired up with you. To Bianca Maris and The Shit No One Tells you about writing for pairing us up.

Thank you to my romance crit group, Sydney Birch, Stephanie Paul, and Haley Catherine. You've read so many openings of this book, and I appreciate the feedback on every single version. Thank you for reading all my books. Thank you for your time and your texts and your encouragement.

Thank you to Robin Blackburn. Your feedback and support are

invaluable. Whenever I have a down writing day, I snuggle the highland cow Henry you sent and I feel a lot better. Just love you! Thank you to my early beta readers Helly Teller and Olivia Jackson. Your feedback went a long way into shaping the book that this became.

Thank you, Katie Naymon for reading some early chapters and encouraging me to lean in on the yearn.

Thank you to my developmental editor, Jo Thurlow. Your feedback was so helpful and expertly delivered. Thank you to my copy editor Jenny Rarden for your humor while pointing out my mistakes. Thank you to my proofreader from Sun and Spines Editorial Andie Smith. You all made this story shine.

A huge thank you to all my beta readers: Maggie Mulloy, Wendy Wake, H.M. Geiser, Hannah Halcrow, KC Selby.

Thank you to all the writers that have come on my podcast and shared your process with me and offered encouragement in my own writing.

Writing has truly changed my life and in true Snoop Dog fashion I'm going to thank me. For showing up, for striving to do better and for finally making a decision. Not an easy feat for a Libra through and through.

ABOUT THE AUTHOR

Nicole Barton received a BFA in mixed media studio art. With a degree in the arts and no solid plan, Nicole has had the opportunity to hold many different jobs; video store manager, barista, photographer's assistant, toy store clerk, and yoga instructor at a retreat in Puerto Rico are just a few. Hands on research for her books.

Currently, when Nicole's not writing, you can find her working at a title one elementary school library, crafting with her little girl, or hosting the podcast, *So I Wrote a Book...Now What*, where she interviews fellow authors about their revision process.

instagram.com/ncbartonwrites